WATERMARK

WATERMARK

Michael Hewes

ISBN-13: 9780692643075
ISBN-10: 0692643079
Library of Congress Control Number: 2016902744
Samntoff Press: Gulfport, MS

For Kay

1

Matt Frazier had a tendency to overthink things. Not deliberately. It was just his nature. It got so bad back in high school, his mother loaded him up with work and sports and made him join the debate club, the drama club and even the math club, for Pete's sake, to try to tone down his fixations. Typically, he turned an issue over and over in his head until he came to a satisfactory resolution or developed an alternative explanation. If he could do neither, he beat the horse to its ugly demise and then, with some reluctance, let it go. The latter occurred only after Shelley finally called bullshit after having had enough of his obsessive behavior.

Matt also put a lot of faith in his gut, and his instincts dictated his actions nearly as often as objectivity did. Performing mindless tasks allowed the cognitive pieces to fall into place, and Matt found clarity while mowing the lawn or driving. He sometimes wondered if Janice, his secretary at the Bing, ever thought he had lost it when she arrived at work to find a blinking phone containing multiple, rambling, stream-of-consciousness voice messages he'd leave after hours during a long drive back home to Gulfport.

Matt was now on such a drive, sitting behind the wheel of his truck, feeling his anxiety grow as the Michelins on his Ford F150 thump-thumped over the cracks in the Highway 49 asphalt. His mind raced and his head hurt. It felt like his cap was cinched up a half size too small, so he pulled it off and readjusted the strap on the back, but it didn't help. He grabbed two Tylenols from the glove compartment and washed them down with the remains of the Diet Coke he had purchased earlier that morning. It had been just over an hour since he left his hotel, and he found himself vacillating between the destruction he saw before him and the fact that, yet again, he wasn't going to get to see his boys. Or his wife, for that matter, but she didn't care much to see him lately anyway.

A few days earlier, he'd driven up to the Bing's central office in Jackson for a series of depositions, and the plan was for Shelley to bring Fin and J.W. over from her mom's house in Meridian one evening while he was up that way so they could visit for a few hours. He was able to get a full day of testimony in without a problem, but midway through day two, the court reporter asked if they could reschedule so she could go home and prepare for the storm. The hurricane, which had been slothing its way through the Caribbean and the southern half of the Gulf of Mexico the prior week, had changed direction yet again, and Gulfport was suddenly in its crosshairs. The Weather Channel talking heads predicted the storm would eventually beat its way through the rest of the state before turning into North Alabama and continuing to points beyond before dying out somewhere near New Jersey. The forecast provided Shelley an excuse not to drive the hour or so to Matt's hotel. And if he was honest with himself, Matt couldn't blame her.

So, instead of getting to spend some much-needed time with his sons, Matt occupied the afternoon by topping off his truck and doing some stocking up. He strapped four full five-gallon gasoline cans in the bed, along with a chain saw and generator he picked up at Lowe's. The store was busy, but the crowds were generally well-behaved and manageable.

Then, against his better judgment, he went to Walmart.

When he walked through the sliding glass doors past the Coke machines and the old man with the smiley face button on his vest, it looked like someone had kicked over an anthill. People were all over the place, scurrying from aisle to aisle, talking loudly with lists in hand. The coming storm had complete strangers backslapping and visiting with each other like they were family, the clusters of people finding solidarity as they equipped themselves for the unknown. It was twenty-first century hurricane preparation at its finest: carts loaded with water, batteries, beer, charcoal, cookies, meat, cards, board games, and more beer. The rush created bottlenecks that in turn created lines that stretched deep into the store, and the glacial pace brought on a case of retail rage so bad that Matt's knuckles turned white from squeezing his buggy handle too tight. He thought he kept his cursing to himself but when an over-fed lady with a doughy face and terrible haircut turned around and glared at him, Matt bit his lip and just stared back. She sneered for a second and then went back to flapping her gums in the direction of what was her sister, mother or daughter; he couldn't tell; they looked the same to him. He wished all of them – everyone in the damn place – would just shut up and move their asses out of the way so *he* could get what he needed and get the hell out of there so *he* could figure out just what to do.

He knew it was too dangerous to go back to Gulfport at that point, and he would not be well received if he drove to Meridian – by Shelley or her mom. So he waited it out all night in his hotel watching the power flick on and off as the brunt of the wind and rain passed. At dawn, he stood by, watching the storm's feeder bands dissipate and move northeast. He headed out once he felt it safe enough for him to drive without getting killed by a falling tree or a rogue tornado. He was glad to be back on the road.

———

Matt had lived in Gulfport all of his life, except for college and law school, and had witnessed five hurricanes by his count, varying in intensity from high-grade rainstorms to tree-toppling disasters. People in Mississippi and Louisiana called them "storms" as if downgrading their name could somehow lessen their impact. Matt always found the immediate post-landfall environment unsettling, and this one was no different. Not many people were out, and the ones he saw were most likely locals surveying the damage. The few vehicles heading south had coastal tags; eager residents returning to what they hoped were some missing shingles at best, a tree through the roof at worst. In Magee, a group of trucks congregated around a gas station under a metal roof that the wind had rolled up like a sardine can. Farther south, in Collins, a fire engine blared its arrival off to the east. A row of Kentucky Electric Power trucks, sent two days before to help the local boys restore electricity, lined up bumper-to-bumper in an empty Home Depot parking lot. A manager type in a hard hat carrying a clipboard walked down the line, making notes.

As he drove, Matt noticed the typical hurricane aftereffects, although he couldn't recall ever seeing damage this far inland, which heightened his anxiety. Power poles littered the ground, and most of the pine trees had either snapped in two or leaned to one side from the northern gusts. Street signs were bent and twisted into odd configurations. The larger green-and-blue interstate markers were altogether blown over, mainsails catching the wind and bringing the whole rig to the ground. Abandoned cars littered the shoulder. He heard chainsaws growling in the distance when he slowed at intersections, which just twenty-four hours before had stoplights where power lines now hung slack. While the damage was disturbing, Matt grew more concerned with the absence of news reports coming out of the Coast.

As a kid, when a hurricane blew through, Matt and his family gathered around a battery-operated radio for storm updates and to find out how their friends, neighbors, and the coastline fared. They always found a news update immediately after the first wave passed, usually piped directly from the civil defense director or the emergency management office. Now, over twelve hours after this hurricane made landfall, he should have been able to turn on any station and hear about the storm's movement and its inevitable aftermath. No such luck. He wondered aloud if this one had caused enough damage to disrupt even the most basic public services. The more he thought about it, however, the more it didn't make sense. The last he heard, even as the eye crept onto land, it capped out at a Category III. Dangerous? Yes. Potential for disaster? Absolutely. Catastrophic? Nope. Just not strong enough.

He reached for his iPhone, which had slid off the seat onto the floorboard. By now he was in Hattiesburg, the college town seventy miles north of Gulfport, and as he drove under the WELCOME TO SOUTHERN MISS – HOME OF THE GOLDEN EAGLES sign, he keyed in his password and thought about whom to call. He went to his favorites and out of habit started to hit "Shelley" but paused and tapped "Hop" instead. Surely Hop, Matt's only remaining high school buddy who still lived in Gulfport, could provide a status report. After a few seconds of no ringing, Matt glanced at the display to see if the connection went through. The message said "Call Failed," so Matt hit redial and got the same message.

"What the hell –?" Matt said and then checked his phone. He had a full battery, but instead of bars, got the "No Service" message. It took him a second to realize what had happened. No tower support. *Dammit.* He held the phone in the air as if that would somehow make a signal appear, but seeing no change, dropped it into the cup holder, adjusted his hat one more time and kept driving south.

2

H E DIDN'T REALIZE how hungry he was until a lone policeman and a gaggle of volunteer rednecks, some on four-wheelers, forced him to slow down as they rerouted traffic around a closed section of road near Hardy Street in Hattiesburg. Matt looked to see if any restaurants or fart-marts were open, but nothing doing. Every retail establishment between Jackson and the Coast had shuttered once the storm's path turned towards Mississippi. Many had boarded up the doors and windows with plywood, serving the dual purposes of protecting the storefronts from flying debris during the storm while keeping the two-legged trash away once people started venturing outside again.

He fished a granola bar from his pack and washed it down with a bottle of water. Once the vehicles sped back up, he'd be on the home stretch. On a regular day, even with traffic, he could get to Gulfport from Hattiesburg in just over an hour. He'd made the trip so many times when he was a Southern Miss undergrad he could almost do it with his eyes closed.

His heart sank as he crested the hill before the I-59 overpass. A long line of cars stretched several hundred yards back from what appeared to be a roadblock, and Matt noticed right away most had their engines off. Others had given up and were maneuvering their vehicles back northward. He wasn't quite ready to turn around, so he drove his truck on the gravel shoulder towards the cruiser holding things up, ignoring the sullen glances from people sitting on their trunks as he passed. Matt slowed down and grinned a sigh of relief when he recognized the highway patrolman.

"Sir, you're going to need to turn around and head back into town," the officer said, gesturing northward with his pen without looking up. "Highway's closed for the time being."

"Closed, my ass, you square-jawed knuckle-dragging jarhead-looking bastard," Matt said.

"What –?" The Lieutenant peered into the cab of Matt's truck, then grinned with recognition. "Damn, Frazier, I didn't see you in there. I should have known it was you; I've heard that line before. Pull on over."

The man rerouting traffic was Lance Glenn, one of Matt's old fraternity brothers. Seeing him in full uniform looking all starched and official, Matt couldn't help but think how many misguided Mississippi citizens Lance must have intimidated in the course of his duties. He didn't bother Matt, though. The two had shared too much, and Matt knew most, if not all, of the bones rattling around in Lance's closet. They had even roomed together one semester, and Lance often said those four months were the best days of his life. Matt agreed.

He and Lance had spent many a pre-Shelley college night drinking beer and chasing leg, and at one time they considered themselves quite proficient at both. But the past was the past, and Matt knew that dwelling in that space did not end well for him. He shook it off and parked his truck behind Lance's patrol car. It had been ages since he'd seen his old friend, and Matt wished he'd made more of an effort to keep in touch. The blowback of late from Matt's domestic situation had a ripple effect on nearly everyone he knew, and Lance was not immune from the collateral damage. Matt felt like an asshole and a bit uncomfortable as he slid out of the truck. They smiled when they shook hands.

"How you been, hoss?" Matt asked.

"Good, considering. You?"

"Fine," Matt said. "Considering. Little nervous about what I'll find when I get home, though." He looked south down the empty highway. "What's with the roadblock?"

Lance didn't answer for a moment. He'd spent his early law enforcement years investigating car wrecks and dealing with irate traffic offenders and drug runners, but it never hardened him. Matt could always count on Lance for a good laugh most days.

But today wasn't one of them.

"Road's closed."

"Power lines?"

"Worse, Matt. Either a tornado or a wind shear came through with the hurricane. Between here and Camp Shelby there must be at least 200 pine trees down." Camp Shelby was a small Army base used to train National Guardsmen. "Two kids and a grandma dead in a trailer near New Augusta. Tree fell right on the bedroom side. Road's totally impassable."

"Damn." Matt paused for a second and tried his best to sympathize with the victims, but felt empty. It was tragic, no doubt, but he had his own issues to deal with. He let another moment or two pass before getting back to the point. "Any way to go around?" Matt scratched his whiskers and tried to think of anyone he knew from Hattiesburg he could call on in case he had to spend the night.

"You may be able to take 75, cut through Shelby, and come out the South Gate. I can get some of my boys on the horn and see if they'll help you get through." Lance squinted back at the cars behind him before turning back to Matt. "Although it may start a riot. You need a place to stay tonight?"

"I appreciate it, but if you think there's a chance I can get through, I'm going to risk it. I've been stuck in a hotel in Jackson the past few nights. I need to get home and get in my own bed."

Lance put down his notepad and turned to Matt. "You heard anything from the Coast yet?"

"No. Strangest thing. I couldn't pick up anything on the radio. What's the word?"

Lance's brow furrowed. "I've been told – from boots-on-the-ground troopers, mind you – that a twenty-nine-foot storm surge washed right through Gulfport. Hundred-twenty-per-hour-plus winds, hundred minimum sustained, for four hours straight. There ain't much left along the Coast between Alabama and Louisiana."

A car horn beeped in the distance. "What do you mean, there ain't much left?"

"Homes. Businesses. You name it – wiped out. Heard a report out this morning that the surge was so strong it ripped one of the Biloxi casinos off its moorings and dropped it right smack on top of a Hampton Inn. Flattened it like a pancake."

"Which casino?"

"The Blue Flamingo," Lance said.

"No shit? The whole thing broke loose?" Matt asked, thinking about the implications this potentially had for him, both person-ally and professionally. "Any other casinos damaged?"

"Every one. From what I've been told most are beyond repair."

Every one. Surely Matt didn't hear that right. "Really?"

Lance turned and looked south again and rested his elbows on the top of his cruiser. He took off his Smokey the Bear hat and rubbed his bald spot before readjusting the back strap and pulling the brim down low over his forehead.

"Really."

"What about in Gulfport? How did The Majestic fare?" Matt asked.

Lance shook his head. "No word yet. If I hear something I'll let you know."

Matt didn't like the sound of that. "Thanks, man," Matt said, and climbed back in his truck. "Listen, I better get going." Matt didn't feel like talking any more.

"Okay," Lance shook his hand. "Don't be a stranger."

Matt cranked his truck and put his sunglasses back on. "Uh, once all of this blows over – and I mean all of it – I'd love to have a cold beer and catch up with you sometime."

"You got it. Be careful. There have been a few shootings down there already."

"No worries," Matt said, gesturing to his backpack, "I'm packing."

"I figured as much," Lance said. "Even so, situations like this bring out the worst in some folks."

"Got it. Until next time, my brother."

"Next time." Lance waved him through, and Matt didn't even hear the horns from the cars behind him blaring their disapproval. By this point, Matt's mind was far away from Hattiesburg, pondering Lance's words. Did Lance really say the Flamingo broke loose and ended up on *top* of a hotel? Incomprehensible. And if The Majestic – Matt could barely fathom it – if The Majestic suffered a similar fate, what impact would that have? After all, The Majestic was the largest casino east of the Mississippi – the developers made sure of that and built it *just* a bit bigger than the Borgata in Atlantic City so they could make that claim. It was Gulfport's only casino, and was *the* economic engine that drove the rebirth of the city – and much of the Mississippi Gulf Coast for that matter. Matt estimated The Majestic was responsible – both directly and indirectly – for the employment of thousands of people. And he would know.

The Majestic was Matt's biggest client.

———

Lance was right. The Camp Shelby route did the trick. Granted, it took Matt over an hour to navigate the twenty or so miles on the back roads, but at least he was moving. He was glad to see that most of Highway 49 had been cleared to one lane, and once he got back on the main stretch, it, too, was slow, but not as bad as it could have been, and he made it to Gulfport in decent time.

As he approached downtown, he debated what to do first: check on The Majestic or check on his house. He knew when phones worked again he would hear from The Majestic brass and his senior law partners in Jackson inquiring about the status of the Golden Calf. Surely Delia Farrell, Matt's boss and chair of Bingham Samson & Toflin's litigation department, would want an update. And he fully intended to provide her with one, but since he was closest to the house – and since no one could reach him anyway – Delia and the rest of the world would have to wait.

Highway 49 turned into 25th Avenue once it crossed the Gulfport city limits and continued south until it dead-ended at the port. Matt noticed the degree of damage got worse with every intersection he crossed and wondered what it would look like once he got closer to shore. He lived on Second Street, one block off Beach Boulevard, the east-west corridor running the length of the coast, and now that he had made it into the city, he realized getting to his home would be more difficult than he first imagined. He picked his way down side roads, driveways and back alleys, but downed trees or debris blocked nearly every avenue. The only option he had to even get close was to try and hit the beach and drive due east to his block.

When he finally made it to the waterfront, Matt stopped, shifted into park, and pulled his sunglasses off, as if seeing it with his own eyes would somehow better help him to connect the dots. It was bad enough that all that remained of the harbor straight ahead was the exposed skeletal iron beams of what once framed up the warehouses that serviced the Merchant Marine ships and banana freighters from South America. While that sight was shocking, nothing prepared him for what he encountered when he turned left.

For the first time in his life, Matt had an unobstructed view down the shoreline as far as he could see. He tasted bile and swallowed hard.

Not a single house remained.

3

"**S**HHHIT," HE SAID to no one as his eyes darted back and forth. He could not recall a moment where there wasn't *some* traffic on the boulevard, yet at four o'clock on that Tuesday afternoon, time stood still. His vehicle was the only one out, and he crept forward, his stomach in knots. Matt couldn't access the two lanes closest to the shore. The water had washed under and over the road and seawall, creating craters every thirty yards or so where the asphalt caved in. The westbound lanes, on which Matt was now heading east, sat on a bluff and fared a little better. Nevertheless, the only way to negotiate the depressions was to drive up on the sidewalk and occasionally through a yard.

Matt rolled down his window, and the heat came at him like a blast furnace. He didn't flinch. Instead, he craned his head out and felt the baked air expand deep through his nostrils and down into his lungs, a painful contrast from the frigid A/C he'd enjoyed in the truck's cab for the last four hours. The thickness of the humidity blanketed what little breeze he stirred up from driving. He slid his sunglasses back on and pushed the nosepiece up high. He was already sweating, and the heavy Wayfarers had a tendency to droop down across the oily bridge of his nose. The only sound he could hear, other than his Ford, was the distant drone of a helicopter.

No traffic, no lawnmowers, no seagulls, no dogs, no people. Nothing.

He hunched forward over the steering wheel so his back wouldn't stick to the seat. As he moved on, he noticed the huge black drainage pipes that had popped out of the ground and coiled across former lawns and patios like giant sea serpents baking in the sun. Some trees had toppled, but most of the grand oaks somehow remained standing, bearing what would be permanent scars high up on their trunks or in the boughs where the waterline peaked and the floating debris banged and cut into the wood. The beautiful old homes gracing the beachfront since before Matt's grandparents came to Gulfport – gone, hundred-year-old estates reduced to naught. Only disconnected driveways dead-ending into nothingness, concrete slabs, and random piles of wood or bricks remained as reminders that folks had once lived there.

He saw a fireplace and chimney standing as the lone spire in the middle of an empty lot. Pieces of clothing and bed linens hung from the trees in twisted knots like wayward Mardi Gras beads thrown too high and too hard by overzealous revelers. Lot after lot looked the same, and he soon became disoriented. He had lived in Gulfport all his life and knew the area like the back of his hand. Yet now, driving down a road he had jogged for the past eight years, he couldn't identify any of the connecting streets. The storm had swept all the familiar corners out to sea.

With no beachfront residences blocking his view, Matt could look straight onto Second Street. He squinted further inland to see if he recognized anything. He finally identified Dr. Archie's house, a two-story Colonial built by hand in 1910. Like many historic Southern homes, it had a name: Blossom Lodge. The old man, Matt recalled, let sons and daughters of his friends get married there. He saw that Blossom Lodge had maintained its shape, but now the southernmost façade had fallen away, dollhouse-like, and allowed him to see inside. He felt odd, like he was violating the old house's privacy by catching it in a state of undress. He shook it off and drove on.

As he closed to within two blocks of his home, he regained his bearing by tracking his neighbors' homes aloud in reverse order: "Burrow. Morton. Damn, whose house is that?" He stared at one home that literally had a smaller one pushed inside it, then moved slowly on and passed an overturned jeep. He continued his inventory: "Youngblood. Werby. Koeppel. Mallette." He took a deep breath. His home was the next one.

His heart skipped a beat when he saw his roofline from the beach, and he wiped his brow with his shirt. Tears blurred his vision as he allowed himself the brief hope that the house may have been spared the full wrath of the storm. Why not? After all, it got no water during Camille – the benchmark storm that hit the Gulf Coast back in '69. He pulled up in what remained of Skip Faneca's driveway, and as his truck leveled out on the bank, the magnitude of the situation hit him. Matt stopped at his property and staggered out of the vehicle, eyes straight ahead, his mind whizzing in a multitude of directions, seeking but not finding solace.

Only his roof and the load-bearing walls remained.

He could see all the way through his house. The wooden floor of his den now lay across his neighbor's front patio forty yards away and across the street. Although the roof did in fact seem somewhat intact, the walls supporting it leaned to the right, as if the storm stopped one gust short of pushing the house all the way down. He squatted on a clothes dryer lying on its side, and put his head in his hands. He wept – for his neighborhood, for his friends, for the inevitable dead, for his community, for his wonderful city – and for his family.

He looked up with glassy eyes at what remained, and the gravity of the situation started to creep in. The storm was the bookend to events that had begun months before, and Matt came face-to-face with the fact that it carried a permanence that transcended the loss of a residence. As he sat there, alone, staring at the grass that had already begun to die and turn gray from the salt water that had seeped into the roots, Matt realized then he'd lost much more than just his house.

He'd lost his home.

4

WHEN MATT AND Shelley moved to Gulfport after law school, they rented an apartment for six months before purchasing a cookie cutter in a "planned" community. Although the house was nice and clean and the streets were laid out like a Seaside knockoff, it never truly felt like a home – to either of them. They longed for something with more history, and Matt felt drawn back to Second Street. Growing up, he enjoyed riding his bike in the neighborhood during his sojourns to his grandparents' house. People were always outside working in their yards or enjoying the shade of the live oak canopy running the length of the street. Even as a kid, Matt felt a sense of belonging there.

One of his favorite places to visit was Ms. Lynnie's house. She lived alone in a comfortable cottage just a few blocks past the park. She was an avid gardener who took great delight when Matt arrived on his bike with a gleam in his eyes and a sack in his hand, hoping to grow who knows what. Ms. Lynnie didn't care what he brought – flowers, vegetables, shrubs, seeds – it didn't matter. Matt could plant anything in his corner by the fence where the honeysuckle and jasmine had taken over the pickets, and it never bothered her that he would get filthy dirty. He liked her because she liked to talk about normal things and did not speak down to him like some of the other grown-ups. He would dig for hours, and she would reward him with ice cold Barq's longnecks or Fanta orange drinks on the porch steps. She even let him take the empties, which were worth ten cents apiece at the A&P. She also kept Hershey bars in the fridge and didn't balk when Matt asked if he could eat the whole thing, dirty fingers and all.

Matt's mom called after Ms. Lynnie died, and through letters, phone calls, follow-ups, and negotiations, Shelley and Matt bought the home from Ms. Lynnie's children, who seemed happy to pass the house on to a somewhat familiar name.

Historical was what they wanted, and history is what they got. When they walked through it after closing, the interior looked nearly identical to how it did during his visits as a child. Shelley's desire for updating quickly overcame any lingering nostalgia, and he and Shelley began a year of renovation and remodeling, doing much of the work themselves. Although difficult, it was a true labor of love, and they often ended their weekend of stripping, painting, refinishing and dry walling by sharing a box of chicken and a six-pack in the back yard, using empty five-gallon paint buckets as chairs. They called it the Sunday Night Special, and the evening usually wrapped up with their returning to their temporary apartment for a quick tandem shower and some pre-child love making, after which they would pass out on the bed for a night of deep, dreamless sleep. "Heck of a way to start a work week," Matt would comment before dozing off.

Their efforts resulted in an incredibly comfortable, modern-yet-vintage bungalow they called home. It was current enough for their tastes and needs, but still retained the kind of charm that comes only with age. It was also large enough for a young family, and procreate they did. Shelley gave birth to Finley just over twelve months after the paint dried, and John Welty followed nearly three years to the date. They often talked of growing old together in that place, but the storm's wrath put an end to such musings.

Of course, Matt could not blame it entirely on the hurricane. After all, his actions – not Mother Nature's – prompted Shelley to leave with the boys earlier that summer.

And they had not come back.

Matt turned to the house. He had no idea how to even begin explaining this newest misfortune. It would add yet another layer to an already untenable situation. What few conversations he'd had with Shelley since his return from Nevada were strained at best – knockdown drag-outs at worst. The wound was still terribly raw, so much so that she never mentioned what happened – not even once. Matt thought he could at least get her back to the table if he had a chance to clear the air and explain everything, but she would have none of it.

At least she hadn't brought the kids into it, or at least he didn't think she had. His exchanges with the boys were always bright spots, dimmed only by his inability to tell them exactly when he would see them again. Perhaps, he thought, if he could only find something that survived, it could provide a link to the past he and Shelley could both share and possibly open a door or two. Some common ground would do them good and could be a catalyst for discussion, if nothing else.

Their cottage had twisted, turned, and eventually moved off its foundation, leaving part of the structure resting on the old crawl space and the other half pushed ten feet into the front yard. The area that he once called the laundry room had spilled out into the front yard, and the garage sale refrigerator they used for beer, soft drinks and extra juice boxes lay on its side, partially opened. The center of the home had broken apart, and the space once occupied by a kitchen and den now held mud, broken joists, and belongings – some of which Matt didn't recognize. As he walked around to the side, Matt thought of Dorothy's home after it fell on the Wicked Witch of the West, but instead of candy-striped stockings and red ruby slippers poking out of the crawl space, he saw the lid of his red Weber grill and an iron floor lamp with the base twisted over to the side. Matt found two of his ties, one loafer, his bathrobe, and someone else's jacket matted up next to a withering azalea. Somehow, one of Shelley's bras had twisted around a broken windowsill.

When he made it around the front, he stopped for a moment to take in the neighborhood. Across the street, one of the homes fared better, but the others didn't do so well. One looked oddly out of place, now that it had separated from its garage; another had a massive rectangular hole where the side porch had ripped off, taking the living area wall with it. The majority of the remaining homes had been reduced to piles of rubble, although some still had roofs.

An odd smell hung in the air, and Matt couldn't pinpoint the source. He thought it smelled like old mud, wood rot, and some other unknown. It didn't quite smell like death, but it didn't bring happy thoughts to mind, either.

Matt stood for several minutes just looking, but still not believing. He didn't even recognize a lot of the things that had washed up; many of them floated in with the surge and ended up in his yard when the water retreated. A stereo speaker with the cable trailing from the back. A Star Wars action figure case shaped like Darth Vader. A baseball trophy with the batter's head broken off. A sleeper sofa on its back with the foldout bed extended, bent and partially sticking straight up. A Tigger Halloween costume, its fur matted and discolored from the mud. He walked around the side of his house and put all his weight on the pitched wall to see if it would cave in. After several attempts with not even a budge – and feeling somewhat safe – he walked around the front, turned and stepped through the open breezeway that at one time sheltered the front porch leading into the den.

He made his way by navigating and jumping between the joists and pieces of brick crisscrossing the two-by-tens. No furniture remained, no cabinets, no appliances, no sinks and, in many rooms, no floors. The wall studs retained small strips of sheetrock up near the crown molding, and electrical wires hung down from gaps in the ceiling. A layer of mud covered the ground. No more artwork, no computer, no television – not even the kitchen refrigerator – was anywhere to be seen.

Matt focused and scanned the interior for something – anything – recognizable. At first, he saw little, but as the initial shock wore off, Matt noticed that some things, although small, could be recovered. The first item he found was one of his granny's sterling silver serving spoons – given to him and Shelley as a wedding gift. Upon further digging, he located three knives, eight forks, and two teaspoons. He suspected he had hit the mother lode and made a plan to come back to that area with a rake and a shovel. Right now, though, the sludge was too thick, and the glass shards made it too dangerous for him to dig anymore with his bare fingers.

He kept poking around in different rooms and eventually found a set of intact coffee mugs and a McCarty pottery rabbit, one of many Shelley collected, unscathed. He noticed that the old cross above the doorway that once led to their bedroom remained in place. He found a blue carrying case of Fin's Hot Wheels pushed up against a door facing. Matt pulled a bent-up wire magazine rack from under a pile of bricks and loaded it up with whatever else he could salvage; before too long, his makeshift basket filled up with odds and ends, most in their pre-hurricane condition. He came to the remains of a door hanging on to its upper hinge and immediately recognized the corner of a frame wedged between a couch pad and their old cast iron tub. He picked it up and turned it over, and for the second time that day, his throat tightened up.

This was it.

It had been their first "professional" family photo, taken on the beach in Ocean Springs. Shelley and Matt sat in the sand wearing khaki pants and white shirts with Fin and J.W. strategically posed in front of them, Fin's hand resting on J.W.'s chubby leg. Fin's big brown eyes melted Matt's heart, and if he looked closely enough, he could see a tiny bit of drool at the corner of J.W.'s toothless grin.

Matt stepped out from under the roof and sat down on a hunk of concrete to take a closer look. It was mud-smeared, discolored, and some of the emulsion had worn off, but all things considered, the photo was in fine shape. His hands traced Shelley's face first, then Fin's and J.W.'s, and his thoughts went back to when it was taken. It was a Friday afternoon. He left work early, so they could arrive in time to get set up before the sun went down. They spent almost an hour posing in various spots along the beach. As the sky darkened, the family took a barefoot stroll down the area where the sand met the water, and wrapped up the night with some barbecue at The Shed. On the way home, he and Shelley held hands while the boys dozed off in their car seats. Of all the things he had recovered so far, this by far meant the most. Matt stood up and carried the photo out to his truck.

He placed it behind the seat and pulled out a bottled water, then walked around to the back of the truck, dropped the tailgate, and sat down and faced the beach. The Gulf was as still as the air, and he wondered how this could be since it had been so angry just hours before. At any other time, Matt would have thought it peaceful, but not now. He felt betrayed by the surf. He sipped and pondered and pointed his face up to the sky. A sudden noise made him freeze.

Matt knew the metallic double-clicking sound that broke the silence – he had heard it many times in his blind up in the Delta. But this was no duck hunt, and before he had time to react, a shotgun blast rang out behind him.

5

MATT HIT THE ground and rolled on his stomach, curse words flying out, first in surprise and then, realizing he had not been shot, in anger. He scrambled partway under the truck, peering between the tires, hoping to get a bead on the feet of the shooter. Spent buckshot pinged off the truck and fell down around him. Then an angry, hoarse voice hollered:

"State your business or I'll shoot again."

Matt had placed his Smith & Wesson snub-nose .38 in his backpack and thought for a second about crawling around front to get it, but he wasn't sure where the shooter was and didn't want to risk exposing himself. He replayed the voice in his head. Did it sound a tiny bit familiar?

"Take it easy," Matt called out, as loud as he could from his position. "What do you want?"

"I asked you first, you sumbitch, and I ain't askin' a-gin. STATE YOUR BUSINESS." Only this time it sounded more like "bidness." Matt grinned with recognition and yelled back.

"Hank, it's me. It's Matt. Put that damned gun down, you crazy old bastard."

"Who? Wha- well dammit, boy, why didn't you say so? Heard that tailgate drop and thought it was more thiev'ry. Come on out where I can see you, son. C'mon out."

Matt peered around the fender and saw Hank Mallette standing on his front sidewalk with a .12-gauge angled over Matt's roof. The sight of the old man with his Carhartt overalls tucked into his boots and his boonie hat pushed back on his head tickled Matt, and his mood lightened for the first time in days. Much to Matt's surprise, he even started laughing. "Damn, Hank," Matt said, still chuckling as he pulled himself out from under the truck. "You scared the shit out of me."

Hank stood about six foot five and had a gray-white grown-out beard, which he rarely took the effort to groom. His hair was a shade darker and notable if, for nothing else, general lack of attention. Matt wondered how often a brush, comb or razor got close to Hank's head. The one time he asked about it, Hank said he brushed his hair once a week, whether he needed it or not.

Hank approached Matt, grinning through his beard, Mossberg tucked under his arm, and Matt noticed Hank's eyes were a little red. Instead of the usual handshake, Hank opted for a full-bore bear hug. He held it for a few seconds, causing Matt to remember just how cockstrong this old bastard was.

"Sorry about your home, son," Hank said, patting Matt on the back. "Terrible thing. Terrible thing."

Matt pulled back and pointed next door. "How'd y'all do?"

Hank wiped his nose with the back of his hand, sniffled, and paused a second to collect himself before responding. "Whew. Dammit, boy. Been slingin' snot all morning."

Matt nodded and rested his hand on Hank's shoulder.

Hank looked at Matt, blinking furiously, and then turned to his house. "First floor's shot to shit. You get about halfway up the stairs, though, it's the damnedest thing. No damage whatsoever."

"Sarah?" Matt asked.

"Not good, not good." Hank often said things twice. "In there somewhere, trying to sort through what's left. Best I let her be for now, if you know what I mean. Our foundation's fine, so we'll be okay, just have to gut the first floor and redo it. 'Spect we'll live upstairs in the meantime. Spoke to Shelley?"

"No. Phone's dead," Matt said. Hank, living next door, couldn't have overlooked Shelley and the boys moving out if he'd tried, and

Matt had even talked to him about it a little. Hank was fond of Shelley, and not having the boys around to take fishing perturbed him greatly.

"I meant before all this," Hank said, waving his hand over his head and at the street behind him.

"Can't say that I have recently." Matt changed the subject. "Hey, y'all didn't ride this out *here*, did you?"

"Sure did. Rough going. Thought the water'd never stop risin'. Thankful the Good Lord finally pulled the plug. Me and Sarah watched it come up and just take over the neighborhood." He spat on the ground, and Matt noticed the tobacco stain on his beard next to the corner of his mouth. "We ended up tying ourselves together with belts up in the attic in case we got washed out."

Matt looked at him for a second. For this old salt to take a measure like that spoke volumes about the storm. "How close did it get?"

"From what I could tell, water was about eight feet in our house. Scary stuff, Matt. Scary stuff. I never seen anything like it." Again, Matt thought, this must have been a mother. "House was shaking like a A-rab in a igloo. Thought at one point the roof was gonna come down on us."

"Hard to believe, Hank."

"Damndest thing, Matt," Hank said, his eyes suddenly distant. After a few seconds of silence, he shook his head, hocked real loud and spat again, then dug the spent tobacco from his cheek and flung it on the ground. He glanced back at his house. "Sarah ain't too happy with me chawin' again," Hank said, under his breath.

"I can't imagine why," Matt said and nodded at the shotgun. "Think you'll need that?"

Hank blew into the barrel, reached into the bib pocket of his overalls, grabbed a handful of shells and reloaded. "Seen some looters pokin' round the street before you got here. Shame someone would take this tragedy and use it for mischief." Sarah stuck her head out to make sure she could get a visual on Hank. She saw

Matt and waved at him with gloved hands before ducking back inside with a push broom.

"You need any food?" Hank asked. "I got a whole closet upstairs full of MREs. Lots of MREs." Hank enjoyed the preservative-packed military-issued, ready-to-eat meals during better times, and this wasn't the first invite Matt had received. It was the first time, however, Matt accepted the offer.

"Considering the fact that there's nothing open between here and D'Lo, I guess I'll take you up on it," Matt said, following Hank into his home and up to the second floor.

"They're better'n they used to be. Little tiny jars of Tabasco in most of 'em. Makes any meal taste better. Tabasco'll do that, though, be careful when you shake it; it will tear the ass out of you if you use too much." Hank opened up the door to what used to be a walk-in closet. It was stacked from floor to ceiling with supplies. "Think a case will do?"

Matt's jaw dropped and he whistled. "Damn, Hank. You expecting an invasion?" Hank was an ex-Navy SEAL who moved with Sarah to Second Street after serving two tours in Vietnam. He told most people he moved to Gulfport to work in nautical engineering. Truth was, after he got out of the Navy he spent over three decades designing and manufacturing black ops boats for the military in a nondescript American Marine machine shop off Seaway Road in East Gulfport. He had been known to bring his work home with him on occasion, but Matt had no idea just how thorough Hank had been with his collecting. Not only did the closet contain ample rations, there were also rifles, pistols, scopes, and ammunition arranged in racks and shelves, along with radios, batteries, flashlights, water purification kits, blankets, flares, and what looked like a harpoon. Hank grinned and winked at Matt. "I don't expect to have any trouble on my watch. Like my old D.I. used to tell us, 'Far better to have and not need, than need and not have.'"

"I can see that," Matt said. "He must've had quite an impact on you."

"Quit starin' and take what you need."

Matt obliged and started back to his truck with the case of MREs, a flashlight, a blanket, a small Igloo cooler of ice – one of several Sarah had pre-packed in advance of the storm – and a two-way radio.

"Keep the radio on channel seven," Hank said. "If you need me, just key it up and I'll get to it eventually. Receiver's got a sleep function on it to save the juice. Keep it on there or you'll drain the cell battery."

"Hank, I don't need a radio –"

"What if you blow a tire or your truck breaks down? Now's not the time to get stuck. Not the time. Now let me help you load this."

Hank followed Matt back across the front yard. They both looked down the street, and again the magnitude of the damage awed them. Neither said anything for a few minutes, and Hank ran his fingers through his beard and pulled on his chin, as if he was picking off a tick.

"Thanks again for all your help, Hank."

"Not a problem, son. Where you layin' your head?"

"I'm going downtown and check on the office. If it's habitable, I'll set up camp there. Your talk about looters has me concerned."

"Hmm. Fair enough. If not, you can rack here." Sarah again appeared at the doorway. "See that? I'm in the doghouse if I don't go see what she wants. If you come back tonight, radio me first." Hank chuckled and tapped on the gun barrel. "Otherwise, you may hear from Ol' Blue again."

Matt smiled back. "Will do." Hank pulled a box out of his pocket with *Remington* scrolled across the lid. "Take these for your piece." Matt started to protest, but Hank had already begun walking back toward the house.

"You take care of yourself," Hank said, "and your family." He glanced over his shoulder. "I mean it."

Matt watched him go back in, and by Sarah's body language, Matt could see Hank visited a little too long for her liking. "Will do," Matt said again, mainly to himself, and threw the ammo on the front seat.

He leaned on his truck and considered more excavating to see what else he could find. It was getting late, though, and, without the benefit of any lights, he needed to go ahead and get to his office before sunset. For a split second, and out of pure habit, Matt thought he better lock the house up before he left. When he realized how ludicrous that sounded, he just shook his head, took another look around, and climbed in the truck.

6

OWNTOWN GULFPORT SAT a little higher above the seawall than
Matt's neighborhood, and from what he could tell in the twi-
light, the damage near his office, though substantial, was not catastrophic. He pulled up to his building, eased around a downed
streetlight, and parked. The bronze plaque that read BINGHAM,
SAMSON & TOFLIN, PLLC still hung above the door.

The building, which at one time operated as a mom-and-pop
general store after World War II, rose two stories. The ground
floor contained the reception area, conference room, break area/
kitchen, and restrooms. A landing at the top of the stairs separated
the two lawyer offices: Matt's to the left; his office mate and law
partner's to the right. Both overlooked the street.

The first floor wasn't gutted, but it had taken a lot of water. The
furniture ended up in an odd, wet, muddy stack in the middle of
the room, as if a burglar had come in with the sole purpose of rear-
ranging the place, dropping a load of dirt on the floor and running a sprinkler on top of it. It smelled wet, but hadn't yet turned
musty. On the wall, an ominous line registered the high water-
mark. It came up to Matt's waist. After moving a soaked Oriental
rug, which had somehow made its way across the room from its
prior resting place in the lobby and up the first four steps in the
stairwell, Matt loped up to the second floor to see how it fared.

The closed offices blocked any available upstairs light, and
Matt had to hold his keys close to his face to find the right one.
He inserted it into the lock, felt the heavy tumbler turn, and

shoulder-bumped his swollen door to get it to open. The pre-dusk glow coming through his windows illuminated the room and spilled out onto the landing. As his eyes adjusted, Matt checked out his office.

"Well, I'll be," he said to himself. "Hank was right. Looks just like I left it." He dropped his backpack on the couch and did a quick inspection of the room. Everything seemed to be in place. It was stuffy as hell so he opened a window to let the air inside and the view caught him off guard. He could look south all the way to the beach in one direction, and north just past the railroad tracks in the other. A small path had been cleared to allow vehicle access, but the rest of the street looked like a war zone. "Damn." He leaned out to try to get a better look at the harbor, but the only thing he could make out were a number of overturned truck shipping containers that had likely been stored off the main pier.

Having neither water nor electricity, Matt decided he'd better use the remaining light wisely, so he finished unloading his truck and set up camp. He peeled his clothes off, stripped down to his boxers, and inventoried the MREs. He tore into one of the hard, brown plastic bags labeled Chicken a la King. It wasn't great, but it was palatable, and Hank was right. Copious amounts of Tabasco added a welcome kick. He felt full after eating just the entrée and set the rest aside. Using bottled water, he scrubbed his hands and face and brushed his teeth with a toothbrush he kept in his desk drawer.

With his flashlight, he looked at himself in the mirror of the small bathroom in the hallway just outside his door. His brown hair, which always turned lighter in the summer, was wet and darker around his forehead where he washed up. He hadn't yet truly begun to age, but years of living under the sun were starting to show. He was still tan, at least around his face and on his arms, but the crow's feet around his brown eyes seemed to exhibit some permanence. A few grays had recently made an appearance above his temples, but he could see them only if he looked closely. He stared for a few seconds, flexed his mouth and cheeks, spat into the sink, and rubbed his whisker shadow before turning back to his office.

For good measure he propped a chair up under the knob in case any looters decided to make their way to his office. He also made sure the .38 was loaded and placed it, the box of shells Hank gave him and the flashlight on the bookshelf within arm's reach. Then he folded out the couch that sat against the wall and looked out into the darkness. Without electricity and almost no traffic, the night turned the city an inky black. He propped himself on the windowsill and stared at the stars, trying without luck to identify any constellations other than the Big Dipper. The stillness conflicted him – soothing on one hand, yet completely illogical on the other. Gulfport should be active, if not buzzing at this hour. Instead, no cars traveled on the roads; no phones rang; and no voices sounded from the street below.

He didn't know how long he stayed there and stared, but after some time, a heavy weariness came over him, and he stretched out spread eagle on the thin mattress. For the first time since his return earlier that afternoon, he felt a slight breeze waft in from the Gulf that chased some of the heat out, although not enough to dull the sheen on his skin. His phone glowed 8:51. He couldn't remember the last time he'd gone to bed this early. But what else was he going to do? It wasn't like he could read, call anyone, work, or watch TV. Besides, it was so dark he could barely see his hand in front of his face. He tried to adjust the couch pillow but had little luck finding even a marginal degree of comfort. He said a short prayer, remembering things he remained thankful for, and tried to discern God's will amidst this chaos.

As sleep closed in, Matt's thoughts turned, yet again, to his family. He ached to hold the boys and wondered what they were doing at that moment. He blinked into the darkness and, like he had done nearly every day since he returned from Las Vegas, cursed his actions and lack of judgment that led to his self-inflicted solitude.

7

MATT JERKED AWAKE on the pullout couch, glistening from the heat ushered in by the morning light. He forgot where he was for a second or two, then, remembering the hurricane, dropped his head back to the pillow, and threw his arm across his face to block the glare. He felt the urge to just lie there, but self-preservation outweighed self-pity, and he figured he needed to get back to his house to see what else he could recover before someone else recovered it for him.

He yawned at the ceiling, stretched his legs over the arms of the tweed couch and swung up into sitting position, resting his feet on the dark floor. He checked his watch: 6:45 a.m. What little breeze there had been during the night was no more, and he felt sticky all over. Matt reached for his phone, but a quick glance told him he still had no signal. He *really* needed to speak with the boys – for his well-being and theirs. He shook some bottled water in his face, grabbed a Little Debbie cupcake and stretched. He slid on his shoes and a pair of shorts and walked downstairs to take a leak in the alley out back.

Emergency vehicles and National Guard Hummers worked their way between the light poles and signs that spilled out across the right of way. Matt seemed to remember hearing helicopters during the night, and sure enough, when he glanced up, he saw three Blackhawks flying down the shoreline. He heard a siren way off in the distance, and a fine wisp of dark smoke rose a few miles north. A group of soldiers lined up near the beach, looking at a map and pointing. One was taking pictures.

Matt wanted to see more of the city, and with all the debris, he figured his interests could be best served by walking instead of driving. He ran back upstairs and dropped a few waters in his pack and pulled it on his shoulders. He slid his gun in his pocket and locked his door on the way out.

The situation looked even worse up close. A sailboat hull rested in a storefront window, its broken keel jutting up and casting a long shadow across the entrance. Banged-up and overturned vehicles transformed the sidewalks and roads into one large municipal junkyard. Debris was everywhere – in buildings, on buildings and under buildings. The city stunk of wet dirt, open sewage and rotting trash. Matt saw his first dead animal – a black Labrador pinned under a stretch of twisted chain link, and he turned away.

The dog nearly got Matt killed. He kept thinking how much the animal must have struggled in those last minutes, fighting the water as it overtook him. Head down, Matt started to cross the street near the post office. He was wondering if he should go turn and check the dog's collar to see if he could get the name or number of its owner when out of the corner of his eye he saw a large vehicle bearing down on him. Matt dove back towards the sidewalk just in time to avoid getting hit. Apparently the driver of the big Suburban hadn't been paying attention either, based on the driver's failure to honk and the length of the skid marks before the truck finally came to a stop. Matt popped up, madder than hell, but when he realized the near-hit was probably more his fault than anyone's, he waved an apology at the man, a haggard-looking redheaded fellow that reminded Matt of Sam Trotter, the tooth-challenged handyman who repaired lawnmowers down off 28th Street. Matt couldn't hear the cursing through the window, but the driver's twisted face said it all. Matt tried to act as contrite as possible, and it must have worked, because once he finally looked at Matt, he sped off, with not so much as the finger. Matt dropped his hand and glanced at the tag. It wasn't local. He watched the truck navigate around a turned-over set of blue and white post office drop boxes and move out of sight.

Matt sidestepped a large armoire with one missing door and struggled up a piece of angled asphalt. Over the next two hours, he continued through the city, trying to determine what made it and what didn't, before coming nearly full circle and ending up at the beach. The shoreline was empty, and the low tide left large sections of oak branches and trees embedded in the wet sand. He didn't hear one seagull or tern, nor did he see any pelicans skimming the surface. He sat down on the seawall and just stared. The beach, like the rest of his city, was still. He eventually turned back and faced the tree line. Of all the things he saw that rang out in his mind, it was what he didn't see that affected him the most.

He'd never considered that the Gulfport he knew could disappear in a matter of hours. He thought of the shared histories in all those old homes and felt sad that no one – him included – ever got to say goodbye. Wood, brick, steel, and mortar made up the structures, but they were much more than just the sum of their materials. They were places of first walks, birthday parties, and tire swings. They had welcomed veterans home from wars, the sick from hospitals, and many a couple were married in those yards. The trees were perfect for picnics and water balloon fights; the grandeur of the ancient gardenias, ligustrum, and camellias created magical places to hide Easter eggs or play hide-and-seek. The porches provided shelter for neighbors and strangers alike and served as staging areas for first kisses and nervous handholding. Yet these homes, ancestral museums in their own right, were now just memories, and most of their inhabitants – at least for a little while longer – remained blissfully ignorant of their losses.

He walked down into the sand to check out a large pile of driftwood the storm deposited just outside the receding tide. He flung a piece back toward the sea and looked at the rest of the gnarled, wet branches piled together like a rained-out funeral pyre. He pulled out a peculiar-shaped piece that looked interesting and considered taking it with him, but a glance toward the direction of his office building interrupted his thoughts. To his surprise, there was a familiar white Yukon parked in its usual spot – to the right of the front door.

He had company! Matt stood and retraced his steps at a much swifter pace. He looked forward to catching up with his law partner and friend and would be glad to have someone else to visit with.

"Hey, partner, it's me," he yelled as he darted up the stairs. "It's Matt!" he said again, as he reached the landing and saw the door was cracked, a slice of light falling into the foyer. "Hello?" He knocked but heard nothing. Matt felt the hair on his neck stand on end.

"You in there?" he called out.

Not a peep. *Something's not right.*

"Well, don't jump up and come running," he said, forcing a laugh as he opened the door. When Matt looked in, he stopped, gasped, and almost fell down trying to get back out of the opening. His breaths came in short, fast bursts, so much so he got dizzy from hyperventilation. He tried to steady himself on the banister at the top of the stairs. He glanced in again and felt as if he might pass out.

Blood, hair, and bone fragments covered the back of the office chair and some splattered remnants stuck on the back wall close to the ceiling. A body lay slumped over his desk, gun next to his hand.

"Oh no," Matt whimpered. "Oh no, oh no, oh no." Matt slammed the door and took off down the stairs. He burst outside and ran down the sidewalk, not going anywhere in particular, but away from his building. He misjudged the distance of a hole in the concrete and landed short, banging his shin onto the jagged rock and splaying him out into the street. He rolled over, unfazed by his bloodied leg, and continued running. He heaved in and out so deeply that the pain in and under his ribs overtook his throbbing leg, and caused him to lean to one side. He tried to scream for help, but he could not produce much noise of any type. When a squad of National Guardsmen finally stopped him, Matt crumpled into a heap on the ground, his eyes wild, his face wet and shiny with tears and sweat.

It took them some time to calm him down enough to tell them what happened, and, even then, as they dressed his wound, he could barely communicate what he had seen.

Down the street, blue lights strobed, and later, Matt could not bring himself to do much more than stand outside and gape – like the rest of the onlookers – as they wheeled the covered body out on a gurney. His law partner, friend and office mate was under that sheet, yet Matt still could not believe it – and would not have believed it if he had not seen it himself.

Jeff McCabe was dead.

8

THE NEXT COUPLE of hours felt more like an out-of-body experience than a passage of time as Matt could feel himself slowly detaching from the world around him. It was similar to dreams he'd had that seemed so vivid and detailed on the surface but upon further introspection had no depth. He often tried to stop his dreams in the middle to try to inspect them more deeply. Read a sign. Look in someone's eyes. Take in the environment. It never worked. Words washed out into nothingness; faces never materialized; the surroundings constructed in his semi-consciousness turned out to be nothing more than window dressing. This was how it felt now, only this was reality. He recalled sirens – loud, noisy, blaring all around him for what seemed like a long time. Lots of huddled, random people, some in uniforms, some not, and nearly every one turning and looking his way at one time or another. He recalled multiple fire trucks and one singular ambulance. An especially somber man walked in and out of the building taking notes flanked by police officers and men in suits also taking notes. Occasionally someone would offer Matt some water or something to eat, but mostly they just left him alone. As the first responders started to leave, someone led Matt to the front seat of a squad car, which took him to the police station. Despite his condition, he was told he had to give a statement and they thought it best to do it away from all the chaos.

So there he sat, on a state-purchased tan and cream colored naugahyde loveseat in the office of George Halliday, Gulfport's Chief of Police. The chief was not exactly a stranger, as Matt used to hang out with his son Tim back in high school. He had one of the best driveways in Gulfport for basketball, and Matt and his buddies played many a pickup game there. Chief Halliday was running late because he was giving the Governor a VIP tour of the destruction, so Matt had to wait it out and listen to an eager corporal blather on about how the President may come down in a few days. Matt would have thought this cool at one time, but now he pretty much didn't give a shit.

He had never, ever felt this depressed. He came close when he got home that terrible afternoon and found his family packed up and gone, but this was something altogether more complex. The shock and loss from the hurricane was bad enough, and now finding his law partner dead was too much. Matt was done crying. Now he just felt like giving up. It didn't help that he was left in the room with a rookie cop who looked and sounded like he should be serving corn dogs at the state fair. Matt wished the guy would just shut up, but he kept droning on an on about his *jawb* and how he hoped to get a picture with the *guv-uh-ner*. Matt tried to ignore him and turned inward, telling himself that this too, would pass, but when it didn't, his emotions ran from hysteria to anger to exhaustion, and any random remembrance of either Jeff or Shelley could trigger a spike or dip, one way or the other.

Mercifully, his new friend got called out, presumably to fetch coffee for someone more important, and Matt no longer had to clench his jaws to keep from saying something he shouldn't. He found an old Field and Stream sitting on a side table and flipped through the pages to try to occupy his mind. A dispatcher (nice and quiet this time) brought him a lukewarm Sprite and a small bag of M&Ms then left. He ate them one by one. The police station's generators were fully operational, and he was surprised to find that the air conditioner, which had cooled him off, now made him rub his arms to try to get the goose bumps down.

After what seemed like an hour or so, Chief Halliday showed up along with his driver and a secretary who took notes. Chief Halliday carried himself in a manner befitting his position – crisp, polished, media-trained – and despite the fact that his city was in shambles, he looked like a bright penny. Even his boots were shiny and polished. He moved some papers off the couch and took a seat right next to Matt.

"It's been a long time since I've seen you, son," Halliday said with a big smile, his pearly whites in full display. When Matt didn't respond, Chief Halliday put his lips together in a sympathetic pucker, as if he was trying to say "hmm" and lowered his eyebrows. "Sorry for your loss."

"Thanks, Mr. Halliday."

"Call me George." Matt always found it weird calling the adults he knew as a kid by their first name. He'd always be Mr. Halliday or Chief Halliday, no matter how old Matt got.

"I'll do my best," Matt said.

"Now tell me what happened."

Matt walked Chief Halliday through the day and tried to explain everything he could recall. Matt went even further back and started with his return to Gulfport, his night at the office, his walkabout the next day, and finally the dreaded discovery. The girl, sitting in the chief's chair, wrote in her pad the whole time. She stopped writing and wiped an eye when Matt discussed the gory details. No one spoke but Matt, and there were few interruptions.

"Anything in the building seem unusual?"

"What?"

"Anything out of the ordinary catch your eye?"

"Well, yes. Jeff with the back of his head missing was certainly an attention-getter." Matt felt nauseated.

Chief Halliday took a deep breath, blinked a few times and nodded. He put his hand on Matt's shoulder and squared up. "I didn't mean to sound so cold, Matt. That was not my intent. We always have to ask questions about the scene, even in cases of suicide."

"What?"

"I'm sorry you had to go see all of this, Matt," the Chief said. "I checked out the office myself and it's an awful sight. You know Jeff was a friend of mine, too."

"Suicide?"

"No one knows why people do this to themselves, but some folks just can't handle catastrophic events as well as others." He turned to Matt. "This is the third that's been reported since yesterday."

"Really?"

"One in Ocean Springs – elderly man. Single mom in Bay St. Louis."

"No, that's not what I meant," Matt said. "You – you really think Jeff *killed* himself?" Matt knew in the back of his mind since he found Jeff that this was a potential, if not probable, explanation, but until now had not been able to bring himself to fully consider it. In fact, if he really thought about it, it made the most sense. Regardless, to say the word out loud made him sick to his stomach.

"I do, Matt. Seen many crime scenes in my day, and this one fits the bill. No foul play. Coroner called it first."

"I don' t see how. Not him. I just don't put Jeff in the category of someone who would commit… "

"No one ever does, son," Chief Halliday said, "in fact…"

Matt realized immediately he was about to get yet another speech, and this one seemed too polished to be off the cuff. Chief Halliday had likely used it on many occasions throughout his career to counsel and comfort families and friends on the surviving end of a tragedy, but Matt was in no mood to hear it. He pretended to follow along and turned inward again to try and reckon with the fact that Jeff had shot himself. He nodded as Chief Halliday continued his diatribe by walking through the various stages of grief, using large hand gestures to make his point, but Matt was elsewhere. He kept returning to the moment he found Jeff, as much as it disgusted him, and couldn't figure out why his mind kept recycling those images. Something nagged at him, but just like in his dreams, details once again failed him. The image of slumped-over Jeff short-circuited his thought process, and he just couldn't conjure up anything else. He realized it was hopeless so he turned back to the speech and realized that the room had gone silent.

"Son," Chief Halliday asked, "you okay?"

When Matt looked up, all eyes were on him, and he wondered how long he had zoned out. He kept his face long and forlorn for impact, then stood and shook Chief Halliday's hand. He mustered out a few words of thanks as earnestly as he could and asked if Jeff's wife had been notified. The secretary piped up and told him that after many unsuccessful efforts, they were finally able to reach Cathy McCabe through Red Cross and FEMA emergency channels. Not surprisingly, she was too distraught to talk, much less drive. Cathy's sister was to bring her down the next day or two from Tupelo, where she stayed during the storm. As Matt was leaving, corn dog ran him down and told him that a team had been dispatched to clean up Jeff's office, and that Matt might want to give it some time before he returned. The young police officer then showed Matt a picture of he and the governor on his phone taken right before the governor flew back to Jackson. Matt was not impressed and was perhaps a little too strong with his response although, again, he didn't give a shit at this point.

They dropped him back off at his office, and he was finally dismissed. His truck was still parked next to Jeff's Yukon, and Matt stared at it a few minutes, thinking about the day. He had heard when a friend or loved one committed suicide, those left behind were often angry. But Matt wasn't mad. He was bewildered. Confused. Disbelieving. But not angry. Regardless, he had no intention of staying at his office so he headed back to Hank's. He grabbed the handheld radio and dialed up the old man on Channel 7, just as he had been told. He already learned the hard way Hank had a shoot-first-and-ask-questions-later outlook on things.

It wasn't a philosophy Matt wanted to test again.

9

WHEN HANK AND Sarah greeted him at the door with a pat on the back and a warm hug, Matt knew the bad news had already spread. Matt told them the same story he told Chief Halliday, even though neither asked him to, but he felt Hank, with his background, wanted to hear what little details Matt could offer. "Made me realize things can change in an instant, Hank," he said. "Three days ago, life was normal for Jeff. Most of us, for that matter." Matt looked out the window, and no one spoke. He dropped his head. "I sure miss my family."

"You need to speak to 'em," Hank said, clearing his throat. "Call 'em."

"Can't." Matt tapped his phone. "Nothing. Plus, Hank, Shelley doesn't want to speak to me."

"Aw, shit. The hell you say." Hank got up and walked out of the room. Matt looked over at Sarah. She patted him on the knee.

"What's her number?" Hank yelled from the other room.

"What?" Matt asked.

"Her number. Where's she stayin'?" Hank marched back in carrying what looked like an oversized cell phone with a large, black antenna the size of a cigar poking out the top.

"What in the world?" Matt asked.

"Satellite phone. Borry'd it from the shop. Nipponese, so you know this sumbitch works. Now give me that number." Matt looked over at Sarah who shrugged her shoulders with a "go ahead" look on her face, so he called out Shelley's cell, and Hank entered it on the satellite phone. Hank handed the receiver to Matt and nodded to Sarah. "We'll be outside."

Matt didn't have time to collect his thoughts before the ringing began on the other end. He hadn't spoken to Shelley since the storm. Where should he start? The house? Jeff? When he heard the voice on the other end, all scripted dialogue flew out the window.

"Hello?"

"F-Fin?"

"Daddy?!?"

"Hey, buddy!" Matt barely got the words out before the lump in his throat choked him up. He could hear Fin yelling on the other line, "Mommy, Mommy, Daddy's on the phone! Daddy's on the phone!" Shelley said something he couldn't understand and then he heard J.W.'s voice in the background, also yelling something gleefully imperceptible.

"Oh, I'm so glad to hear your voice," Matt said. "I've been missing you, my man. How are you?"

"Good. Daddy, are you okay?"

"I'm fine."

"When are you going to come see me again?"

"As soon as I can." Matt hadn't cried in two consecutive days since elementary school. He found the section on his shirt with the least amount of dirt and wiped his eyes. "I miss y'all so much."

"I miss you too. Mommy said the hurricane was really scary. Is my swing set okay?"

"May have to get you a new one. That one was getting worn out anyway, right?"

"We've been trying to call you, but you never answered."

"Well, I tried to call you too, but I couldn't get the phone to work. I'm so glad you picked up just now, though. Are you taking care of J.W. and Mommy?"

"Yes, sir. Daddy, J.W. wants to speak to you." Matt could hear Shelley helping J.W. with the phone, which brought even more tears to his eyes. J.W. was just over two, but on most days Matt could make out what his younger boy was saying. It was always easier face to face, though.

"Hey, Daddy." Again, Matt's world came into focus with those two words, and he felt the full impact of being absent from his sons' lives.

"Hey, J-dub."

"I'm at Mimi's."

"I know you are. You having fun?"

"Yes, sir."

"I miss you, buddy."

"I miss you, Daddy. We're going to Chick-fil-A." He pronounced it *chifeeyay* but Matt understood him.

"You are? I wish I could go." He wasn't just saying that. He really wished he could go.

"Me too. They have ice cream." Matt smiled. J.W. was an ice cream hound. "Bye-bye."

"I love you, J.W."

J.W. was already off the phone, and Matt heard Fin telling him they were getting a new swing set.

"Hey." Shelley's voice sounded cool and a bit anxious.

"Hey," Matt said, trying to hold back the avalanche.

"We've been trying to get you, but couldn't get through. What number are you calling from?"

"Hank has a satellite phone he is letting me use. I haven't had a signal since I left Jackson." He stumbled getting the last part out.

"Matt? Are you okay?"

With that question, Matt let go. The events of the prior week blindsided him, and Jeff's death had finally pushed him over the edge. He didn't even try to stop it. He gushed for what seemed like a long time before he was finally able to calm down enough to tell her about the city and the neighborhood. Each recitation was worse than the last, and by the time he got to the house, he heard a brief gasp and the familiar feminine sigh Shelley let out after a long cry. She could barely get the words out.

"Is there anything left?" she whispered.

"No, babe, not much." *Babe? What the hell?* Matt kept talking so it wouldn't hang there. "I got a few things out of the yard and dug around to see what else I could find. Some of Granny's silverware – "

"Any pictures?"

Matt felt defeated. "No, although our big photo on the beach kind of made it."

Shelley said nothing. He wanted to be there to hold his family, to provide counsel and let them know it would all be okay. He wanted to sit the boys on his lap and hug Shelley all at the same time. He wanted them to walk hand-in-hand through a park, somewhere – anywhere, for that matter as long as it was not in Gulfport and as long as all of them – *all* of them – were together. But all he could do was rest his elbows on his knees, keep the phone to his ear, and wipe his eyes. Then he took a deep breath.

"That's not the worst of it, Shelley."

"What do you mean?"

"I left the office this morning and took a walk to check out downtown. You know, see how it looked."

"Yes?"

"When I got back." He stopped and took a breath. "Whew. Okay. When I got back, I found Jeff in his office."

"And?"

"He – he's dead Shelley."

She shrieked. "Dead? Jeff? Oh, dear God. What happened?"

"They say he shot himself," Matt said, his voice turning husky.

He heard another gasp, and a few moments passed as she processed what Matt said. He heard Fin ask Shelley if she was okay before she finally got back on the line.

"Oh, Matt. I'm so sorry. So sorry. Why?"

"Don't know. No note, no nothing. Police chief thinks it was the storm. He lost everything, too, based on what the beachfront looked like. Maybe it pushed him over the edge."

"Did you even know Jeff had stayed down there during the hurricane?"

"No. I figured everyone scattered once they realized they were in the cone. You know how it is once that happens. Maybe he decided to hang back. Hank and Sarah stayed."

"They okay?"

"Yeah. A little shaken but fine."

"So sad about Jeff," she said through her tears. "So sad."

"I know. I can't believe it myself," Matt said, trying to regain his composure. "Don't think his service will be till next week. Funeral homes are all backed up."

"You said *you* found him?"

"Yes. It was awful."

"Are you okay?"

"Am *I* okay?" *She asked about you.* "Frankly, no, I'm not," Matt said. "But I will be. It would do me some good to see you and the boys, though."

"Can you try and come up here tomorrow, then?" Shelley asked. "They want to see you, too." For a second it felt like a pre-Vegas conversation. Okay, so Shelley wasn't telling him how much *she* missed him, but the fact that she'd invited him to Meridian was a good sign.

"Nothing would make me happier," he said. "But right now it's not even possible. There's no gas. Not one station open down here, and from what they say, there won't be any for days. Plus, I owe it to Cathy to be here when she arrives."

"Poor Cathy," Shelley said. "You probably should stay at least until she gets there."

"Can you come down for the service?" Matt asked. "You could bring Fin and J.W."

"Gas stations are empty here, too," Shelley said. "Although that'll change soon, I heard. I'll come, but I don't think bringing them is a good idea. I don't want their first post-hurricane experience to be tied to a death."

No. "I know, but –"

"No. Not for that."

"But Shel –"

"Let's talk about it later. Where are you staying?" Shelley had a way of taking control of a situation, and as much as Matt's heart disagreed, he knew she was right – the boys were *really* young to endure this on top of their parents' separation. Besides, this was the first discussion they'd had in what seemed like ages that was not all vitriol. He didn't need to blow it.

"I was at the office last night. Not too bad," he said. "Couch isn't very comfortable but it served its purpose. But I can't bring myself to go back there right now. Hank said it'd be no problem if I crashed here at his house."

"Stay with Hank as long as you need to," she said. "Have you thought about coming back up to Jackson temporarily, until everything's under control on the Coast? Bet Delia would be glad to have you working up this way."

"Maybe. I still need to go through what's left of the house and see if I can recover anything else. And with all the looting I want to keep an eye on the office. It's all we have left. I'll probably wait until the service before deciding what to do. I'll try to take some pictures of everything and get them to you when I get a chance. You should see how bad it is down here, Shel."

"I'm not sure I want to. Is it as rough as it looks on the news?"

"Worse," Matt said, and cleared his throat. There was an awkward silence. *What now?* Matt knew what he wanted to say but left it alone. "Look, I don't want to burn up whatever time Hank has on this phone," he said, sensing the discomfort. "I'll call you in a few days when I know more, okay? My phone should be working soon and if not, Hank'll let me use this one."

"Okay. And Matt, I'm really sorry. Jeff was a good man."

"He was indeed, Shelley."

"It was nice talking to you. Be safe, okay?"

"I will. Let me speak to the boys one more time."

Matt told Fin goodbye and that he hoped to see him soon. J.W. got on the phone but accidentally hung up mid-sentence, which happened often. Matt grinned, then turned off the satellite phone and put it down. He stared at the floor, soaking it all in. It had not been an ideal conversation, considering the subject, but at least it didn't end with a fight; Shelley even said it was nice to talk to him, although that could have been nothing more than an effort to lift his spirits. The more he thought about everything, the more tired he felt.

He dragged himself up to Hank's big La-z-Boy, kicked off his boots, and clicked on the oscillating fan Hank had jerry-rigged up to the generator outside. He picked at the dried blood at the cuff of his sock and thought he should probably eat something, but didn't think he could stomach food at that point. He unfolded the recliner until he was horizontal and stared up at the ceiling. He couldn't ever remember feeling so utterly exhausted. As the fan turned back and forth, Matt couldn't escape the image of Jeff lying across his desk. At first it saddened him, but the more he focused on the scene, the more something nagged at him. *What is it?* Matt probably wasn't in there for more than two seconds when he found him, but still, even in that brief moment, something seemed off, out of place. In the weightless moments between consciousness and sleep, a light that had gone off earlier in Matt's brain when he was pretending to listen to Chief Halliday burned a little brighter. He tried to reach out and latch on, but fatigue beat him to the punch and the glow retreated.

It was close to midnight when he finally conked out.

10

THE NEXT MORNING, Matt awoke in a fog. He could feel the weight of grief and bite of despair pulling at him, and he thought it best to stay busy to keep his emotions at bay. He grabbed a banana and hunted down Hank's rake, put on his work gloves and walked up the sidewalk. His house looked just the same as the last visit, and Matt's emotions hadn't changed much either. Disbelief. Awe. Longing.

And he was hot. Africa hot. Already.

Second Street had much more activity now, relatively speaking. News crews from the major networks were set up in front of the "good" destroyed houses, and Matt saw Robin Roberts, a Coast native herself, broadcasting in front of a *Good Morning America* van less than a block from his lot. Inspector squads walked up and down the street spray-painting a big "X" on the front of what was left of the homes. According to one of the crew members, each quadrant of the X contained a code which identified the date the building was searched, any hazards – gas leaks or otherwise – and a body count if applicable. Matt suspected some of the houses down the street had a number in that final box.

A camera crew found Hank next door, and by Hank's grand gestures and the growing crowd, Matt could tell Hank was putting on a show. Hank hadn't bothered to buckle up his overalls, leaving his bare barrel chest and belly exposed to the world. He was basking in the attention. He looked so unconventional Matt had no doubt he would make the cut on someone's newscast. Hank pointed Matt's way, and the cameras followed the angle of sight, but Matt stepped out of view. Matt was neither in the mood nor did he intend to waste any time talking to the press, especially since he still had work to do. He set his sights on the spot where he found the silver the day before and began digging. The sun had soured the mud, and it had started to smell, but Matt bore down anyway.

By the time he took a break a few hours later, dirt, sweat and grime covered him head to toe, but he took pleasure in the fruits of his labor. In addition to finding the digging therapeutic, he recovered, by his estimate, a good bit of the heirlooms, including some serving spoons and a carving knife. When he thought about it, he could count on one hand the times Shelley and he had used the "good" silver. He swore if she ever joined him under the same roof again, he would make it a point to break it out more frequently.

He burrowed some more, and his efforts led him from the area where his den used to be to the hallway entrance. Several collapsed floor joists blocked his path, so he had to get a shovel to wedge open the gap. After some grunting, he forced open a space big enough for him to wiggle through and continue following the trail.

He was rewarded for his efforts. When the house moved off its foundation and eventually settled onto the ground, it created a cavity that provided an oasis from the damaging effects of the storm. The space took on some water, but all the jostling on the outside didn't affect the contents. Matt not only found more silver, but also discovered several pieces of their wedding china in pre-storm condition. He also found Fin's favorite Lightning McQueen melamine plate, some of J.W.'s sippy cups, and two framed photographs that, in a prior life, sat on the kitchen windowsill. In one, Matt could see Fin and J.W. grinning out of a hug from Pluto at Disney World. At least Fin was smiling; J.W. looked scared. The other frame held a picture of Matt and Shelley in Times Square.

Matt didn't see anything else in the hole and wasn't comfortable reaching in any farther. He didn't think he'd encounter moccasins this close to the salt water but didn't want to take any chances, so he grabbed his Maglite from his truck and aimed it down the crawl space. At first all he saw was mud, but as his eyes adjusted, he focused on a photo album. He squatted there for a moment and gauged whether he wanted to slide his tired ass up in there to recover some photos from an album he didn't recognize – and likely didn't own. But if a neighbor found some displaced item of his and Shelley's lodged in their house or yard, he hoped they'd go the extra mile and return the favor. So Matt had a look.

"Dammit," he said to himself, going into the hole. Mud already covered him to the point that the dirt lines in the deeper creases on his skin looked like thin streaks of paint. Getting dirtier didn't bother him. No, the issue came down to physics and, well, flexibility. The tightness of the space provided little room for maneuverability, and Matt no longer possessed what little athleticism or limberness he had enjoyed years ago. Using what could best be described as a modified low-crawl, and propelled by volleys of alternating grunts and cursing, Matt finally reached the photo album and in one quick jerky movement, pulled it free and tossed it back over his head where it rested on the small of his back. It was a lot of effort for one album and he hoped it was worth the effort. He rested in the spot for a few minutes until he caught his breath. The sweat trickling down from his scalp picked up the mud and grit on his forehead and channeled its way down to his eyes, causing them to burn. He was starting to feel a bit claustrophobic and started to plan his retreat, but he found himself in a quandary. He needed both hands to push his body back, and because of his position, he couldn't figure out what to do with his flashlight, other than throwing it behind him to perhaps speed up the retreat. He quickly decided against that. He damn sure didn't want to be scooting around in the pitch dark.

He ended up balancing the Maglite on his shoulder and securing it as best he could by craning his neck and holding it down with his chin. It worked as planned during the first push – the light bouncing around the closed-in area like a strobe – but just as Matt slid his hands under his chest to move backwards for the second effort, his chin lost pressure and the flashlight rolled into the mud. "Dammit! Shit. Damn flashlight piece of shit." He grunted and reached his hand forward to grab the metal end and looked, for the first time, where the lens was pointing. It was a spot Matt hadn't searched before. Several feet ahead, halfway buried in the sludge was a duffel bag, glistening with mud.

And from what Matt could tell, it appeared to be full.

Matt's cursing turned the air blue as he worked his way back in towards the bag. Sweat beaded off his nose, but he couldn't wipe it with his sleeve as it would only spread more mud on his face. At least he wouldn't have to deal with any spiders. He hoped. He glanced around and couldn't see any webs. The surge probably took care of them (at least that's what he kept telling himself). He twisted and shimmied and moved deeper and deeper in until his entire body was inside the cavity. If the house falls in, Matt thought, no one will ever find my stupid ass. At least not until I cook for a few days. The thought disgusted him and he considered backing out, but by this time he was close.

He moved in another foot, and the air felt more stale as his expired breaths no longer had anywhere to go. He extended his hand until his fingers finally touched the nylon handle. When he got close enough to get a tight grip, he pulled.

It didn't move.

Dammit. He pulled again. Again, nothing. "Fine, then I'll leave you, you cocksucker," Matt yelled at the bag. "Son of a bitch." He started to back out, but gave it one more tug. As he did, the bag made a sucking *schlock* as Matt pulled it free.

Matt continued his grumbling until he pulled himself out, and the fresh air hitting his skin felt like a cool splash. He was soaked through with sweat and mud and was limping because his leg and ass cramped on the way back out. He realized he would rival Hank on the news if a camera caught him now. He spat, coughed and poured his water on his cheeks and eyes to get the mud off. He stood there, breathing, hands on his hips, trying to recover. He smelled like sour mud and body odor and couldn't remember a time when he had ever needed a shower more. Even three-day fishing trips didn't produce this kind of funk. He set the items on one of the remaining floor sections where he had scattered the dining implements. Mud caked the bag, which appeared to be a good-sized North Face duffel, and, as Matt noted audibly yet again, a *heavy sonofabitch.*

He pulled the bag close and tried to open it, but a small luggage lock secured the zipper to a metal D-ring. He poured some water on the lock to wash the mud off and tugged, but it didn't give. "You have got to be shitting me," Matt said, glaring at the hasp. He pulled again until his sweaty hand slipped and scraped on the combination dial. He jerked his arm back and shook his hand off. He flipped the bag over and examined the handles, but couldn't find a name tag anywhere. Matt squeezed it to get a read on the contents. The thickness of the nylon combined with the dried mud hindered his efforts, and, since he was ready for a break anyway, he dropped the bag, picked up the photo album and traipsed to the front of the house where he could sit down.

He hopped on what remained of his front porch, his legs dangling inward over the area where his foyer should have been. When he opened the album, he saw a young man in a brown polyester leisure suit with bad, bad sideburns next to a lady who appeared to be about the same age with an equally offensive beehive hairdo. The photos had "1974" printed on the white border and, considering what they had been through, appeared to be in remarkably good shape. Matt thought the man looked vaguely familiar, but he couldn't quite identify him. He thumbed through the photos, not wanting to pry, but also a bit curious. He found Christmas pictures, pictures of a formidable land barge Pontiac or Oldsmobile, and garish outfits on pretty much everyone. Even the dog looked dated. What a decade, Matt thought. He started to close it until a page about halfway through got his attention. The fashion-challenged duo stood before a white house in their Sunday best. The paint color had changed, and Matt didn't recognize the twisted wrought-iron ornamentation that doubled as stair rails back then, but he had no doubt about the occupants. Matt glanced at the couple's photo again, this time, he grinned with recognition. Cathy must have created quite a stir back then.

It wasn't much, Matt thought, but an album full of old photographs provided something familiar in this alien land, and just might bring Cathy back to a better place. Matt put it away when he heard a car door close and a voice call out to him.

"Matt? Hey, darling, is that you?"

He wheeled around and smiled at the familiar face walking up the sidewalk.

It was Delia.

11

WHEN MATT MET Delia Farrell for the first time in Jackson during his Bing orientation, he made a slightly off-color joke about LSU and Ole Miss football that neither she nor anyone else in the room had been prepared for. Delia's no-nonsense reputation had not made its way to Matt, and he had no idea he had committed what most deemed a serious faux pas before one of the lead rainmakers in the firm. It could have blown up in his face, but Delia found it not only funny, but refreshing to encounter another lawyer who actually addressed her without barriers or filters. That was the beginning of a long friendship that buoyed Matt throughout his career with the Bing. Not everyone was happy with it, and many thought he curried special favor because of it, but he didn't care – plus, it wasn't exactly a cakewalk serving under arguably the best trial lawyer in Mississippi if not the Southeast. From the beginning, she made sure he met the milestones expected of someone of her caliber and worked his ass off. But it was good work and she slotted him in jobs that had great opportunities for growth. She even introduced him to numerous high-level corporate contacts, and as a result, he started developing his own client base, which was almost unheard of for a midlevel associate. He sometimes wondered if Delia, who never had kids of her own, took to him on a maternal level, and if so, he was good with that. He just felt fortunate to have someone as respected and influential as Delia as a confidante and a mentor. Delia served as the chair of the Bing's litigation department, and her reputation was not only of someone who was a tough-as-nails advocate, but also of an incredibly smart and exceedingly fair companion so long as you were willing to work as hard as she did. He hadn't seen her since, well, since Las Vegas, now that he thought about it, and she was a happy sight for his weary eyes.

Matt jumped up and greeted her with a hearty hug. He didn't care how dirty he was or how bad he reeked. Delia didn't either, apparently, because she squeezed him back, stink and all. Delia stood barely five feet tall with heels; wearing tennis shoes, her head hit him about chest high. She might have weighed only a hundred pounds soaking wet and been thirty years his senior, but she was no shrinking violet and held onto him like a steel trap. She pulled away and looked up. Her eyes were kind and her voice soft. She looked him square in the eye.

"How are you, honey?" she asked.

Matt looked back at her and felt a lump in his throat, then looked down saying nothing. Delia gave him a little nod and squeezed him again.

"I'm so sorry about Jeff," she said.

"Thanks," he said, clearing his throat. "How'd you find out?"

"Cathy called me. She wanted to make sure everyone at the firm knew."

"How is Cathy?"

"Sounded pretty broken up, as you can imagine. We didn't speak long. Said she'd head to Gulfport soon but didn't have the energy to make the trip yet."

"I plan on being here when she arrives. I found something of hers in my house that may bring her some comfort."

"Oh yeah?"

Matt showed her the binder. "Washed in from the storm. Photo album of Cathy and Jeff when they were a young couple."

"Washed in, huh?"

"Yeah. There's stuff all over the place."

"Anything else of theirs?"

"Nope, but I found some items of mine," Matt said, motioning. "At least, here on my lot, I have something to dig through. Not so for Cathy. All the homes fronting the beach are gone."

Delia wrinkled her nose and looked down the street. "Good grief, the news reports just don't do it justice. This looks like Armageddon."

"It's bad, isn't it?" Matt asked, scratching his head and digging a piece of dirt out of his ear.

"You weren't here during the hurricane, were you?" Delia asked.

"No. Drove down the day after it hit."

"Where have you been sleeping?"

"Downtown. Our office turned out okay, and I have a foldout couch. First floor is shot to hell, but the second wasn't damaged at all. Once we get power and data lines, we'll be around eighty percent in terms of functioning capacity upstairs."

"Surely you didn't stay there last night –"

Matt flinched. "No. They're supposed to have the place cleaned up by now, though," Matt said, and tried to shake the image out of his head.

Delia put her hand on his elbow. "You sure you're okay?"

He looked her square in the eye. "A little anxious, but considering everything… yes."

"Well, we're going to get you back on your feet. I've arranged for a runner to bring a truck down later in the week to restock you and anyone you think could use it. We're loading up paper goods, food, water, Purell, those types of things. We'll also have several coolers of ice. Anything in particular you need?"

"Gasoline. No way to get gas around here."

"Really? We went without for the first day or so, but stations are slowly opening up again. I'll put gas at the top of the list. I need your shirt size, shoe size, pants size, waist size, and measurements. I will have them stop by S.F. Alman's on the way down and get you cleaned up." She gave him the onceover. "Can't have you running around looking like a hobo."

"Delia, you don't need to do all that."

"Well, I'm going to."

They sat down on the steps and Matt thanked her for taking the effort to come down and see him. She didn't appear to be in a hurry so they spent the rest of the morning talking about the hurricane, Jeff, his family, and the Bing. Between multiple divorces, her inability to have children, and the death of her parents, Delia had weathered several storms of her own and knew how to assess a situation better than anyone else. Matt enjoyed having her ear for a few hours.

She asked about The Majestic, and he suggested they drive by and see how it fared. They tried, but debris from an imploded Best Western still blocked beach access to the east so they couldn't get close enough to see anything. Matt drove to the office, parked, and told her she could go in if she wanted, but he was content to wait outside. At least for another day.

She shielded her eyes from the glare of the sun and looked up and down the carnage on the street. "You stayed *here*?"

"Yes, Delia," Matt said. "Right here."

"Are you not going to get spooked when you go back, considering Jeff's –"

"I'll just try not to think about it. Like it or not, it's my home for the time being."

"You sure it's safe?"

"Oh yeah. I can secure it pretty well. And I don't travel alone, if you know what I mean."

"I trust you've talked to the police."

"I have. Gave a statement."

They spent a few more minutes talking about the office and after Delia decided that she didn't want to go inside either, they drove back to Matt's lot. Neither of them said a word; he was lost in his thoughts, and Delia seemed to be awed to silence by the destruction. She stared out the window as he parked behind her car.

Matt broke the stillness. "Delia, I just can't rectify death in my mind. I've known him for years. You have too. Rock solid all along. Suicide doesn't fit the picture."

She nodded and slowly faced him. "Hard to believe. Maybe this storm had something to do with it."

"I understand. But everyone down here has been impacted in one way or another. What could have been so bad for him that..." He felt that vague sense of unease again in the pit of his stomach as he looked past her.

"Matt?" Delia asked.

"I know this sounds crazy, Delia, but I think there's more to this."

Delia's eyes grew wide. "What are you saying?"

"I don't know exactly, Delia, but my gut tells me Jeff didn't kill himself."

"But didn't the police say –"

"Yeah, I know what the police said," Matt said, "but they haven't really had the time to properly investigate, right? They have a thousand things going on right now, and Jeff is just one number in a long list for them. I knew him better than almost anyone else. He didn't kill himself."

"Strong words, Matt." Delia squinted her eyes up and puffed out a breath. "Look, this is just us talking," she said, lowering her voice and biting her lower lip. "Any personal problems you were aware of? Cathy? Money? Girlfriend?"

"No, and that's just it: Yes, Jeff lost his home, but he still had a good job, good marriage, and even a backup place to live. Far as I know, they had no problems, either."

"Enemies?"

That, Matt knew, was a good question. He looked at her and sucked in air between his teeth as he thought about how to answer. "Enemies," he said after a moment, then shook his head. "Again, always the chance this was an angry client," he continued, "but I just can't think of anyone who'd want to hurt him. But I still don't think he'd do this to himself."

"Well, you think long and hard before you make those thoughts public. If you're wrong, this is only going to make the recovery period worse for Cathy."

"Yeah, I hadn't thought of that. What should I do?"

Delia gazed off past him and shook her head. "I don't have an answer for you, Matt. I wish I did, but I don't. The best thing I can tell you now is to roll with what the police have told you. At least for now."

"Yeah, I guess you're right," Matt said, climbing out of his truck. "No use rattling any cages at this point." Delia pulled out her keys. "You sure you have to leave now?"

"I think I can help you more from Jackson than I can down here. Now that I know what you need I should be able to get your supplies in a few days. Plus, no offense, but it's not like there's an extra bed to go around."

"Why Delia," Matt said, "I didn't realize you were so high maintenance."

Delia laughed. "Perhaps I should clarify. The bed's not the issue, honey. If I have a hot flash in a room with no air conditioner in the middle of August in Gulfport, Mississippi, you're going to wish 'high maintenance' was your biggest problem."

"I really didn't need to hear that."

"You asked." Before Delia got in her car, she squeezed his hand and turned to him. "Now let me flip it. Do you want to come back up to Jackson and get away for a while? This is a lot to handle alone."

"I'm fine. Got friends down here."

"I'm worried about you."

"Don't. Now you're starting to sound like Shelley."

Matt could tell Delia was about to say something in response, but true to form, stopped herself and shifted gears. "Give it some time and let all the dust settle, okay?" she asked. "Let's talk again after Jeff's service. Speaking of which, do you know when the funeral will take place?"

"Not yet."

"Well, once you find out something, let me know. I'll send out an e-mail. I'm sure a big contingent from the firm will come down."

"That'd be great."

"Don't expect Tripp Massey, of course. That chicken shit fool won't set foot south of Mendenhall if he knows I'll be here," Delia snorted before climbing into the car. She muttered something else as she cranked the engine, and the words kept flowing until she rolled down the window, her face crimson and hard. "Seriously, you let me know if you need a place to stay in Jackson – you'll be welcome there long as you want."

"You know salt water runs in my blood," he said. "Can't be away from the beach too long or I'll have withdrawals. But I really appreciate all this, Delia."

"We'll talk. Bye."

"Bye." She waved, pulled out, and faked a half-smile. Matt couldn't have been more grateful that she'd driven down to the Coast for him. He was sorry she'd mentioned Tripp Massey at the end – it soured the mood. The bitter rivalry between the two senior Bing partners was no secret in Southern legal circles, but Delia, ever the professional, refrained from publicly discussing the rancor and ignored his repeated attempts to undermine and embarrass her. Plus, years of high-level litigating made Delia as thick-skinned as anyone Matt had ever met, and he didn't think Tripp's invectives cut too deep.

Until recently, that is. Of late, Matt noticed Delia's private comments regarding the situation between her and Tripp becoming more frequent and more caustic. Maybe she had just had enough and wanted to put an end to it. Maybe she wanted Matt to know how much she needed an ally if she was going to take Tripp on.

And maybe – just maybe – he was getting to her after all.

12

AFTER DELIA LEFT, Matt poked around the house without much luck, and eventually started packing up late in the afternoon. He grabbed the box with the silver in it, the duffel bag and photo album, and loaded them in his truck. Sarah saw him from the door and waved him over. He was covered in dirt and grime, smelled like sweat and soured mud, and had not planned on going to Hank's until after he cleaned up. But the pungent aroma of something cooking drew him in like a dog in heat, and his appearance and cleanliness suddenly paled in comparison to the prospect of a hot meal. No one – *no one* was cooking yet. Hank turned the corner holding a bowl of gumbo and a plate of biscuits.

"Damn, you're a ugly-lookin' son of a bitch," Hank said, spitting out pieces of biscuit when he spoke. "But I reckon I'll let you in." Sarah punched Hank and he winked at her. "C'mon, have a seat. Just in time for chow."

The meal may have been served with paper towels and plastic utensils, but Matt couldn't recall ever partaking of anything finer. His manners went right out the window and he didn't come up for air until he polished off two bowls of gumbo and three biscuits. For a few minutes he forgot about everything, and for the first time since he was back he didn't feel like a cloud was over him.

"I'd be willing to bet," he mumbled, licking roux off his fingers, "that no one within a hundred miles is eating this good."

"I'd a said that before the storm, too," Hank said, nodding to Sarah. "Got to cook what's in the freezer 'fore it goes bad." He pushed the plastic bowl over to Matt. "Eat some more. We thawed out two gallons of gumbo and hate to see it go to waste."

"Better rest before I bust a gut." Matt sat back and rubbed his belly. "How're you cooking all this, anyway?"

Hank smiled again. "Few years ago I picked up a case of M-1950s, left over as surplus from 'Nam. Camp stoves, eight to a case. Thought I might need 'em one day. Sure enough, the time has come. Luck favors the prepared. Yep, favors the *pre*-pared." Matt could tell Hank enjoyed this bit of field-expedient improvisation. Sarah, meanwhile, had pulled two large coolers inside and was organizing the meat and other food they'd pulled out of their massive deep freeze.

"Y'all are too good to me," he said.

"Just now figuring that out?" Hank smiled. "Glad to do it, boy. What all'd you do today?"

"More archaeology. Even though it's a mess, I'm finding going to the house therapeutic."

"Find anything good?"

"I think so," Matt said. "Got some old silver and some other pieces I couldn't identify, but I'll hold on to them anyway. In case I find out who they belong to."

Hank wiped his beard. "Lord knows what's out there."

"I tell you, Hank, I got to thinking after I found that family photo the day before yesterday. You know, just before you shot at me –" Matt said this to tease Hank – it would definitely get a rise out of Sarah – and sure enough she came marching into the room.

"I *thought* I heard a shotgun the other day –"

"Just a warning shot, honey. I never aimed at the boy. Shot it straight into the air."

"From where I was crouching, you could've fooled me," Matt said with a grin. Hank grunted out a laugh, and Sarah smiled.

"You know, Hank," Matt said, turning serious again, "if I could go back in time and have just ten minutes in that house – ten minutes – I could get nearly everything of value to me."

"Well, if my aunt had balls, she'd be my uncle," Hank replied.

Sarah slapped him across the shoulder. "Hank! You should be ashamed of yourself for talking like that. And what in the world are you doing with your overalls?" Hank shrugged at her and Matt realized Hank's hand had disappeared behind the bib. "Scratchin'," Hank explained with a grimace that reminded Matt of his old dog's strained face when Matt rubbed his chest. "Scratchin'."

Sarah spoke up again, this time with her back to them both, as she tied up a garbage bag. "Ignore Hank, please, Matt. He knows not what he says – or does." Hank started to speak, but Sarah cut him off as she walked back towards the coolers, drying her hands off with a dish towel. "We all wish we could go back and do things different."

Hank jumped in before she could go any further. "You want to go for a ride tomorrow in the a.m.? Out in the Gulf, I'm talking about. Been needin' to get back on the water. Would do us both some good."

Matt looked out the window and let his gaze pass over the beach to the ocean. The waves were now lapping in over the scrub. He still felt pissed off at the sea and hadn't considered going back out anytime soon. "I assume your boat made it?"

"What do you think?" There was pride in Hank's voice. "Damn right *Big D* made it."

Boating had always been the ultimate escape for Matt, and perhaps getting away from the ravaged coastline for a few hours would let him decompress, or whatever the mental health experts called it. If nothing else, it would let him see firsthand how the barrier islands fared. "I guess I'm in, Hank. Do you think we ought to give it a few more days, though, to make sure the debris and –"

"It's a date. We'll leave at 0800. You staying the night here again, I 'spect."

This was a statement, not a question. Matt held his hands out to his side and looked down. "Uh, I don't think Sarah wants me in your home like this, Hank."

Sarah let out a little laugh. "You do remember that I live with Hank Mallette, don't you? Plan on sleeping here. I've got your recliner ready."

"You're better than a Holiday Inn," Matt said. "And much more hospitable than Hank, I might add."

"You'll think hospitable after a day as my deck hand tomorrow," Hank said. "*Big D* could use a swabbie."

"You be quiet," Sarah said to Hank, then ruffled Matt's hair. He picked up the scent of lavender. "Matt, you'd better get some sleep before Hank thinks up another chore."

"Will do. Let me see if I can clean up first. Be right back." Matt drove until he found a broken water line and stopped to give himself a makeshift bath right there on the curb. While not ideal, it served its purpose. He drove back to Hank's wearing nothing but boxers. He hung his wet clothes outside near Hank's porch and stretched out in their recliner. He thought about retrieving the duffel to give it another shot, but it was locked in the truck, and Matt was too tired and too comfortable to climb out of the chair.

The bag would have to wait.

13

THE SOUND OF chain saws outside woke Matt up, so he got dressed and strolled into the kitchen. Hank was brewing a fresh pot of coffee and looked suspiciously like he had taken a shower. Twenty minutes later, they drove down Industrial Seaway Road to American Marine, Hank's former employer. Seaway ran parallel to the Back Bay, which connected to the Gulf of Mexico via a series of canals and passages.

Due to the confidential nature of its affairs, American Marine operated out of a large, nondescript warehouse tucked between an asphalt plant and a tug repair business. Once painted light gray, the American Marine exterior had faded over time to a dull, heavy white. No sign on the building gave any indication as to what went on inside, nor were there any windows. Matt had driven by the building before and even ridden out there with Hank once, but Hank always made him stay in the truck.

"They weren't supposed to do this, but I guess they figured they could make an exception for me," Hank explained.

"Do what?"

"Let me store *D* at the shop. Wild Bill wasn't going to do it, but I twisted his arm. He finally agreed when he realized how bad this storm looked, although I owe him a dinner. He'll prob'ly want a steak, cheap bastard."

"And I assume 'Wild Bill' is the …"

"Manager, head boss, dickhead, whatever you want to call him. Best boat man I ever seen, though. Did time with him in Da Nang."

They pulled into the oyster shell and gravel parking lot, and Hank headed toward the door. He looked back at Matt sitting in the truck. "What the hell you waiting for?"

Matt shrugged, grabbed his things and followed.

A few seconds later, Hank squinted down at a keypad and poked it over and over again.

"Sonofabitch." Hank said. Then he said it again.

"What's wrong?" Matt asked.

"Can't see close up worth a shit and don't have my glasses with me. You try."

"Hank, I don't know if I'm supposed to have access to..."

"HM1961. Punch it in."

"HM1961?"

"Got to pick our own password so they can track ins and outs and let us know if somethin' ain't right. HM – well, that's obvious, it's me." Hank's back stiffened and he raised his chin. "1961. First SEAL teams formed in '61."

Matt nodded and keyed the pad. Nothing happened, so he keyed it again. The combination didn't seem to work, and he remembered his phone problems after the storm and stepped back. "This place have a generator? Not sure you have power."

"We got a generator." Hank stopped and held up his hand for quiet. "I don't hear it humming, though. I have a backup key to the boat bay doors. Stay put."

Hank returned from his truck swinging a key ring, and he motioned around the back of the building. After stepping over a pile of wet insulation, a few pieces of orphaned aluminum siding, and a bait shop sign that had blown up against the building, they came upon a large, metal roll-up warehouse door. Hank balanced on the pilings and glanced around the area real quick to see if anyone was around.

"You ain't supposed to be here, so don't look at nothin' inside," Hank said under his breath. "I could definitely lose my privileges if they knew I brought you. Most of the classified stuff got stowed anyway for the storm. If anyone asks, though, you were never here, and you ain't never been here."

Hank knelt down and unlocked the manual slide, which kept the door secure if the power kicked out. He and Matt lifted the door enough for Hank to shimmy under. Within a few minutes, Hank began pulling a hanging loop chain to roll the door up the rest of the way. Sweat covered Hank's face by the time Matt ducked inside.

"Hotter'n two rats fuckin' in a wool sock in here," Hank said, using the band of his hat to mop up the beads of water running off his forehead into his eyes. "I'm sure the first thing Wild Bill'll want to do is get the power back on. His ass won't put up with having to hand crank this thing, and he damn sure won't come to work if his office don't have no A/C." Hank banged on the green lift button for good measure to see if it worked. He spat out a few more words, and then Matt took over and gave Hank a rest.

More sunlight poured in with each stroke. Matt recalled Hank's admonition, but he immediately looked around when he got inside anyway. At first glance, it resembled any other dry boat storage facility with the only exception being a cut-out dock and bulkhead that took up about a quarter of the space. A small office, a gas pump, and a Coke machine occupied the ground level. Most of the offices were on the second level, connected by railed gangplanks.

Nearly all of the boats had been placed high and dry prior to the storm, and the forklift used to lift the boats hung by a crane over the water inlet. Three boats remained in the water, moored so they could rise and fall with the surge without coming loose. Matt recognized *Big D* tied up next to two boats that looked like close cousins and started toward it, but Hank made his way up the metal stairs nearest the front entrance.

"Left my keys for *D* in Bill's office in case he had to move it," he said. He pulled the key with the floater fob off a rack hanging over the computer and threw it to Matt. Then he scooted down the stairs, went past Matt, and climbed into *Big D*. "Let's go, boy."

Several years back, the U.S. Navy awarded American Marine's sister company, Southeast Marine, the contract to manufacture the Mark V Special Operations Craft. The Navy designed the Mark V SOC as a SEAL team insertion vessel. At 80-plus feet, it could carry and deploy multiple teams. The boat's V-hull design gave it good handling qualities in rough water, and its shallow draft allowed for close-to-shore operations. The five gun mounts at the front of the boats allowed for any combination of heavy or light machine guns, and the dual 12-cylinder diesels in its belly made it fast. Really fast.

Hank never worked on the Mark V's, but they fascinated him nonetheless. After the first Mark V came off the line and went into service, Hank began fulfilling a lifelong dream of designing and building his own boat. He used the Mark V as an inspiration. Three years later, Sarah broke a bottle of champagne over *Big D's* bow, officially christening it on its maiden voyage. Hank named it after Johnny "Big D" Donegan, the Navy DI who trained Hank and eventually befriended him upon graduating from SEAL school.

By Matt's eye, the difference between the Mark V and *Big D* came down to size. Both appeared to have V-hulls; the silhouettes were similar and – as a nod to his prior career – Hank kept one gun mount for good measure. He called it his hood ornament. *Big D* came in around fifty feet shorter than the Mark V, and Hank installed one 12-cylinder diesel instead of two. It looked a bit stubby from the outside, and several of the blueblood sailors and boaters initially turned up their noses at it. Those who got the privilege of riding in it, though, sang a much different tune. The boat ran so smoothly that even rough seas had little impact. *Big D* ran circles around boats twice its size and larger, even if the other boats had twin props. No one ever saw *Big D* out of the water, which only added to its mystique.

When they started untying the lines, Matt glanced from *Big D* to the other two boats in the water and back. The three appeared almost identical, although one had a large .50 caliber machine gun mounted on the gun post. Then he gave Hank a knowing look and couldn't resist teasing him a little.

"What's going on here, Hank?" he said. "I thought *Big D* was one of a kind."

"Prototypes," Hank replied, leaning on the gunwale. "Can't talk about them – hell, you ain't even supposed to be lookin' – but let's just say old Hank knew what he was doing when he built this one," he cackled, knocking on *Big D's* hull. "The legacy of *Big D* may live on for some time. Some time, indeed."

Hank cranked the boat after Matt unwound the last rope from the cleat and stepped in. It roared to life, and Matt could hear the prop churning the water. The savory tang of diesel hung in the air, reminding Matt of overnight fishing trips with his cousins on the *Vanalburtlee,* and he wondered if that old wooden lugger had fallen victim to the surge like so many others. He put on his sunglasses, plopped down on the seat next to Hank's, and scratched the scab that had crusted up on his leg.

He could tell by the look on Hank's face as he guided the boat out of the slip and trolled into the bay the old man was pleased to be back at the helm. Sunshine crept onto the deck as *Big D* cleared the building's shadow, and Matt leaned back and propped his feet up on a cooler. That old bastard was right, Matt thought with a smile.

It felt good to be back on the water.

14

"GOT TO BE careful getting through here," Hank said, pulling the throttle back as they worked their way through the channel. "Look at all this shit."

Debris littered the water as far as Matt could see. Every few feet he spotted beams and posts from destroyed bulkheads poking out near the shoreline. Floating remains piled into the mouths of inlets, in some cases creating mini-dams and garbage repositories. Trash also clogged up the marshy areas near the shore, much of it fabric or paper trapped in the reeds. Masts, bows, and the occasional prop from sunken boats cut the surface, and oil slicks formed liquid rainbows that shimmered across the water near the drowned vessels. After *Big D* scraped something neither of them could see, Hank told Matt to sit at the bow and watch for anything else that could damage the hull.

"We'll be okay," Hank said, cupping his hand to block the sun as he looked down at his depth finder. "They haven't had time to do any dredging, so we need to watch out. Should clear up once we get out front."

"I'm on point," Matt replied. He tried to stay focused on the water but couldn't stop looking around as they passed empty warehouses and washed-out buildings.

"How'd y'all do, Chazmo?" Hank yelled to a group of men standing by a shed missing its bottom three feet of siding. A man in a red baseball hat turned and thumped his cigarette on the ground.

"All right, considering," he yelled back. "Moved out most of the equipment before it rolled through."

"How 'bout your home?"

"Still there, but a little wet."

"Doris?"

"Aw, she's all right. We ain't lost nobody, so I reckon that's good."

"Okay," Hank replied, "you need something, you let me know."

Hank repeated this conversation with various friends and colleagues in one form or another time and again as they puttered down the canal. By this stage post-storm, most had assessed the damage to their homes and were now returning to their workplace for an inspection and check in. Although many appeared shell-shocked, the response was generally upbeat.

"You know all these people, Hank?"

"Most of 'em. Good, hard-workin' folks."

"Ever do business with any of them?"

"Sometimes. We try to get our raw materials locally whenever possible. You deal with people in your industry long enough, you develop a kinship of sorts. Some can be sons of bitches, but most are all right."

Matt thought about that. He'd practiced law going on eight years now, and other than Jeff and Delia, he barely knew more than the first names of his professional colleagues. Yet here stood Hank, who knew personal details about people he probably saw just a few times a year –

Another vibration and loud scraping sound under his feet jolted Matt. "Sorry, Hank," he said, and looked down at the water but couldn't see anything. Whatever caused the noise had passed. "I swear I'll pay more attention."

"You're the worst navigator I ever had," Hank said. "Now, here, make yourself useful." Hank took out a small Nikon pocket camera and threw it to Matt. "Take some pictures."

"What are you, a news boy now?" Matt asked.

"Shut up and snap," Hank said, "trying to document all this for posterity's sake." Hank revved the throttle as the bay opened into the Gulf just inside the Biloxi line. The debris started to thin once they got into deeper water half a mile out, and Hank turned southwest and opened it up. Although the Gulf didn't appear too choppy, Matt repositioned himself on the chair anyway in case he got bounced around.

They saw nothing unusual at first. The channel markers and the buoys had washed out, but Hank had traveled the route so many times he no longer needed them for direction. Plus the GPS worked, and a quick glance at the monitor told Matt exactly when they would reach their destination. Then Hank pointed at a pile of what looked like inflated floaties bobbing in the water. Hank tried to go around them, but they surrounded the boat.

"What the hell are those?" Matt asked.

"Chickens," Hank said. "Supposed to be going to Russia. They were all in cold storage at the Taylor Warehouse on the dock when the storm flattened it. Spread them all over creation."

"Nobody's going to believe this," Matt said. When they drew close enough, he leaned over and took some pictures, then grabbed the net and scooped one from the water. The birds had been sealed in bags, and when the warehouse went down tens of thousands of frozen chickens floated out to sea. Three days baking in the August Mississippi sun had turned the meat and skin into a greasy gelatinous mass held loosely together by tendons and bones. The escaping methane from the decomposition puffed up the bags like macabre balloons.

"Warning you, boy," Hank said. "Don't touch that..."

Matt hadn't planned to, but once he pulled the net close enough to inspect the bag's contents, it was too late. Just the sight of it made him gag, and when he flipped the net over to dump the bag back into the water, he missed and it bounced off the rail and burst. Some splattered on Matt, and when the stench hit him, he retched and dry heaved.

Hank laughed. "That'll teach you." Feeling satisfied that he had captured the moment, Hank returned to his post and continued driving. "Curiosity killed the cat," he yelled over his shoulder. "Speaking of which. Hello, Cat Island. Hel-lo."

Matt shivered and looked up. They had arrived.

15

A SERIES OF BARRIER islands spans the Mississippi Sound from Louisiana to Alabama. They vary in size from small outcroppings of sand and scrub vegetation to atolls miles long with their own thriving flora and fauna uniquely adapted to survive the harsh sunshine and unpredictable weather. Some, like Ship Island and Horn Island, lie several miles off the coast. Others, like Deer Island, are so close they can be reached with a short swim.

While locals often debated whether the islands actually offered any protection in the event of the storm, one thing no one disputed was the positive impact the islands had on pleasure boaters, fishing, and sightseeing. Tourists took large ferry boats to Ship Island National Park for a day of tanning, swimming, and sandcastle building, while island marshes provided fertile fishing grounds for sportsmen seeking reds and specks. Larger boats went even farther out to Chandeleur – a string of small islands forty miles out (and fifty miles long) – for three- and four-day fishing trips.

Of all the islands in the sound, however, Cat Island had always been Matt's favorite. Named after the raccoons that Spanish explorers mistook for cats back in the 1800s, Cat Island was almost as far out as Ship Island – about eight miles – but situated a little farther west. Of importance to Matt, it wasn't overrun with vacationers and didn't even have a pier. One had to either own a boat or know someone who had a boat to get out there. Cat Island stretched out like a sideways "T" or shark's tooth, as Matt liked to think. The long stem of the "T" faced west, and the cap arched, umbrella-like, from north to south. The curvature created semi-protected areas and petite wharfs on both sides of the stem where the respective arcs met in the middle. Perfect spots to drop anchor and relax.

The slash pines and live oak trees covering Cat prior to the storm still looked fairly thick to Matt, even if many now had a slight northern lean from the constant wind. The sand on the beaches seemed a little closer to the trees, although trash covered most of it as far as Matt could see. Apparently, their open water reprieve from the wreckage had come to an end now that they were approaching a land mass. Even so, Matt couldn't imagine how debris could track eight miles out to sea without sinking or being broken apart, yet it made it in full force.

"Can't escape it, huh, Hank?"

An entire roof, shingles and all, sat between stacks of wood, broken pieces of furniture, and a pile of cushions and mattresses. Boats and pieces of boats also littered the beach. Matt thought it looked a lot like the trash piles on the mainland, and he pointed out a full pickup truck lying upside down in the sand.

"Would you look at that?" Hank said with a whistle. "You believe all this washed this far out?"

Even the chicken floats had started to back up against the shoreline, and Matt couldn't imagine how it would look – or smell – when the whole flock arrived. "Let's go around to the south side, Hank. I wanna see Smuggler's."

A small, natural cut ran behind the trees and scrub on the shore of the south side. Hidden by several sand dunes, it was just wide enough and deep enough to maneuver and conceal a medium-sized boat. The trip rewarded those who took the time to navigate the inlet with a small, private beach nicknamed "Smuggler's Cove" by the lucky few who knew about it. Most boaters in the area, even those dropping anchor just offshore, weren't even aware of its existence. Matt and Shelley had spent several nights there. He even took Delia out to Smuggler's once on the *Queen* – one of The Majestic's charter boats – during a fishing trip with The Majestic's in-house counsel, and she fell in love with it. He confided to her that Smugglers' was where he retreated when he needed to get away from it all. And now he couldn't think of a time when he needed it more.

Much to Hank's and Matt's pleasure, this side of the island had not been sullied too much. The debris coming from the coast either stopped when it hit the north side or drifted past the island and out to sea. Hank had to be careful making the turn around the arm of the "T" due to the sandbar and a large, partially-sunken barge and tugboat. Matt's eyes strained for the dune heralding the entrance. It remained, but the battering of the wind and rain shrunk it and made it even more unremarkable than before, which, to Matt, was not necessarily a bad thing.

"You think it's safe to take *Big D* in?" he asked.

"Let's get a little closer and see," Hank said. "So far so good."

The inlet leading to the cove itself didn't seem to have changed much, and Hank chanced it and eased the boat down the waterway. When Smuggler's came into view, Matt could barely contain himself. Other than some broken-up vegetation on the sand and blown leaves and sticks on the ground, the area looked clean. Hank maneuvered the boat through the passage with little effort, and soon Matt climbed over the side. Hank grabbed two MREs and they sat down at the foot of one of the live oaks. Soon the food was gone and Hank, with a full belly and a shady spot, fell asleep.

Matt didn't think he would be able to snooze but closed his eyes anyway. The cool breeze cleared his head, and he could feel himself finally relaxing. He took advantage of the down time to try to figure out just how – and when – he could get to Meridian to see Shelley. The lack of fuel was his biggest problem. The cans he had filled up in Jackson would get him there, but there was only enough fuel for a one-way trip. He decided he would call her from Hank's satellite phone when they got back to see if the pumps in Meridian were up yet; if so, perhaps he could drive all the way in or talk her into meeting him halfway in Hattiesburg. He pulled the brim of his hat down low and tried to shut out the noises coming from Hank long enough put together a coherent plan. Within minutes he, too, was out.

A loud snort jerked Matt awake, and he squinted over to the source and found Hank still sleeping. According to his watch, they'd been out for over an hour. He rubbed his eyes and started picking up the remnants of the MRE packets. The commotion stirred Hank.

"Hoooo-wee!" Hank said. He sat up and rebuckled his overalls. "I don't know about you, boy, but I have charged my batteries. Bring it on."

"You ready to roll?"

"I reckon." Hank stood then, snorted, stretched and yawned all at once. "I reckon."

They headed back north toward the Coast, neither of them interested in exploring the other islands right then. On the trip back they passed more chicken bubbles gathering along the shore and several more still floating. Matt thought of the people they'd seen checking on their businesses on the ride out that day and asked Hank to pull up alongside The Majestic once they got close enough to see how it looked.

"Important to you, huh?" Hank asked.

"You could say so," Matt said, as The Majestic loomed over him. He walked to the bow to get a better look and leaned on the gun post. "Yeah. You could say so."

16

GAMBLING HAD ITS furtive start on the Mississippi Gulf Coast in the mid-1800s but didn't become legal until over a century later when tourism, the bread and butter of the region, began its decline. Beach Boulevard, the primary artery shuttling visitors and locals up and down the shoreline, dwindled into near obsolescence upon completion of Interstate 10, the freeway running from Florida to California. Suddenly, golfers, sportsmen, sun worshippers, and other potential revenue generators bypassed Mississippi's coastal towns in favor of New Orleans to the west or Gulf Shores and Destin to the east. Local politicians, their own profit potential notwithstanding, saw casinos as a way to revitalize the declining revenue base, and they pushed hard for legislation to make it happen.

To quell the protests from the Baptist and Pentecostal constituents in the central and northern parts of the state, legislators proposed casino development only on the navigable waters of the Gulf Coast. Limiting the casinos to Mississippi's southernmost border would, in theory, keep the corruption from infiltrating deep into the inland back yards and communities of the more pious residents. Not everyone was convinced this was a great idea, though, as it didn't fully consider the calamitous effects a hurricane or tropical storm could have on the casinos and the surrounding areas.

As a result, potential gaming suitors dispatched public relations firms, engineers, and lawyers from the capitol to the coast in an effort to reassure the lawmakers and locals that the state-of-the-art mooring systems and cofferdams needed to contain the structures would minimize, if not eliminate, the risk of damage in the event of a storm. It worked. The governor signed the bill with much fanfare and press coverage, and a decade later the coast had eleven casinos - massive behemoths built on secured barges that gave no appearance of being waterborne.

The majority of the casinos were concentrated in Biloxi. Gulfport had just one – The Majestic – and it more than lived up to its name. Its Biloxi cousins, due to lack of any substantive zoning restrictions, paid more attention to sparkle and signage than detail or design, and were lined up side-by-side on the shore like Yankee tourists in garish pantsuits. But The Majestic incorporated elements invoking both Southern heritage and modern eloquence. Mature magnolias and moss-laden oak trees harvested from a Louisiana estate lined the cobblestone drive leading up to the entrance. Large, plantation-like columns gently heralded the entrance to a five-diamond, LEED-certified hotel. Its restaurants bore the names of Emeril and Cat Cora, and The Majestic's nightclubs rivaled the best Vegas had to offer. Marketed as a destination resort, The Majestic had architects and designers who spared no expense to create an environment that was both hospitable and profitable, and soon the casino resort turned into *the* place to see and be seen for up-and-coming yuputantes and social climbers.

When the casinos first opened, many of the coast residents ventured in with mixed emotions. While the coast desperately needed a new industry to jump-start the economy, its people were fiercely protective of their culture and thus speculation ran rampant about whether the casinos would tamp out the coast's unique personality. As it turned out, the local fears were unfounded. In fact, the casino management played it very smart and did everything feasibly possible to embrace the lifestyle. They sponsored social events and affliction balls for the largest charities, hosted Mardi Gras receptions and deep sea fishing tournaments, and spent more money on advertising the Mississippi Gulf Coast in one year than the chamber of commerce had the past decade. The Majestic launched its opening with a free Jimmy Buffett concert on the beach. Most importantly, the casinos stocked their work force with locals, which in turn grew the economy and municipal tax rolls.

Jeff McCabe was one of the coast natives who embraced the casinos from the beginning. On one hand, Jeff saw the potential business opportunities on the litigation and regulatory front that come when a new industry sets up shop, and on the other hand, Jeff discovered that *he* actually *liked* the casinos. The bright interiors, the constant activity, and the action on the floor energized him. Jeff even embraced the pinging of the slot machines that greeted him when the elevator doors opened, and he certainly took no offense to the outfits barely covering the cocktail waitresses. Over time, he became a regular, taking advantage of the generous incentives, shows, and buffet deals. He also enjoyed playing craps and blackjack – when Cathy would let him. Eventually, he developed relationships with directors of some of the establishments, and when the general manager of the Dixie Cavalier – one of the earlier riverboat-type casinos – mentioned the need for some legal work, Jeff gave him his card. The Dixie ultimately retained him to handle zoning and run-of-the-mill labor and employment issues. After he helped the Dixie clear some unanticipated regulatory hurdles, they rewarded him by giving him a large bulk of their litigation. Jeff's status as a casino advocate grew, and when the Bing identified the need to open a coast office in order to have a local presence for The Majestic, Jeff McCabe's name topped the list. Delia Farrell and some of the other principals made Jeff a lateral partnership offer based on reputation alone. The consideration flattered Jeff; the price was right; and, after clearing conflicts, he accepted the position. The McCabe law office officially became a part of the Bing.

While Jeff's professional history with The Majestic was tied somewhat directly to the Bing, Matt's history with The Majestic was inextricably linked to Jeff – and it began with a game of a different sort – baseball. Having no kids of his own, there was nothing

Jeff liked to do more than coach Little League, and over time he became a bit of a legend in the Southeast for consistently rostering championship teams. It was during one of these early seasons that Jeff and Matt first crossed paths – specifically, during tryouts. Matt, while not unathletic, was not a superstar either, yet Jeff saw something special in that gangly nine-year-old and picked Matt during the draft because, as he would say later, Matt was "coachable." Matt lived up to Jeff's expectations, and midway through the season ended up taking over at shortstop after the starter, a much bigger kid, snapped his leg after getting cleated trying to turn a double play. Jeff spent the next four years coaching Matt – all the way through Babe Ruth – and Matt ultimately made the varsity team at St. John's. He even lettered in his junior year, and he had Jeff to thank for it.

When not playing ball, Matt spent his high school summers working as a runner at Jeff's law office in Gulfport. After he graduated from college, Jeff wrote the recommendation letter to Ole Miss Law School on Matt's behalf. Just after graduation, Jeff hired Matt as the Bing's first Gulfport associate, and before the ink dried on Matt's Bar results, he was in court arguing motions for The Majestic. Matt tailored his practice to better serve The Majestic, and with Delia's oversight and Jeff's tutelage, started to develop a reputation of his own, which in turn brought him even more work. At the time the storm hit, ninety percent of Matt's billable hours were tied one way or another to The Majestic – which Delia kept telling him was a good thing. And Matt believed it.

Until now.

From the beginning, Matt had never bought into the rhetoric that the colossal floating buildings could survive a named storm unscathed, and much to his dismay, this hurricane proved him right. The hotel's slate roof and large columns had held firm. But Matt couldn't yet see the lower floors that held the casino, the convention halls, most of the restaurants, and the hotel's expansive lobby. The Majestic had recently added a sports bar on the south side of the resort overlooking the water, next to the private pier built for high-roller guests to park their yachts. The Majestic's three charter boats – the *King*, the *Queen*, and the *Duke* – also had designated slots on the pier.

Hank drifted closer and cut the engine, and the sudden silence added to the gravity of the situation. Matt moved to the front of the boat to better assess the damage. The bulkheads were gone, and the occasional remaining piling provided the only linear indication that a pier once existed. A gaping hole in the south side, where the Seaside Restaurant used to be, ran deep inside and up through the second level. Gaming tables and slot machines lay piled and scattered about the gaming floor, and the barge on which the casino superstructure sat listed slightly to port. Considering what he'd seen lately, Matt knew not to be surprised, but he couldn't believe how bad it looked up close. The Majestic, with all of its size and "hurricane hardening," as the contractors called it, took a beating like every other structure on the coast. Hank turned to say something, but Matt was snapping away.

"Damn, it's pitiful, ain't it son?"

"Sure is, Hank. My boss will want to see this. Terrible."

Hank couldn't think of anything to say in response, so he took the camera and started snapping some photos while Matt looked on. After a few minutes, Matt motioned he was ready to leave. Hank motioned back. "You got the wheel, son."

Matt nodded and turned *Big D* in the direction of the entrance to the bay. He was pleasantly surprised Hank let him finish out the trip. It took some of the sting out of what he'd just seen. He felt the urge to open the boat up, but with hazards everywhere – above and beneath the surface – he knew not to. Instead he turned his attention to making sure he didn't hit anything and finished the rest of the trip in silent concentration. They didn't encounter any problems on the way back, and he switched places with Hank as they turned into the dock. Hank pulled *Big D* into his slip where they unloaded and drove home.

"You stayin' here again tonight?" Hank asked as he stopped next to Matt's truck.

"Nah. I've burdened you enough. Time I go back to the office."

"The office? You sure, boy?"

"I'm sure."

Hank looked Matt up and down, put one hand on Matt's shoulder and nodded. "Suit yourself, although you know you ain't botherin' us. You good on food?"

"I'm good." Matt said and picked up Hank's camera. "You mind if I take this? I may try and download some of those shots."

"Long as you need it, son," Hank said.

Matt looked at his house, yet again, with incredulity. He knelt down next to the refrigerator turned over in the front yard and reached his arm inside. He made a teethy face as he strained for a grip, and when he felt the box, he smiled and pulled out a mostly full twelve pack of Diet Coke.

Back at the office, Matt unloaded the photo album and duffel bag and brought them both upstairs. The smell of bleach coming from Jeff's side permeated the hall and burned his nostrils, making him cough. Jeff's office door was still closed, thankfully, and Matt left it so. Even with the cleanup, Matt had no intention of going in there anytime soon.

He checked the bathroom to see if the city had made any progress with the water service. Finding none, Matt took one of his spare one-gallon water jugs and gave himself the best washing he could. He rinsed his hair and cleaned out all his cracks and crevices. He could taste the salt from the sea spray as the water trickled down his face. He pulled a spare pair of boxers out of his suitcase left over from his trip to Jackson, and walked back to his office shirtless, the cool wood floor creaking under his weight. He actually felt refreshed for the first time in days and slapped his belly a few times as he plopped down on the couch. He had scrubbed his body, his hair, and his teeth, and although the world had turned upside down, a decent breeze from the south had finally picked up, and the draft coming through the window eased his mind. Matt looked around. If only he had a cold beer.

Then he remembered the Diet Cokes and rinsed out a coffee mug on his desk in what was left of the slushy ice that remained in the cooler. The *shh-glick* sound the can made when he pulled the tab up echoed in the empty room, and he poured the drink over the cubes. Matt cupped the mug with both hands and sipped his first icy drink since the storm hit. The pops from the carbonation fizz-tickled his face. It was delicious.

He jimmied open a can of tuna, ate it with his pocketknife and picked up Hank's camera. Matt hadn't realized it but Hank had been up and down the coast documenting the aftermath. He spent a few minutes going through the photos. The roads, people, bridges, and what remained of the houses looked uniformly bad in every one. Matt kept scrolling backwards and stopped when he got to Hank's pre-storm pictures. It looked like a different world. Green. Bright. Colorful. Happy. He went back further to see what else was on there and smiled when he saw Hank's photos of Fin and J.W. from Fin's superhero birthday party. Matt stopped at a picture of a young Batman and Spider-Man – both boys grinning through masks way too big for their heads. He wondered where those costumes were now and continued to click backward, but the sound of footsteps on the stairs outside the door made him freeze.

"Hank?" Matt called.

No response.

Matt stood up and listened closer. Sure enough, someone was in the building. He picked up his gun from the arm of the chair and stood behind his desk, pointing it toward the door. Whoever it was, they didn't consider stealth a high priority.

Matt tried again, this time a little louder. "Hank? That you?"

After a few seconds of silence, a loud knock sounded from the hallway. "Hey bro, you in there?" Matt put the gun down and rubbed his face with relief.

Thank the Lord. It was his old buddy, Hop.

17

MATT FRAZIER AND Jason Hopkins first met in seventh grade when they tried out for the St. John junior high basketball squad. Although both made the team, their borderline skills kept playing time to a minimum, and they spent many an hour warming the bench discussing *Star Wars*, debating which restaurants had the best cheeseburgers, and providing commentary on the virtues and mysteries of the fairer sex. Their shared interests soon developed into a friendship that carried them through high school and college.

Hop was Matt's only buddy who'd avoided marriage altogether. As the heir apparent to his dad's construction business, he lived a carefree lifestyle in a downtown loft with a beach view three short blocks from Matt's office. When Matt returned to Gulfport after law school they picked up where they'd left off, and Hop became a frequent guest at their house, so much so that Fin and J.W. referred to him as "Uncle Hop." Matt hadn't heard from Hop since before the storm and embraced his old friend when he opened the door.

Hop looked him up and down. "Damn, I didn't know it was that kind of party," he said. "Put some clothes on, dude."

"Don't you worry about my lack of attire," Matt said. "Lucky I didn't shoot first and ask questions later."

"Hell, I didn't even know you were here until I drove by just now and saw your truck. Didn't expect you'd be *here*." Hop looked across the hall and made a face. "Where it all happened, you know?"

Matt pulled on a t-shirt. "I actually crashed on the couch a few days ago. It'll probably be a little weird tonight, but this is the only place I can call my own for now. I feel like I need to be here."

"If you say so," Hop nodded and looked around. "Nice digs."

"Yeah, right. Welcome to my new home. You're now in the living room-slash-den-kitchen-bedroom and, I guess, now that you're here, the guestroom."

Hop looked out the window south to the horizon. "At least you now have a beach view."

"No kidding. Got it the hard way, though."

"Yeah, you did. I checked out Second Street yesterday. Unbelievable. Seriously, this shit is crazy."

"That's one way to put it," Matt said. "How'd you do?"

"If I had power back, blindfolded you, and walked you up to my loft, you'd think nothing had changed once you got inside. Of course, a look outside brings you back to reality…"

"Well, good for you."

"Though I feel sorry for Ms. Kari, who lived on the first floor."

"Ms. Kari?"

"She was relatively new. Lost everything. Hell, Matt, you haven't been over to my place in months."

Matt smiled. "Was she one of your, uh, conquests?"

Hop raised his eyebrows and shook his head. "Hell no. She's AARP."

"Your point being?" Matt said, as deadpan as he could muster.

Hop rolled his eyes. "Hasn't been that long. At least that's what I keep telling myself. How're my nephews?"

"They're good," Matt said. "They were in Meridian the whole time. Spoke to them a few days ago. They have no idea what went down."

"That's probably best, Matt…"

He knew what was coming next before Hop spoke the words.

"…things the same between you and Shel –"

"The same. Something to eat or drink? Not much on the variety front, but I got plenty."

"Nah, I'm okay. Cranked up my generator after the water receded, and my fridge never lost its cool. I stocked up before it hit. You need to come by and eat a real meal sometime."

"I might, although Hank's been taking care of me. Or, should I say, Sarah is."

"That dude is always prepared, right? Speaking of boy scouts, have you spoken to Lance?" Hop asked. He and Lance became friends after Hop tagged along one year down in Perdido on what became their annual boys' trip to the Flora-Bama Mullet Toss.

"I actually ran into him on my way down, right in the middle of a logjam on 49," Matt said. "He tried to warn me how bad it'd be, but I didn't listen."

"You got to figure he of all people would know."

"I suppose so," Matt said. "You got phone service yet?"

"Nope."

"Me neither." Matt clicked on a battery-operated lantern that cast a webby glow over the room.

"Actually, this isn't all that bad," Hop said.

"Home, sweet home. Have a seat," Matt said, pointing to the couch. "Move that bag out the way if you need more room."

"Will do." Hop picked up the duffel and frowned at its weight. "What the hell is this, anyway?"

Matt explained how he found it. "You should've tried pulling that bastard out," Matt said. "Buried half-deep in the mud."

Hop got up and lifted it by the straps, curl-style. "Nasty-looking for sure. Pretty heavy. What's in it?"

"Don't know. Locked."

Hop tugged at the zipper. "Shit, it's just an old luggage lock. Got any pliers or anything?"

"Not here."

"Want me to try and open it?"

"Sure. Kind of curious myself."

"Gimme a sec." Hop set the bag down and started down the stairs. He returned a few minutes later with a Leatherman's tool. "This lock is so small, I bet I can get it with the wire cutter."

Hop positioned the tool and gave it a good squeeze. After grunting for a second he stopped, shook his hand off, and checked out the metal. "Dammit." Hop squeezed again, and this time Matt could see a vein bulge on his temple. Hop stopped, looked at the lock again and took a deep breath.

"Almost there, bitch." This time, he squeezed with both hands so hard he raised up on his toes. His hands jerked with the *click* of the hasp breaking, and he pulled the lock off. Hop backed up, wiped his brow, and grinned. "You want to do the honors?"

Matt was standing over him by this time. "Sure." Matt tried the zipper but it didn't budge. He blew on it to clear the dust off, but it still would not give. "Dammit. Hold on a second." He grabbed a Clorox wipe and ran it up and down the zipper line, turning the cloth a dirty brown. He dried the pull with a paper towel and repositioned himself to get better leverage. When he gave it an effort this time, the zipper flew, causing Matt to catch himself. The bag gaped open, and Matt jumped back, arms flayed out to the side.

One of several tied up bundles dropped off the couch onto the floor with a "thud."

"Whoa," Hop said softly.

The fact that the brick appeared to be made up of hundred dollar bills should have been enough to turn Matt's head, but he didn't lock on the cash. It was the adornment on top of the package that caught his gaze.

Affixed at the tie point was a familiar looking, if not uncommon, item. Casino workers and high rollers called it a "pumpkin" – an orange, $1,000 chip. While a pumpkin itself was a strange sight to see outside of a gaming floor, to Matt, the real surprise was the logo stamped in the center: a purple, gold, and green crown with the name of the casino scripted underneath.

It came from The Majestic.

18

MATT AND HOP looked at each other, mouths drawn and wide-eyed, before turning back to the bag. Matt opened the duffel wider and found several other bundles, each wrapped in cellophane, each tied with a burlap cord, and each with an orange, thousand-dollar Majestic pumpkin affixed to the outside. Next to each chip was a number written on the clear plastic with a Sharpie. Hop pulled them out one bundle at a time and arranged them in order from one to six on top of the big ottoman Matt used as a makeshift table. Matt got up, pulled the shades down, and double-checked to make sure he'd locked the door. He couldn't believe his eyes and paced back and forth, looking at the bricks laid out before him.

"Oh shit. Oh *shit!*" he said. He picked up one of the bundles and balanced it in his hand, Indiana Jones style. He didn't know whether to be excited or nervous and decided he was a little of both. He stared up at Hop, half grinning, half bewildered.

"Tell me again where you got this? You sure you didn't rob someone?" Hop asked.

"No, no," Matt said. "I *found* it. Seriously."

"*You* found it?"

"Yes, when I was digging out in my house. I started going through there, you know, seeing if I could recover anything. And – and I came upon this bag."

"In your house?"

"Yes, in my house. Well, kinda. I mean, you've seen my house, right?"

"Do you know whose it is?"

"No, I don't. That's just it. No idea. I checked to see if there was any info on it. *Nada*. It ended up on my lot next to some family silver and a photo album. You saw Second Street. There's so much crap spread out from all over the place, there's no telling," Matt said, holding up another brick and touching the pumpkin. "And what the hell are these on here for?" he said, mostly to himself.

"Looks like we got a gambler. That's a heavy chip. Drug money?"

"I don't know," Matt said. "I would think so, but why would they stick a $1,000 chip on top of it?"

"Bonus?" Hop said. "No telling. I need a drink. You got anything?"

"What do you think?" Matt opened his bottom drawer and pulled out the remains of a fifth of Wild Turkey. He filled two Styrofoam cups and passed one to Hop. "Gobble, gobble. Now let's see how much we got here."

Each stack contained what appeared to be all hundreds, and Matt and Hop made sure they kept the bundles separate before untying them. They counted out each bundle – twice – and tied them back like they found them. Matt jotted down the amounts for each stack on a legal pad. Numbers one through three had the highest amounts, ranging from $350,000 to $700,000. Numbers four through six contained lower amounts, ranging from $75,000 to $125,000. All told, they had two million in cash staring them in the face, plus the six grand in chips. Matt stepped back and tried to take it all in.

"I could certainly get a head start on rebuilding with that," he said.

"You ain't bullshittin'. I could use a little change myself," Hop said. "So, what to do? Keep it? Bank it? Cops? What?"

"I don't know, Hop." Matt said. "I'd really like to think it's ours, but I feel weird even saying that, you know? I mean, we *can* keep it, right? We found it."

Hop swished his drink and took a sip. "We?"

"Should I – we – call the cops?" Matt asked.

Hop was always looking to joke around. That was his nature, and a big part of why Matt liked him so much. But he went quiet for a long moment then licked and bit his lip. "I guess *you* could keep it?" he said. "I mean, hell, you found it on your own lot."

"Could I? I don't know, *I don't know.*" Matt said. "If it is drug money, why not? I mean, who's going to file a report about missing drug money?"

"Good point," Hop said. "But… Something about this doesn't smell right, Matt."

"Not right now, I agree, it doesn't. So…" Matt stood, thumped his index finger just below his nose, and turned to Hop. "I tell you I could really use this…" His eyes were alive with prospects. Matt snapped his fingers. "So here's what we do. We keep our mouths shut and sit on it awhile, just you and me. Hang on to it till the clouds clear, then if nothing's said we can enjoy this. Maybe even buy that big Boston Whaler we've been talking about for years." Matt hoped the reference to their dream fishing boat would bring him around. "Work for you?"

Hop stared at the money again, and Matt could finally see Hop's gears turning. "You know me," Hop said quietly. "I'm not one to lecture on morality, so that ain't what this is about. Just saying, though, someone out there's having a bad day about now. A *bad* day. Why not just go to the police?"

"Sure, we could do that. But the cops have their hands full," Matt said with a gesture at the drawn blinds. "Plus, if this is dirty – which it *has* to be – we'll never see a dime of it if we turn it in. Not like there'd be a reward or something."

"Well, we can't ever be caught flashing those chips around," Hop said.

"Won't have to worry about that any time soon. The Majestic's gone, for all practical purposes." Matt began pacing and sipping. He wasn't going to say anything to Hop, but he'd already run the pumpkin scenarios in his head. He first thought about approaching some of his Majestic contacts and telling them that a few high-dollar chips washed up in his yard. But that would raise suspicion and may warrant further investigation.

There were more serious reasons the pumpkins gave him pause, though. When criminal activity had been suspected at The Majestic in the past – when the occasional dealer colluded with a customer to cheat, or when an employee was found stealing from one of the retail stores – Jeff and Matt usually got involved to ensure, procedurally, that everything was handled properly. But Matt heard nothing from The Majestic prior to the storm about missing or stolen chips. And, considering the denomination of these chips, news of their absence most certainly would've reached his desk or Jeff's; the thousand-dollar chips were logged and monitored, and someone always knew when they were in play or out of the till.

Which made Matt wonder if someone at a higher pay grade could be involved, perhaps someone on the inside. If something shady *was* going on, Matt wasn't sure he should share his find until he'd spoken to Delia about what kind of damage control might be needed. But even telling Delia about the pumpkins would require Matt to show his hand and probably disclose the existence of the real money. That, of course, went against his primary objective – keeping the cash. By the time he turned to Hop his drink was almost gone.

"Let's do this," Matt said. "Let's try to poke around town over the next few days, put out some feelers to see if anyone's asking about – or has heard about – missing money. If someone *is* looking for it, word'll get around fast, don't you think?"

Hop pursed his lips. "Okay. But it just makes me a little nervous. And by the way you're wearing a hole in the floor, I can tell you're not exactly at ease, either."

"I *am* nervous." Matt sat down on the couch to speak with Hop at eye level. "But look, as long as we don't break any laws, what does it hurt to wait till the smoke clears? We won't touch it – not one dime – until we decide what to do. Fair enough?"

Hop nodded ever so slightly. "Okay. You've talked me into it. You're the smart one, after all. This could be all right."

"I agree. But we can't tell anyone. Yet."

"Got my word," said Hop. Then they shook on it like old times, and Matt felt some relief wash over him until Hop spoke up.

"But what about Shelley? You gonna tell her?"

Matt groaned and rubbed his temple with his hand. Hop had a great point. With all of her trust issues, he had to tell her, eventually. "Of course I will," he said. "But let's give this a few days and come up with a solid plan. I just dropped the house *and* Jeff on her, which was rough. Plus, if it goes bad, I don't want her involved."

"What do you mean 'if it goes bad?'"

"I don't want to tell Shelley it's ours if, ultimately, we don't get to keep it. That's all."

"As long as you tell her," Hop said, then raised his eyebrows and looked around the office. "Do you think it's safe to keep all this cash here?"

Matt thought about it for a second. He felt pretty confident he could hold onto it without a problem. "I don't see why not," Matt said. "I don't think anyone would think they'd find much interesting in a law office."

"Agree, but if you want somewhere more secure I can take it. I have a gun safe in my closet we can use."

"I'm fine with keeping it here so long as you are," Matt said, surprised that he resented Hop for even suggesting the money should be kept at Hop's place. "Maybe we'll both have clearer heads in the morning. Give it time to marinate. I can store it out of sight right here under our nose." Matt inched the padded cover of the ottoman to reveal a concealed storage area underneath, being careful not to knock the money off the top.

"Didn't know you had that," Hop said. "Works for me."

"Good deal," Matt said, still thinking. It made sense to Matt to leave the money at the office. If this thing turned sour down the road, the focus would be on Matt, not Hop. And, when it came time to break up the spoils, Matt did not want Hop to have an excuse for getting more than his cut. Plus, toting that bag out in public – even for a few minutes – was too risky.

"How about Triplett-Day for breakfast?" Hop asked. Triplett-Day had been around since Matt could remember. Not only was it the drugstore of choice for the locals, but it also operated an old-fashioned soda fountain in the back that served breakfast and lunch during the week. "We can get a window seat and keep an eye on your office while we're eating, if that makes you feel better."

"Mr. Day back up for business already?"

"Word is he's gonna try and open tomorrow. Saw them hooking up a generator on my way here and stopped by for a sec."

"Great. Eight-thirty?"

"Nineish," Hop said. You're too much of an early bird."

"See you then." Hop picked up a stack of bills, stared at it, then tossed it back in the pile. "This is weird, man. Weird."

Matt walked Hop downstairs and saw him off. Then it was quiet again – too quiet. He couldn't tell if it was the alcohol or not, but he suddenly felt paranoid and looked up and down the street before going back up to the office. He'd only known of the cash for a few hours, but here he was obsessing over it – which made him feel off-center and unclean. He picked up the duffel bag and examined it one more time. Someone *had* to have left a name – or another clue – in sight. Right?

The bag was still dirty so he walked into the foyer and slapped it to get the rest of the caked mud off. After the first few strikes, a cloud of dust enveloped him, making his hands a powdery clay color. When he turned the bag over to clean off the other side, a small, brown manila envelope, not more than three inches long, fell out. Someone had written the number "7" on it. Matt looked around, picked it up and quickly stepped back inside and locked the door. He opened the tab on the end, blew in the envelope, and shook it. A brass key fell out in his hand.

Matt examined it. The key had no numbers or marks, and it looked too small to fit a door or a car. A circular paper tag with *PBT 117* printed on it hung from a string on the end. He suspected it went to a safety deposit box but had no clue as to the bank, as there were no other distinguishing marks. Matt thought about trying to chase down Hop but decided it could wait until the morning.

He looked in the bag to see if anything else was in there, and, satisfied it was empty, rolled it up and shoved it under his couch, out of sight. Matt returned to the money and still couldn't believe the spread before him. It felt like waking up on Christmas morning to find a full stocking. He admitted to himself he was a little excited about the opportunities that came with an influx of cash, but he realized there were a lot of problems as well, not the least of which was how he would explain this good fortune to the feds. Laundering was out of the question; he did not intend to spend middle age in jail. But how else could he sit on this much without alerting anyone? He thought about it for a minute then set it free. He could worry about that at a later time; he had bigger issues to deal with in the short run. He picked up the bundles, one by one, and their weight felt good in his hands. He lined them up in the bottom of the ottoman side-by-side and layered file folders, books, and magazines on top of them in case anyone peeked inside.

He picked up the remnants of his drink, sat back on his couch, and smiled at the fact that he was resting his feet on a cool two million and change.

19

MATT HAD ALREADY slid into a booth by the time Hop rolled in for breakfast. The smell of fried country ham and bacon in the air made Matt's stomach rumble, and he took the liberty of ordering coffee for two as Hop worked out the cobwebs.

"Sorry I'm late, bro," Hop said, puffy eyed and yawning. "Still too early for me." He smelled like alcohol and put both hands around his mug.

"Take a little something extra before you went to bed last night?" Matt asked.

"A snort or two of Gentleman Jack pairs nicely with that crap you served me. Always helps me sleep," Hop said, stirring his coffee and looking around. "Thought it'd be more crowded."

"Word's not out yet. But by this time tomorrow we won't be able to get in the door. Almost feels normal, doesn't it?"

"Almost." They both grabbed menus from the clips built into the napkin holders and looked them over. Everything looked good to Matt, but he went with his old standby.

"Scrambled eggs and bacon. Well done and crispy," he said to the waitress who looked and acted like she was from another era.

"You got it, honey. Already wrote it down that way." The waitress turned to Hop and gestured toward the menu. "What about you, sunshine?"

Hop cleared his throat. "Uhh. Just bring me what Matt ordered. Same for the bacon."

"You sure are a sight for sore eyes, Peggy," Matt said as she scribbled. "Good to see things moving again."

"Good to see you boys, too," she said with a gap-toothed smile and walked to the prep area. When the food came, Matt and Hop attacked their breakfasts as if they hadn't eaten in a week. Matt loaded his eggs and bacon into one of the sliced cathead biscuits and ate the whole thing in a matter of minutes.

"Unbelievable," Matt said. "Best breakfast ever."

"Napworthy," Hop mumbled.

Matt fumbled in his pocket and leaned over the table. "I want to show you something," he said, keeping his voice down. "And keep it out of sight."

He pulled out the key and slid it between the plates. Hop lowered it to his lap and looked down. "A safety deposit box key. So what?"

"Fell out of the duffel bag."

Hop looked up and whistled softly. His sleepy eyes came alive and he adjusted his Cubs cap. "Last night, right after you left," Matt said. "I found it when I was packing everything up. Safety deposit box, huh?"

"I'd say so."

"Any idea what the tag means?"

"Well, 117 is obviously the box number," Hop said. "No idea about PBT." He gazed off into the distance and repeated it to himself. He coughed and slid the key back across the table. "Nope. Doesn't ring a bell."

Matt put it back in his pocket. "Me neither."

Peggy returned with the bill and topped off their coffee. "Sorry to hear about Jeff, hon."

"Thanks," Matt said. "I appreciate it."

"Bad news travels fast," Hop said, slurping his mug.

"Yeah. It does," Matt said, mainly to himself. His stomach twitched. "Let's talk about the plan we came up with last night."

"Plan? We have a plan?" Hop asked.

"Okay, so I admit it's not much of a plan," Matt said. "And I know stealth is not your forte, but try to dig around as quietly as you can, anyway. Ask some questions. Listen for a change. Maybe you'll turn up something. I'll do the same."

"Okay," Hop said. "I'll throw out some feelers, but I don't expect much return."

"You got power yet?" Matt asked.

"Nope. Other than what limited wattage the generator throws off. You?"

"No," Matt said. "But whenever we do get some juice and can get back online, the first thing we should do is try and run down PBT or PBT Bank. Once we have internet access we can look for leads. In the meantime, let's keep our ear to the ground."

Hop swirled his drink and finished it off. "Will do. I'll let you know if anything comes up." Hop looked at his watch.

"Where you heading?" Matt asked.

"I told the old man I'd go check out some of his rentals. I guess I better do that so he'll get off my ass."

"Sounds good," Matt said. "Talk to you later."

———————

Matt went back to the office and debated about what to do next. He still wasn't ready to go back into Jeff's office, but he certainly didn't plan to sit around by himself and let the depression creep back in. He killed an hour or so washing what clothes he had left using bottled water and soap. As he was draping them over the windowsill, a familiar sound chirped from his desk.

His phone was ringing.

He looked at the screen and saw Shelley's name, but when he picked up, Fin was on the line. Matt grinned from ear to ear, and they chatted for what seemed to Matt like thirty minutes. Fin told him everything and more that was going on his world, and Matt gave him abbreviated explanations about Gulfport and answered the best he could when Fin asked him about his school and where his friends were. The conversation was proceeding better than expected until Fin asked Matt when Matt was going to come visit him at his new home in Meridian.

His new home in Meridian? Matt could feel his face flush with anger. He took a deep breath and was glad Fin couldn't see him. "Hopefully, you'll get back down here soon, okay buddy?"

"Okay."

"I love you, man. Let me speak to Mommy."

"Okay, Daddy. I love you, too. Mommy!" Matt could hear Shelley warning Fin not to wake J.W. Then she was on the phone. Her greeting sounded warm enough.

"Great conversation with Fin," Matt said. "Quite the chatterbox. I miss him like crazy."

"I heard y'all. He misses you too."

Matt paused. Then, unable to help himself, he continued with what had suddenly become an urgent matter. "Shelley, he asked when I was coming to see him at *home*. Since when did he start calling *Meridian* home? You never said this move was permanent, and you'd better damn well not be telling the boys that shit if you are."

"What are you talking about?"

"Home. He asked when I was coming *home*," Matt said, enunciating each word and feeling his patience wear dangerously thin. "Should be the other way around, should it not?"

"I don't know why he'd say that. I guess being up here so long, now, and Mom doing up his new room with Buzz Lightyear..."

"His new room? Your mother's behind this. I should've known," he said through clenched teeth.

"Matt, let's not go there. Not now."

"Damn right I'm going there. This pisses me off. I've been down here trying to dig out of this shit for almost a week now, Jeff's dead, and you haven't made the first effort to even try and come down here for just *one damn day*. And now, when I finally get to have a halfway decent conversation with my son, he says some brainwashed bullshit like this. We have to have some boundaries here."

"Oh yeah?"

"Yeah, Shelley. I'm sick of this shit." He felt himself digging the hole and wished he could take it back but it was too late. He couldn't unring that bell.

"Oh, you're sick of it? *You're sick of it?* I can't believe I'm hearing this, Matt," Shelley said. She was crying now. "Really? *You're* the victim? You're the one who could have – would have – *screwed* that bitch if not for your drunken incompetence in Las Vegas."

And there it was. First time she'd addressed it directly – or even said the words Las Vegas – since he sent that dreaded text from that awful hotel. Matt didn't know what to say. She snuffed out all of his anger with one sentence and he had no other option but to capitulate. "Shelley, I – I'm sorry."

"How dare you talk to me about *boundaries?* How dare you. You broke my heart, Matt. You have no idea how much you hurt me."

He could barely understand her sentences through the tears. He wanted to hang up. He wanted to start the conversation over without being blind with fury. He knew she was right. He suddenly felt tired again. "Look, I didn't mean to start a fight, Shelley. I know I was wrong. I just –"

"Tell me what happened."

"What?"

"You never told me what happened!"

"I tried to but – I told you. I screwed up. I went too far. But honestly Shelley, as bad as it sounded, I never truly crossed –"

"Start from the beginning," Shelley said, regaining her composure. "Tell me everything."

"Everything?"

"Everything."

So he did.

20

I T HAPPENED JUST a few months before, but to Matt, it seemed like an eternity. Delia had dispatched Matt to Las Vegas to assist her in a trial involving The Majestic's parent company, Majesticorp, after it had been sued by the Hojaru Casino Corporation – HCC to insiders – for alleged trade secret and copyright infringement violations. Majesticorp owned three casinos: The Majestic in Gulfport, The Monte Premi in Atlantic City, and its newest and largest resort, The Panacea, in Las Vegas. According to Delia, HCC's Board was upset that it had just sunk a ton of money into its newest casino, the Belle, only to discover shortly thereafter that The Panacea, a nicer, even more modern – although *remarkably* similar – resort just across the street was pinching the Belle's business. HCC had to stop the bleeding, so it sued Majesticorp. Because The Panacea's design mimicked The Majestic's antebellum theme, and because the Bing handled all of the legalities associated with The Majestic's construction in Gulfport, Majesticorp called the Bing in – Delia specifically – to help prove that The Majestic's design and theme predated the Belle and thus show HCC's claims lacked merit.

This was Matt's first exposure to a large, out-of-state trial, and Shelley encouraged him to go, even though he would be away six weeks or more, depending on the judge. Delia had told him he could come home for a weekend midway through, which would help a little on the home front, and he and Shelley were in complete agreement that saying no would be a huge mistake – there might not be another blue-chip opportunity like this if he turned Delia down. He was assigned to work up documents, prep witnesses, and help Delia behind the scenes; she would be first chair and lead trial attorney. A local Nevada firm provided ancillary support.

Even though Matt was relegated to working in the windowless, converted conference room in The Panacea that served as the trial "war room," he was grateful to Delia for hand-picking him, and was glad to assist the other lawyers. The Nevada firm had two lawyers, three paralegals, and a graphics team; Majesticorp also had its own set of in-house counsel there, morning to night, observing and assisting. Everyone knuckled down, and sixteen-hour days were the norm. The only nights they got off were Fridays – and the down time was mandatory. When the week came to a close, the trial team cast aside their briefcases, closed their laptops, and hit the town, starting off with a nice dinner, and on to one – or many – of the multitude of Vegas watering holes.

During Matt's second week, Delia paired him with an in-house Majesticorp lawyer named Robyn Frost. They worked together to prepare corporate witnesses for testimony and to finalize and supplement direct- and cross-examination outlines. Matt was glad to have the help, as there just weren't enough hours in the day to do everything expected of him. Plus, she was funny and cute in a nerdy schoolgirl kind of way, and Matt enjoyed having someone his age around. After two weeks working side-by-side, they developed a comfortable rapport that made the time away more bearable.

As they turned the corner into the fourth week of trial, Matt counted the days before he could fly home to see his family. He thought it would be wise to check with Delia before booking his flight, and his instincts were right – the lawyers looked unusually dour as they gathered in the war room that Tuesday afternoon. Matt looked up from his computer and asked what was going on.

Delia set her briefcase down on the floor. "Rough one," she said with a heavy sigh. "HCC had a good day."

Everyone listened as Delia explained how the witness, a Majesticorp executive, had mistakenly referenced a critical document previously excluded by the court. HCC's lawyers immediately requested a sidebar and argued that since Majesticorp opened the door, the document had to be explained. The only way to clear it up, they argued, would be to call the witness who drafted it. The judge agreed.

"When are they calling him?" Robyn asked.

"Monday," Delia said.

Matt felt his chest tighten. "Whose witness is he?"

Delia turned to Matt, her face all business. "Mine. I'll need some help on that outline this weekend." *Not this weekend. Please tell me I didn't hear that right.* "Go ahead and start pulling his employment records," Delia continued. "We can start running through them Saturday morning."

Matt swallowed hard and said he'd get right on it after stepping out for some fresh air. It was clear Delia didn't remember the weekend pass – and that made him furious. But he knew better than to let it show and tried to be inconspicuous as he walked out of the war room. Robyn tried to follow him out, but he waved her off.

He called Shelley from a Starbucks a block away and ripped into Delia. Shelley, true to form, let him vent for a few minutes and then put a positive spin on it: she told him he was making an impact or Delia wouldn't have asked him to stay. She said a few more weeks was nothing, and the additional time away would make the reunion that much sweeter. But Matt knew she was saying that only for his benefit.

Matt's mood darkened as the next three days ticked by. The week, which was supposed to end with the trip home, wound up with Matt and Shelley getting into a blow-up over a comment her mother made about the kids watching too much television. Matt realized later that he'd picked the fight out of sheer frustration, and it only drove him deeper into his funk. When he tried calling Shelley back after cooling off, she didn't answer, which put him even more on edge.

Per tradition, the trial team made Friday night plans and asked Matt to join them. Delia delivered the invitation personally, realizing Matt was feeling a little homesick. Matt declined, but Delia insisted he go. She even recruited Robyn to try to convince Matt to join them. He didn't know what was more depressing: sitting in his hotel room all alone feeling sorry for himself or going to dinner with a bunch of people he didn't care to be around. They eventually talked him into it. Morton's was on the rotation, but Matt was in no mood for a steak, no matter how good, how prime, or how expensive, so he didn't order anything he couldn't drink.

The longer he sat at the table listening to them clink their glasses and flap their gums, the more he regretted the excursion. He kept thinking of what he would be doing if he had gone home, and tried to push away thoughts of eating out with J.W., Fin, and Shelley. He would take McDonald's with his family over Morton's with this crew any day. He realized he was being petulant but didn't care. Matt found solace in the Pinot, and by the time the group had finished their main course, the buttery wine had softened the rough edges. Matt nibbled on some bread and leftover appetizers and made sure the waiter kept his glass full. He turned his attention to Robyn so he wouldn't have to feign interest in the other conversations.

By the time they left, the steakhouse was several thousand dollars richer and many Cabernet, Chardonnay and Pinot bottles lighter. Matt decided to return to his room and crash. Everyone else wanted to go to a club for more drinking and dancing, and against his better judgment, Matt agreed to go out for just *one* more round. When they got to the bar, Robyn, of all people, ordered shots, and, over the next two hours, Matt's alcohol-induced stupor grew deeper with each pass of the waitress. The evening culminated in Matt's being stone drunk at a corner booth in a penthouse bar in The Oasis. By then, Delia had turned in for the night, as had most of the other lawyers. Only Robyn remained. She excused herself to go to the restroom, and Matt thought it would be a good time for his check-in text to Shelley.

Lng nt. Hdng to hotel. Drnk2 muuch. Love you & mis y ou. Will call. Tmorrw.

The phone vibrated a minute later. Matt checked the screen.

Luv U lots. B Careful. Nite.

Matt and Robyn had one more drink, and Matt asked that they go back to the Panacea because he could barely keep his eyes open. He knew it was time to leave an hour earlier when Robyn started to look appealing, but he couldn't muster the initiative to go back to his hotel until the return message from Shelley jerked him back to reality.

He needed to get out of there.

Robyn had a car service pick them up, and when they got into the Lincoln, she sat next to him instead of the window. She smelled like Crown Royal and cigarettes.

"This turned out to be an okay night, right?" She moved even closer, and he could feel her breast pushing into his arm.

"I guess," Matt said, looking out at the Caesar's fountain. He felt her hand on his shoulder and her fingers combing through his hair. Instead of stiffening and pushing away, he relaxed and tried to rationalize through the alcohol just where the hell she was going with this. She leaned up and kissed him on the neck. He could feel his heart thumping beneath his shirt and her breath on his neck. His mind was racing, and he couldn't stop it.

"What are you doing, Robyn?" Matt whispered, his face close to hers. He felt nervous but it was an excited nervous.

"Just trying to help you feel better." She pulled his head close and kissed him right on the lips. Her tongue pushed through, and he closed his eyes.

In a split second, Matt thought about pulling back, but the haze of tequila slowed him. This could get extremely ugly, and Shelley certainly would not approve. That said, this was a one-time thing, plus he would never get caught, plus he felt he deserved it after being stuck here alone, plus it was no slight against Shelley; all he would do is kiss this girl, who was not bad looking – and had great tits, by the way – and then call it a night. Plus, he thought, it did make him feel better.

What the hell. I'll just blame it on the booze.

Matt pulled Robyn into his arms, and they stayed locked up until the driver interrupted them to tell them they had arrived. He removed his hand from her thigh and smoothed down his hair. By the time he stumbled out of the car, Robyn was already halfway to the lobby. Matt shuffled after her, caught her just inside the glass doors, and tried to hug her from behind, but she pulled away.

"Hey," he slurred. "What're you doin'?"

"I'm sorry," she said, turning to him. "We shouldn't have. I – I can't do this."

"Sorry?" Matt asked. "What?" At this point, Matt figured he had already danced across the line and convinced himself that going on just a bit longer would hurt no one. He hadn't really committed any major fouls; no buttons undone, no zippers pulled, no clasps released. Just some groping and kissing in the car and frankly, Matt could go for a little more. He held on to a chair to steady himself.

Robyn dabbed the corners of her eyes with her pinky fingers. Matt closed one of his to get her into focus. Was she crying, or about to? What had he done to make her upset? There was no mistaking something was wrong, although Matt couldn't make sense of it.

"Please, don't be mad..." he tried and reached out to her again.

"We can't, Matt," she replied. "I'm supposed to... want to, even, but we can't. I mean, I thought it would be a quick job, but..." She moved close and seemed to speak very softly. *Supposed to? Quick job?* Matt asked himself as the room rocked back and forth. His thoughts came slowly. "What...?"

"You're a good guy, Matt. You have a family who loves you."

"C'mon, Robyn . . ."

"No, Matt. No." She wiped her eyes with the heels of both hands and pushed her hair behind her ears. "I like you, Matt. I really do.

I didn't expect this to happen . . ." Her voice trailed off, and she covered her mouth with her hand. After a second, she kissed him on the cheek, shook her head, and got in the elevator. Matt stood there for a minute and thought about what to do. He sidled up to a barstool in the hotel bar and ordered a beer. It didn't taste good, but he choked it down anyway.

"Chicks," Matt said to the bartender, tapping the top of his longneck to the side of his head. The bartender nodded and wiped the bar off. Perhaps a few minutes in her room would allow her to reevaluate her position on whether she needed some company. Matt dialed her cell phone, but she didn't answer.

"I know you're up," Matt slurred to himself, so he hit the "Messages" icon on his phone and sent her a text.

R – I had los of fun ttonigt especially on way back. Am feling lonely here. If youw ant company, my romm 1105. Let me know

He sipped his beer and looked for peanuts or something to munch on – he suddenly remembered he'd had nothing to eat all night other than some bread and a few bites of calamari. Right then his cell phone vibrated. It startled him, and he nearly knocked it off the bar trying to grab it. Maybe Robyn was still in the elevator when he tried to call and didn't hear the phone ring? But she'd sure answered his text quickly. He peered at the phone.

Matt. What is the meaning of this? Where are you? This scares me. Call me NOW.

Matt frowned at the message and tried to decipher it. He began to text back, but first double-checked the recipient. His eyes widened.

Shelley.

———

"And that's it?" Shelley asked.

"That's it," Matt replied. "I tried to call you right then but you never picked up."

"Yes I did. You were so drunk you could barely talk so I hung up."

Matt didn't even remember talking to Shelley, so he didn't respond.

"So what happened to Robyn? How were things between you two lovebirds back at the war room the next day?"

"Fine. I mean there was nothing the next day, Shelley. According to Delia, she got pulled away on another job. I never saw her again." *Thank God.*

Matt didn't tell her that when his plane touched down a few weeks later after the trial ended he hoped and prayed to find a car waiting in the arrivals lane with two little boys craning their heads about for Daddy, with their mother at least willing to talk. Instead, he found no one. He didn't tell her that he was absolutely devastated upon arriving home to find a one-sentence note from Shelley informing him that she was moving in with her mother. He didn't tell her that he tried multiple times to call her and how sorry he was but each time he called, she either didn't take the cell or her mother blocked him on the land line. And he didn't get to tell her it was the biggest mistake of his life and that he loved her and that he would do anything to have one more shot at what they used to have. And when the phone was quiet on the other end, he wondered if, perhaps, he should tell her all those things. But Matt couldn't even hear Shelley breathing anymore, and he thought she'd hung up.

"Hello?"

"I'm here."

"Oh. Okay. Well, that's it. Never saw her again, never heard from her again, nothing – nor do I intend to."

"Well I would hope not."

"Can I – can we – start this conversation over – before it's too late? I never should have said anything about boundaries. I was out of line."

"I won't argue with you there. You were out of line," Shelley said. "And I don't want to fight either. This isn't good for us. Or the kids. It's just, with all you're dealing with, and with all of my emotions – it's not easy being here, either – I just don't know. One side of me wants to drive down there and jump in your arms, but the other side keeps thinking of that text from Las Vegas. I wish I knew what to do."

Jump in my arms? He swallowed hard. "I don't know what else I can do, Shelley. Tell me, please. That night during the trial was months ago. It's over. There is nothing else that I know to do – that I can do – to get us back on track."

She sniffled but didn't chime in, so he kept going.

"We have to get through this, one way or the other. I have to, and you have to. God forbid if you decide to end what we have and what we've shared over the years, I'll find some way to deal with it, but before you do, please give me another chance. I just miss you so much. So much. Let me try and make it work. I'll do anything."

"I just can't work through it yet, Matt. I'm not ready." All-out crying again.

"Okay – but. Okay." Damn, he wanted to hold her. He wanted to tell her how much he loved her. He could feel the emotion pulsating through on her end, and he sensed a breakthrough. It rattled him to the point that he had to hold his phone with both hands to keep it from shaking.

"I'm sorry, Shelley. I'm sorry." Finally got to say that. *Good.* "And I want you to know –"

"I know, Matt. I know. Let's talk again Sunday. I can't do this right now," she sniffed. "Bye."

Dammit. This time she did hang up, but she wasn't mad for a change. At least now he appeared to have a potential opening on the reconciliation front. He planned to continue where he left off the next time he got the chance.

Defeated and exhausted, Matt collapsed onto his sofa bed and kicked off his shoes. He stared at the ceiling and tried to remember the last time he tucked in J.W. and Fin. He couldn't recall whether he read them a book or made up a story, but the mere thought of saying goodnight to his young sons made his heart ache. Matt realized at that moment he had to do something – *anything* – to get his family back under the same roof. He felt a plan coming together, but it had not fully materialized in his head. He knew one thing for certain, though.

It had to start with Shelley.

21

MATT AWOKE AT daybreak thankful for a dreamless sleep. He thought about calling Shelley back, but he felt pretty good and didn't want to blow it by seeming too eager. For once he bowed to discretion and found it suited him. He checked in with Hop, who had nothing to report on the mystery money front, so he packed up his digging gear and headed back to the house. He didn't find a whole lot worth saving this round except an old antique iron dog that previously guarded their hearth. Matt saw a metal paw sticking up out of the mud next to a set of concrete stairs and dug it out. It was dirty and slightly bent, but he put it in his truck anyway. He took extra care to check out every nook and cranny to see if anything else washed up that could be linked to the duffel bag but came up empty-handed. He shone the flashlight into the hole where he found the loot to make sure he didn't miss anything and, as he suspected, it was empty.

Matt treated Hank and Hop to lunch at Triplett-Day. Matt's prediction had been right; word had spread fast about its opening, and it attracted quite the crowd. Hop hadn't caught up with Hank since the storm, and they visited for over an hour. Hank let it slip he had an operating field shower, and Matt made an appointment for that afternoon.

Seeing the crowd made Matt happy. He ran into other people he knew whom he hadn't seen since before the storm, and it felt like a high school reunion for the Gulfport residents. The discussions always ended up the same. How are you; how is your family; how did your house do; do you have plenty to eat, let me know how

I can help; we're lucky to be alive; and God bless. Matt never tired of saying it. He ran into his Sunday School teacher and found out Trinity was having a service the next day. He planned to go.

He was surprised he hadn't heard anything from Cathy, so he called and left her a message to let him know when she got to town that he was available to help out. Now that his phone was up, he tried to search "PBT" on Safari but was disheartened to get an endless buffering signal, so he set it aside.

Matt took a change of clothes to Hank's. "Don't hog all the hot water," Hank said, as he showed Matt how to operate the shower in his back yard. "Actually, it ain't all that hot. Don't hog all the warm water," Hank said, adjusting himself.

"I won't."

"You only got five minutes. Five minutes."

"Got it, Hank. Leave me alone."

"Be sure and wash your balls."

"Dammit, Hank."

"And your arse."

Hank walked off, cackling. Matt stepped in and felt the water hit his face. He was outside, and the sun was just setting. The converted blue tarp provided the four walls of the shower, and the shower itself was yet another rigged-up military contraption of Hank's. But it felt wonderful. Matt shampooed his hair, washed off with soap and then just let the water hit him until Hank called time. Hank hung a fresh towel on a nail supporting the tarp. It smelled like Downy, and when he buried his face in it, Matt realized how much he must have reeked the past few days. A fresh towel and clean clothes – and underwear – made Matt feel human again. He thanked Hank, accepted a turkey sandwich from Sarah, and went back to his office for the night.

Matt looked forward to the next day. After all, he was going to church.

Matt realized soon after he woke up that he had no proper clothes to wear, but he figured no one else would either, so he put on the same pair of shorts he had on the day before and dug a white t-shirt leftover from his trip out of his suitcase which he had worn only once under a suit.

Matt and Shelley made it a point to go to church every week-end if they were in town, but he hadn't gone since she moved out. He didn't feel like subjecting himself to the stares and glances of those who'd heard some of the story but not all of it. He knew people had been talking about them. That's just the nature of the beast, especially in a town like Gulfport, where community circles run small, insular, and tight. Couples in their social and Sunday School groups had split in the past, and the rumors and discussions flew around so fast no one could tell what was true or not. He didn't feel like being judged and didn't want to explain anything to anyone. He figured there'd be members who'd ask – quite inno-cently – why Shelley and the boys weren't with him. Matt didn't want to tell a lie in a place of worship, but he didn't want to tell the truth either. It had been easier for him to just stay at home.

Today, though, was different. Matt felt a longing for church. He felt the need to share in the fellowship of this aftermath with his fellow members, and he really wanted some direction and comfort from above. The situation with the money was weighing heavily on him, and he could feel it like a yoke around his neck as he drove through Bayou View. That, coupled with losing Jeff, left him feel-ing like a cork in the water – floating and directionless, subject only to the whim of the day's tide. He had read in the Bible and in other stories about people actually feeling spiritually thirsty. Matt had never felt "thirsty," per se. Nevertheless, he paid attention to the sermons to the extent possible and occasionally picked up a nugget or two, which he tried to weave in to his week. He wondered if the feelings he had as he turned into the parking lot amounted to a longing, a thirst, or just plain loneliness. He didn't know, but he knew he needed something.

Matt felt humbled when he walked through the doors. Trinity didn't yet have power either, but the natural light illuminated the sanctuary in a way that Matt had not seen, or at least observed, before. He had never appreciated how magnificently the stained glass threw bright colors over the walls and pews. The dust particles floating up and up through the beams of light gave off tinted flashes and made Matt felt thankful for this unexpected display of the mundane turned spectacular by a hand unseen. His strongest emotions rose up, however, when he saw the people. Although most had lost their homes, and no one had power, gas or an effective, reliable means to communicate, word of a church service had somehow gotten out. Matt could not see an empty seat, and he eventually had to squeeze in on the end of a pew close to the front – and he never sat up front.

During a normal service, the occasional small, quiet conversation percolated here and there before the call to worship bells rang, but most of the time, families and individuals sat silently waiting for the service to begin. Not today. Everyone talked, hugged, and shook hands. The din sounded like a convention center hall. People showed up in whatever they could pull together: t-shirts, shorts, pants, hats, bandanas. One man even had a tool belt on. No one wore any makeup; no one shaved; and everyone looked like a total wreck. Matt had never seen a more beautiful congregation. He got pulled right into the crowd and did his share of cheek kissing and hand shaking and was hugged more times than he could count.

After a few minutes, a slow hush came over the crowd as Reverend R.J. Curtis took the pulpit. He, too, looked like the rest of the group. He wore old jeans and a Columbia fishing shirt that looked like it had not seen a washing machine in some time. Instead of putting on a robe, he draped a brightly colored vestment around his neck.

R.J. moved to the center of the altar to be better heard and welcomed everyone.

"It's so great to see all of you here," R.J. said with a warm smile, and asked everyone to turn in their pew Bibles to 2 Corinthians 1, verses 2-7. He then read the verse:

Grace and peace to you from God our Father and the Lord Jesus Christ. Praise be to the God and Father of our Lord Jesus Christ, the father of compassion and the God of all comfort, who comforts us in all our troubles, so that we can comfort those in any trouble with the comfort we ourselves have received from God.

Matt read along as if he were hearing this for the first time. *Compassion.* Good. *Comfort.* More perfect words could not have been spoken.

For just as the sufferings of Christ flow over into our lives, so also through Christ our comfort overflows.

Go on, R.J., Matt thought. Setting up for a home run once again.

If we are distressed, it is for your comfort and salvation; if we are comforted, it is for your comfort, which produces in you patience and endurance of the same sufferings we suffer.

This one was out of the park. It was so quiet in the church, it felt thick.

And our hope for you is firm, because we know that just as you share in our sufferings, so also you share in our comfort.

R.J. closed the Bible. "Amen."

"Amen," Matt said, joining the rest of the flock. Never had a Bible verse resonated to Matt like the one R.J. just read. Matt hung on every word, as did everyone else, and the lump in his throat grew larger as Betty banged out the first chords of "The

Old Rugged Cross" on the piano. Not a dry eye remained when the song ended, and, over the sniffles and nose-blowings, R.J. asked everyone to take a load off and have a seat.

"I won't keep you here too long today," R.J. said over the creaking of the pews. "I know everyone has lots to tend to. I thought we would just talk some, share Communion, and plan on doing this again next week. So let's talk."

And R.J. talked. He talked about the sufferings of the people of the coast. He talked about lives lost and lives forever altered. He talked about the stress and the strain this terrible event would have on relationships. He talked about the financial impact, both short term and long term. He talked about hardships now and hardships to come. He talked about how Job must have felt when his world came crashing down. And how Jesus must have felt, day in and day out, until his crucifixion, especially when facing betrayal upon betrayal by those closest to him.

He talked about the light from the people. He talked about how, since the storm, he had observed a sense of respect and care for others like nothing he had ever seen before. He talked about the resiliency of those affected by the storm. He talked about how neighbors who barely knew each other just a week ago now sat down every night in their back yards and shared food, getting through it together while growing and nurturing their relationship and friendship. He talked about walking the streets and hearing as many, if not more, words of encouragement than words of despair. He talked about the miracle of the loaves and fishes and how now, just six days after the storm, Trinity provided hot meals for over 400 people – and the numbers were growing each day. He asked the church members to look around and try to remember the last time – other than Christmas and Easter – this many people showed up for one service.

He asked the congregation what they valued most now that the storm took it all away. Was it their couch that washed out to sea? Was it their clothes or their car? Was it their iPad or their HDTV?

"No, these things don't make the list, do they?" R.J. said. "Look around. Look to your left and to your right. That's what matters. *This* is what matters. You. Your family. Your neighbors. Your friends. I keep asking people, if they can, to identify what material things they missed the most. You know what they tell me? Do you think it's something they bought? Something in that list I just mentioned? No. Do you know what I am told nearly every single time? Photographs. Letters. Children's artwork." R.J. smiled and paused for it to sink in. "Did you hear what I said? *Photographs, letters,* and *children's artwork.* That stuff hanging on your refrigerators or stacked in your drawers. Things you cannot replace from the people you love. It all comes back to the people – you – and the connection you have with each other, the fellowship you share with each other through Jesus Christ."

Matt nodded his head.

"In this age of technological isolation, it took this storm, this horrible, terrible, destructive event, to get us outside again. Working together. Talking to each other. Visiting with each other. Providing for each other. Serving each other. It took this event for some of us – and I don't exclude myself here – to realize what really, truly matters. Now, we have a long road ahead, no doubt about that. But I am confident in the future. My future. Your future. The future of the Gulf Coast. I am confident because I have faith. Faith in our fellow man. Faith we can do it. Together."

Matt now knew why he got choked up when he saw Hop the other day, when he saw Hank after the storm, and when his friends at Triplett-Day asked about him and his family. It was the connections he valued most. He knew then he would do whatever it would take to mend fences with Shelley.

At the Communion rail, Matt prayed harder than he could ever recall praying. He asked for guidance, peace, and reconciliation. When he sang "Amazing Grace" at the close of the service, holding the thick stumpy hand of the lady next to him whom he did not know, he realized then he knew what it was like to be thirsty, and he was thirsty no more.

He called Shelley after the service to tell her about it and to offer up the olive branch, but she beat him to it. Apparently, the events of late had been weighing on her as well.

Shelley was coming down on Friday.

And she was bringing the kids.

22

THE NEXT MORNING, a thundering HWAAAAHHHHHHHHHH jolted Matt right off the couch. With the windows open, nothing buffered the racket and, for a split second, he couldn't figure out what happened. When he heard it again and realized where it came from, he scrambled to his window to look. Sure enough, he saw two diesel locomotives pulling a line of boxcars.

Debris and trash had blocked the tracks since the storm, preventing the trains from running, and some speculated months would pass before the railroad became operational again. The deep rumble of the engine meant progress, and Matt realized just how much he'd missed the train coming by every day. He listened for more, and soon the echoes of the horn rewarded him as the train signaled its arrival farther down the track. He looked at his watch.

"Like you never missed a beat," he said, watching the last of the cars go by. "Seven a.m. sharp. Just like back in the day." He stayed there until he could no longer see or hear the train any more. Down the street, an electric crew on a bucket truck was installing a new transformer. Another good sign.

In spite of the train, or perhaps because of it, Matt woke up refreshed and rejuvenated. He didn't know if it was Reverend Curtis' sermon the day before or the upcoming visit from his Shelley and the boys, but something had put a new spring in his step. When the Bing truck stopped in front of Matt's office two hours later he grinned with anticipation. And Delia did not disappoint. The runners she'd sent stacked nearly every inch of available space in Matt's office with food, water, drinks, books, batteries, sanitizing solutions, and paper goods ranging from toilet paper to Clorox wipes. And it was only the beginning.

He let out a long, low whistle when they unloaded ten five-gallon cans of gasoline and immediately filled up his truck. Matt kept the remaining fuel just inside the first-floor office in case he needed to top off later or share with Hank or Hop.

When Matt thought they were all done, the driver unloaded several large boxes wrapped in butcher paper. Matt recognized the S.F. Alman seagull logo stamp and couldn't believe what was inside. Delia was not kidding when she said she would restock him. Not only did she include brand new suits, shirts, ties, and shoes for work, but she re-outfitted him on the non-work side as well: jackets, pullovers, t-shirts, tennis shoes, casual shoes, hats, underwear, fleece pullovers, sunglasses, and even a new watch. They also packed an overnight bag, a shaving kit, two fleece blankets, and a duffel bag. It truly was a haberdashery in a box. Matt couldn't begin to calculate how many thousands she spent on the sundries. An envelope taped on the box bore his name, and he found a card inside.

From your family at Bingham, Samson & Toflin.
We hope this gets you back on your feet in style.

But the good feeling drained away when he saw the signature line: *Stephen Andrew Massey III.* He picked up his phone with some reluctance.

"Hi! Just got the supplies and clothes," Matt said after Delia answered. "You outdid yourself this time."

"Consider it the least the firm could do for you, honey."

"*You* did it, Delia. Not the Bing. I know it was you."

"Does it matter?" Delia asked.

"Not really. Just thought you should know that someone else took credit for it."

"You have to be kidding me."

"Tripp signed the card, Delia."

Matt could hear her blood pressure go up.

"Son of a bitch," she spat. "He has never lifted one damn finger to help anyone unless it benefited him in some way, too. I knew I should have checked everything before it shipped. Pitiful."

"I know, Delia. I know. I'm sorry. I probably shouldn't have even told you, but I wanted to let you know how much I appreciate what *you* did."

"Nothing for you to feel sorry for, Matt – and I'm glad you called; I wish I could do more. As for Tripp, this doesn't involve you. It's just, well, the way he's been acting lately is almost as bad as he behaved back when I first started out. I took what some called extreme measures back then, and I may have to take some more soon. Did I ever tell you about that?"

"You did, Delia. How could I forget?"

"Well, I'm telling you now it may be time for another adjustment." He heard her take a deep breath, and when she spoke again, she suddenly sounded weary. "Look. I'm sorry for bringing you into this. My problems with Tripp are miniscule compared to what you're going through. The important thing is that everything made it down there and that you're safe."

"Delia, really. It's no problem."

She closed the subject and was moving on. "You good for now, honey?"

"Good to go, Delia. Thanks again. This was above and beyond the call of duty."

"Say no more. Take care and call me anytime."

"Will do."

With that, Delia hung up. The conversation, which should have been one of joy and thankfulness in light of such a kind gesture, instead turned out heavy and awkward. Matt now realized he had been wrong about Delia's hardiness. Tripp's attacks had hurt her – and why shouldn't they? Despite her reputation, she was human too. Plus, it's not like this conflict was something new. Delia and Tripp *had* been feuding since Matt's grade-school days. And it appeared the battle was not yet over.

As Matt understood it, through no fault of her own, Delia got sideways with Tripp the day she started as the firm's first full-time female attorney some thirty years before. At the outset, she had to work twice as hard to build credibility to show she could cut it in the men's club. Just the fact that she was there ruffled feathers, and she further stirred the company pot by logging eighty hours-plus per week out of the gate. When, in just a matter of months, her billables jumped ahead of every other associate's on the payroll, some realized they could sit idle no more.

Tripp had arrived three years before Delia and immediately garnered special treatment since he was the first associate hired at the Bing who had attended Harvard Law School. He took pride in his pedigree and worked hard to maintain his status as the golden child. He was a master at bringing in new business (although some questioned whether he had the chops to keep it) and he had a fraternity of young disciples who hitched their trailer to his wagon in the hope that they could benefit from the coupling.

Tripp was none too pleased at the thought of bringing on someone who had the capacity to steal his thunder – a woman, no less – and made his feelings known in an effort to put a stop to it. He had no such luck. When Delia came and people actually started to like her, he railed even more. His efforts fell on deaf ears as it soon became clear that Delia, even as a junior associate, was building her own client base and in some cases, outperforming Tripp. This only strengthened his resolve, and he recruited some of his like-minded cronies to execute a plan designed to publicly shame Delia and, hopefully, run her off.

The "adjustment" that Delia referenced had long been firm lore. Matt first heard it told in the break room during his second year at the Bing, and every time it was retold he got nervous that Tripp Massey himself would burst in on the session and fire everyone present just for rehashing of the facts.

Matt considered himself fortunate as he counted himself as one of the few chosen ones who heard the story from Delia's mouth. One Friday afternoon after Matt had been with the Bing for about four years, he found himself stuck in Jackson doing rote document review on a commercial litigation case. Afterwards, exhausted and in need of some libations, he shared several glasses of Basil Hayden on the rocks with Delia to try to feel sane again. Much to his surprise, after the whiskey had sufficiently lubricated (and loosened) their tongues, the subject came up. Matt couldn't remember if he breached it or she did, but once it was on the table, Delia paused, leaned back in her chair, and a crooked grin crossed her face. Then, much to Matt's surprise, Delia lit a cigarette, took a long pull and began to speak.

———

It happened one June afternoon during the firm's weekly office lunch after Delia – who had been with the Bing for barely two years – sat down to break bread with a friendly group of attorneys and staff to chat and discuss everyone's weekend plans. As she started to leave after finishing her meal, she thought she heard someone calling her name over the din of the cafeteria crowd, but disregarded it and kept walking. When she heard it again, she stopped in her tracks. This time there was no doubt, and when she turned to face the direction it was coming from, she saw a particularly smug lawyer waving his arm at her. "Hey Dee-lee-uh," he said, "you missed something." He pointed to a pile of trash in the middle of the table left over from his and his cronies' lunch.

Nearly everyone in the firm – attorneys, staff and otherwise – ate lunch in the same room at about the same time on Fridays, and right now Delia felt all eyes upon her. Deep down, Delia knew this moment would come, but she just didn't know when or how. She had a solid contingent of supporters and coworkers who lauded her achievements, and these individuals were truly happy for what she brought to the table. On the other hand, she couldn't ignore the more subtle invectives from the group that snubbed her, and, like it or not, the latter faction was better established in the Bing in both numbers and political clout, and thus kept her allies in check.

Good, bad, or ugly, this was a pivotal moment in Delia's development at the Bing, and she knew then the tone, tenor, and substance of her response would have long-lasting implications. She could either take the more passive route, let it go, and ignore them, or she could hit it square on the nose and let the chips fall where they may.

One day back in elementary school, Delia had come upon an older boy pushing and berating her kid sister, and she faced a similar choice. If she didn't step up, Delia would leave her sister – the only quiet one in the family – vulnerable to future torment from her ill-behaved, mouth-breathing neighbor. That was something Delia could neither bear nor tolerate, and she hesitated for only a half second before striking. When the teachers finally arrived at the scene, they found a writhing, screaming, skinny, hornet of a girl balled up in a mass of hair, earth, torn clothes, and snot on top of some poor soul twice her size. The only thing making more noise than Delia was the boy, and he wasn't making any sense. He was lying on the ground, mouth bleeding. His tears had cut shiny paths through the dirt Delia ground into his face when she raked his cheeks across the gravel in the playground. His shirt was torn from belly to shoulder, and he had a tread mark on his back where Delia had been standing for leverage. Later, as Delia sat in the principal's office missing her other shoe and waiting for her sentence, she scraped his skin out from under her fingernails and pondered her actions. She was scared she would be suspended and dreaded even more what would happen when her mama found out. That paled in comparison, however, to the satisfaction she felt in righting a wrong, and not once did she ever regret her decision.

So when she stopped, set her tray down and looked over at the louts lurking at the table, Delia knew at that very moment, come hell or high water, she would again spill some blood, although likely in the more figurative sense this time. There were four of them altogether, and they sat facing her, all with the same goofy, arrogant tight-lipped smiles, waiting for Delia to respond to the trash comment, which still hung in the air. Delia's feet suddenly felt like they were filled with lead, yet she forced them to move, one in front of the other, until she completed what seemed like the longest walk of her life.

"Excuse me," she said just loud enough for everyone to hear, although it didn't take a lot of effort. The cafeteria was pretty much silent by now. "I said, '*excuse me.*'" Now she said it even softer, but it might as well have been a ton of bricks dropping. The ringleader looked at her as the young man next to him cleared his throat. He still had the haughty smile plastered on his face, but his eyes no longer mirrored the grin.

Now no one in the room moved except Delia. She let a moment pass and then spoke. "Let me be perfectly clear. I am not your helper, your secretary, your maidservant, your lackey, your minion, and I am certainly not your wife – God bless that woman." Out of the corner of her eye, Delia noticed subtle nods and "uh oh" glances around the room and felt the momentum shift – in her favor. "I waste enough of my time correcting your mistakes in the courtroom, and I do not intend to clean up this pile of – of *shit* you and this pack of lemmings left here in the lunchroom." She glared at the other goons but no one would make eye contact, so she moved a step closer. The instigator's smile now faded as the color left his face. Delia remained standing over him and continued staring, breathing, but not saying a word until beads of sweat gathered on his forehead. She leaned in some more and flared her nostrils.

"Well?" she asked, barely over a whisper.

Silence.

No forks clinked, no ice shifted, no chairs moved. Even the women behind the serving line stopped to watch. The table of young lawyers looked around for some support or for some way to quietly escape, but all eyes were now on them, and Delia did not blink. She just stood there, inhaling and exhaling – deeply now. Eventually, one by one, they got up, removed their respective scraps and retreated to the stairwell. The last one to leave was the individual who barked the order to Delia in the first place.

He walked out alone. With his trash.

The man she publicly flogged was none other than Stephen Andrew Massey, III, but most people called him "Tripp."

Two days after it happened, she arrived to find her small, windowless office cleaned out. When she rushed to her secretary in a panic thinking she had been fired, Delia found a bouquet of flowers and an arrow pointed across the hall. Outside the door of one of the larger exterior window offices was a plate with her name on it. Tears welled in her eyes when she saw it.

Later that day, after most of the firm had shut down and gone home, Delia retrieved the box of certificates, awards, and photos her secretary had packed up for the move. She closed the door, turned on the radio, clipped in a barrette to keep her hair out of her eyes, and started laying out her things. She stopped briefly to toast her reflection in the large plate glass window overlooking the highway, turning up a bottle of whiskey she kept in her purse. She stayed there for a few minutes, sipping and thinking how proud her mama would have been to see her at that moment. She watched the rush hour headlights zipping by twenty floors below and wondered where everyone was going and why they were in such a hurry to get there. The opening chords from "Sweet Virginia" eventually lifted her out of her daydream, and she quietly sang along with Mick as she began arranging the office. Delia hung her diploma in the middle of the wall directly opposite from her desk so she could see it when she sat in her chair.

She arranged the flowers on her desk and laughed aloud when she read the card. It said: *Congratulations Delia, our own Steel Magnolia!*, and was signed, simply, *Your Friends.* Matt had seen it before, framed and hanging right below her diploma, but did not appreciate the context until he heard Delia tell the story as only she could.

The lunchroom showdown was to be Tripp's *coup d'etat*, but after it blew up in his face, his merry band failed to maintain their solidarity, and a few even quietly apologized to Delia. From then on, Tripp's crusade was primarily his and his alone. Tripp vowed, publicly and privately, never to forget the way Delia embarrassed and humiliated him on that fateful Friday afternoon.

And as evidenced by events of late, he apparently never did.

23

MATT ATE LUNCH at Trinity and was thrilled to find out the power was back on when he returned to the office. He stuck his head in front of the AC vent to feel the cool draft coming in and kept it there until his nose ran and his earlobes were good and chilly. He checked the bathroom, and water spat out when he turned the knobs on the sink. It coughed and ran brown for the first minute or two, and even though it eventually cleared up, Matt thought it best not to drink it, at least not until he got clearance from the city.

He considered calling Delia back to check in on her, but decided against it. Discussions about Tripp always made him uncomfortable. Plus, if the story of the found money ever saw the light of day, Matt figured he would have to explain to Delia why he failed to bring it up to her each time they spoke, and didn't want to add another tally to the list.

Matt took inventory one more time and tried to figure out what he needed and what he could give away. God knows there were people in need. He even stopped to try on some new clothes, and to his surprise, they mostly fit, although the waistband on his pants had loosened up. He hung what he could on the hooks behind his door and boxed up the rest.

Cathy called Matt later that afternoon. She had come down the day before but had been taking care of other business, primarily with the funeral home and her insurance agent. She sounded tired, and said she would be returning to Tupelo the next day and that she planned to move there permanently after the funeral, which was at least a week out due to the backlog. It saddened Matt to hear her say she had nothing left in Gulfport. She asked him if he would gather any personal items of Jeff's from the office for her to pick up on the way out. Matt agreed, although returning to Jeff's office was the last thing he wanted to do. He didn't mention the photo album; he wanted to surprise her with it in person.

After he hung up, his mind turned, yet again, to the money. Its existence was never far from his thoughts, and he realized he had begun to act like he did when he used to pick up Louisiana lottery tickets on the way back from New Orleans. Almost every time, without fail, Matt imagined what life would be like after the Wednesday or Saturday when they drew his numbers. Would he pay off his house first? What kind of car would he buy? How much would he clear after taxes? Would he quit work? Whom would he tell? How much would he give away? And the questions went on and on until he checked the website a few days later only to find out he didn't win, and usually did not even come close. Even though he knew the odds were heavily stacked against him, he was always disappointed when his numbers didn't come up.

This was different, though. He'd *won* the damn lottery. His proceeds were sitting right here in his office. Yeah, he could make two million dollars work. Even with Hop's take, which Matt figured would be about 25%, subject to negotiation (but not too much negotiation), Matt would come out way ahead of the game. He couldn't stop thinking of what he could do with all of it. Travel. Pay off debt. Buy a new car. Mercedes. How much should he invest? How much would he spend outright? From a home standpoint, he could build back bigger and better than before the storm. Shelley could have every amenity she could ever want.

Shelley. Now Matt realized the doors this potentially opened on the marital front. He finally saw the looser ends of his plan coming together: this unexpected windfall could be the catalyst he needed to get the relationship back on track. If she approved of his keeping it, she would enjoy some of the security and freedom that came with having seven figures in the bank. Matt didn't necessarily want to have to *buy* her back, but if it was the card he had to play to get them together, he would definitely throw it down.

The more he thought about it, the more it made sense. He had to convince Shelley that coming back was right on so many levels. He would share their good fortune, as it were, on Friday.

———

He could delay the inevitable trip across the hall no more, so he finally opened the door to Jeff's office and looked around. The whole room – not just the area near Jeff's desk – was sparkling clean. Even the ceiling had been wiped down, and Matt noticed a hole near the crown molding, where, he presumed, the bullet lodged. The smell of disinfectant still hung in the air, just not as strong as when he first returned. Although Matt tried his best to block the ghastly images filling his head, they came back with a vengeance and in vivid detail for the first time since that dreaded day. Jeff slumped over, eyes open but expressionless. Blood and other gross things, tissue probably, behind him on the chair and on the wall. No computer whirring. No note.

Matt didn't know why he was now remembering; perhaps being back in the room was what he needed to put the pieces in place. Matt recalled the gun on Jeff's desk, and the thought of it made him frown. He had never seen Jeff with a gun. Never known Jeff to own a gun, for that matter. The more he thought about it, he was even more surprised it was a Glock. And not just any Glock, it was a big boy: the G31.

Matt knew it was a G31 because he had researched Glocks months before the storm when he was looking to replace his old Smith and Wesson. He had owned guns all of his life but never a Glock. Lance used a G31 as his service weapon, and Matt even accompanied Lance to the firing range to get a feel for it. The G31 was a big, heavy, high velocity gun that meant business. G31s were serious guns for serious gun people – and Jeff was definitely not one of those types. So what the hell was Jeff doing with one?

Something else bothered Matt about the day he found Jeff, but even with his sudden wave of clarity, he couldn't drill down on it. He plucked a rubber stress ball with *Mississippi Blood Services* printed on the side from Jeff's inbox basket, and plopped down on the couch. He squeezed the ball and let his mind wander back to the day Jeff died.

Matt leaned back and started throwing the ball up, trying to get it to arc just before it hit the ceiling.

Jeff's body sprawled across his desk –

Matt could gauge the distance from the ball to the ceiling by watching the ball's shadow close in as it got higher with each pitch.

The gun lying near his body –

The ball went up and came back down, over and over again. He was in such a rhythm he barely had to look at his hands to catch it.

Trying to get out of the office as fast as he could –

Up and down, up and down . . .

The condition of the office –

Matt stood straight up and caught the ball with both hands. What had eaten at Matt ever since that cop said they were sending a crew to clean Jeff's office finally crystallized: When he found Jeff dead at his desk, it wasn't just the gore and gun that got his attention. It was the room itself. Jeff's office, even in his best days, had never, ever been clean. But that morning it was spotless. Jeff always had more business than he could handle, and his office reflected Jeff's heavy workload. Bankers' boxes and files littered the corners. Trade journals and magazines, mostly unread, filled his inbox. And anyone who stopped by to visit had to move papers off the couch in order to sit down. But his office contained none of the usual mess when Matt found him – and Jeff's office was without a doubt a wreck the week prior; Matt had been in there discussing the depositions with Jeff before he left and had to stand to take notes as all the seats were stacked with transcripts and file folders.

So what would possess Jeff to suddenly clean it up? Especially when a storm was churning up the Gulf?

Matt supposed Jeff could have put everything away in advance of the hurricane. After all, some folks prepare differently than others. Matt left Gulfport a few days before the real storm prep started, so he would have had no idea what went on – but it certainly didn't sound like something Jeff would do. Jeff had a small file closet in his office where he kept the more sensitive files from The Majestic. Matt opened the door, and it looked clean too. Perhaps he loaded up the filing cabinets to get everything off the floor? Matt pulled open one of the filing cabinet drawers to investigate. Instead of being heavy and squeaky with the weight of the papers, it flung open, fast and light until the track extended all the way out and the metal stop banged the divot.

He stepped back. It was empty. Matt checked another. *Empty.* Then another, and another. *Empty, empty.* It didn't take him long to go through the filing cabinets.

There was not a single document in any drawer.

Matt eased back out of the closet, suddenly fully aware, and stared around the room. The boxes were gone; the couch was clean, and the floor was spotless. It almost looked like a new tenant had just moved in.

Matt tried to give Jeff the benefit of the doubt. Maybe Matt *was* overthinking it. Maybe Jeff had an oh-shit moment and realized this hurricane was going to tear through Gulfport like a buzz saw, so he packed up everything and moved it farther inland. Maybe he realized the peril his business would be in if he somehow lost his Majestic files. The Bing did keep a small storage unit off John Clark Road for closed files and old furniture. But if Jeff took those precautions, why did he leave all of his photos and certificates and things hanging on the wall? Why was his computer still on his desk?

Matt sat back down on the couch, now feeling paranoid and suspicious, and resumed tossing the ball, hoping something would come to him. Nothing did, though, and he eventually forced himself to refocus on his original reason for returning to Jeff's office – to retrieve Jeff's personal belongings for Cathy. He glanced at the picture of Jeff on his boat holding up a huge redfish, grinning from ear to ear, and memories of better days distracted Matt's rhythm enough to cause him to miss the ball. It glanced off his hand and bounced along the floor before rolling under the credenza against the wall.

"Shit," Matt said, not quite ready to remove himself from the couch. He sat there for a minute, staring ahead, feeling tired. He eventually stood with a groan and walked over to the spot where the ball disappeared.

Matt got down on all fours. When he was low enough to look, he saw several sheets of paper, some balled up trash and a pen under the furniture. "Well," he exhaled, "can't say he got everything." Matt strained his eyes to find the ball, and when he did, saw it had rolled all the way in and was resting near the baseboard. He was going to leave it and began to straighten back up when something next to it caught his attention. He slid his arm deep underneath the heavy piece of mahogany and had to turn his head to the side to get his hand all the way to the wall. When he finally pulled it back out, he sat cross-legged on the floor and stared at the object resting flat on his palm. He rubbed his free hand through his hair.

It was a casino chip from The Majestic.

And it was orange.

24

A CHILL RAN UP Matt's spine, and he suddenly felt nauseated. His breathing picked up as he tried to remember if he ever saw Jeff or Cathy with a North Face duffel bag or if he ever saw the bag at the office. He couldn't recall either. Nor could Matt think of any time before the storm – ever – where Jeff displayed suspicious behavior. But why would he have a pumpkin in his office? After all, Jeff would be the last person he would expect to be involved in something below board. Matt thought through every possible scenario, and none came back to implicate Jeff. If Jeff were involved in some bad shit, though, maybe it had something to do with his death. Perhaps someone *did* want him dead, which would explain Matt's first suspicion – that Jeff did not – and would not – take his own life.

He got another chill and shook his arms out.

Matt had never been a believer in coincidence, and something inside him told him to dig deeper, so he returned to his office to start where he deemed the most logical place. There were no more hardcopy files – Jeff or someone else had made sure of that. But recently the Bing had decided to become environmentally conscious and had been transitioning to a paperless system. Most everyone thought it was bullshit and that Tripp Massey – who spearheaded the effort – didn't give a damn about the environment. He was doing it only so he could tell his bigger clients up north that the Bing was on board with carbon credits, responsible sourcing, and whatever other buzzwords his highness could come up with. Regardless, Tripp was the chair, and what he said went, so everyone was on board, either voluntarily or involuntarily. Matt found himself thanking Tripp, possibly for the first time ever, if in fact, the electronic files could provide him with an answer. He didn't expect to find much; searching for a needle in a haystack would have been less daunting.

Matt's efforts would be moot from the outset if he couldn't access the server, and he hoped the Bing's network had returned with the power. When he booted his computer up, it whirred for a second and asked for Matt's user name and password. It had been so long since he entered it, Matt had to think about it a second before keying it in. Once he typed it correctly, the Bing homepage came up with a pleasant chime.

"Yes," Matt said. "All right." He cracked his knuckles and clicked the mouse. Out of habit he glanced at his inbox. Over 300 e-mails. *Great.* He quickly glanced at the subject lines to see if any were of importance and concluded they could all wait. Most had to do with the storm, the status of the Gulfport office and, most recently, Jeff's untimely death.

Matt first pulled up Google and checked some of the news sites. He was interested to see what had been reported about the storm and wanted to see if there were any reports of missing cash. He didn't see anything on point on the WLOX or the Sun-Herald websites. He pulled up Drudge to check the national pulse and was surprised how much coverage New Orleans was getting as opposed to Gulfport and the rest of the coast. The flooding in the French Quarter was a terrible thing, no doubt, and he felt for his neighbors to the west, but in many ways their flooding situation was quite different from the all-out destruction caused by the washing machine that ripped up the Mississippi Coast.

He looked at a few more articles, allowed a passing moment of acknowledgment of all the victims, and then returned to the task at hand. He Googled "PBT," but the search didn't hit on anything substantive, although Pittsburgh Ballet Theatre and Pottery Barn

Teen seemed to be quite popular. Matt then decided to direct the search internally.

FileManage was the proprietary software the Bing used to manage its documents. Anyone who logged in to the Bing system could conceivably access every document saved to the server. Documents were assigned individual numbers and could be searched by document number, date, author's name, title, client matter number, description, document type, and/or document history. The FileManage database contained the thousands upon thousands of documents drafted by the Bing lawyers and staff, and the number grew each day.

Matt opened the program, and on the *Description* line of the search page, typed *PBT.* The search icon blinked for a few seconds, and the results came back: *0 Documents Found.* Matt entered *117,* and more documents than he could count popped up. None of them seemed relevant. Most of the *117* references came up as exhibit numbers to depositions or trials, or as sections or subsections of statutes or rules. Nothing rang a bell for Matt, and he quit looking when he realized he could spend the rest of the evening chasing *117* hits.

He tried another angle. Author searches were usually done by first initial and last name, so in the author line, Matt typed in *JMCCABE.* Not surprisingly, the *> 500 Documents Returned* message came up, and Matt scrolled through some of these as well. No surprises there. Various motions and briefs, correspondence, billing statements, and other things of a client nature.

Matt narrowed the search. He entered *117* on the description line along with *JMCCABE* on the author line. One document came up, and Matt leaned into his computer. Nothing more in the description, just *117.*

"Hmm," Matt said, clicking on the document.

A message prompt popped up on the screen. *Access Denied – Unauthorized User.* "What the hell?" Matt said. He tried again and got the same message.

"How could I be an unauthorized user?" He looked at the document profile and found his answer. The document had been saved as a *Personal* and not a *Firm* document. Documents of a personal nature saved in that capacity were usually documents pertaining to a Bing employee's or partner's pay, insurance, evaluations, employee file, or estate matters. They could be accessed only by a Bing administrator or by the individual who created and saved the document as *Personal,* so long as that individual had logged on with his or her user name and password. The only thing that other users could see was the name the document was saved under.

Shit.

He tried another option to see what else would come up. This time, Matt typed *JMCCABE* in the author line and *PERSONAL* in the document type line. Sure enough, a long list came up, and Matt scrolled through them. Matt didn't care about any items pertaining to Jeff's employment, salary or otherwise, but he wanted to see if there was anything sensitive that Cathy might want or need. He also wanted to see if he could link this *117* document to anything relating to PBT.

Matt found a few relating to wills and will revisions, and he made a note to follow up with Cathy on those. He couldn't identify anything like PBT, and it took him several seconds of scrolling even to find *117.* When he did, out of habit, he clicked on it again. No access. He stared at the computer screen for a few minutes. He knew he could do something else to probe the document. He tried to quick-view it, but that didn't work either. Same message. He tried to e-mail it to himself. The document appeared in Matt's inbox, but when he clicked on it, he was denied again. Matt saved the document to his computer's hard drive and tried to open it that way. The save worked, but he still couldn't open it. Then he thought again about the timeline surrounding the events of late, and it came to him. Matt clicked on the document history. Jeff had saved the document almost exactly one month prior to the date he died, and he revised it on four separate occasions during the two weeks prior to the last save date. Then apparently Jeff left it alone.

"Well, well," Matt said. He conducted another search of Jeff's personal files. This time, however, he used the history line and limited the date range to the two weeks referenced in the *117* document history. A series of document numbers popped up. Oddly enough, none had descriptors or titles to speak of, and, as was the case with document *117*, Matt couldn't open any of them. All of them, however, had a final save date that exactly matched the one on the *117* document.

Bingo. So the bag just might be Jeff's after all. Although it would have to wait until the next day; now he just needed Jeff's log-in information.

And he knew just whom to call.

25

"IT HELP DESK. Good Morning,"

"Hey, Ravi. Matt Frazier. How you doing?"

"Oh, good morning, Mr. Frazier. I am great. Good to hear from you finally." Ravi paused for an instant and brought the good cheer down a notch. "I am so sorry about Mr. McCabe."

"Thanks, Ravi. He'll be missed. How's your family?"

"Very good, sir. The hotel in Biloxi should reopen soon, and the others already have customers."

Ravi Asha headed up the Bing's IT department. If anyone had a problem with the network, their computer, or with anything electronic, Ravi was the man. He managed a small staff of computer wonks, but Matt preferred Ravi himself – he always seemed happy to help and found timely, creative solutions even when difficult situations arose. Ravi liked Matt, too; Ravi's family owned a chain of hotels in Biloxi and Hattiesburg, and Matt helped set up their LLC and successfully defended them in two premises liability cases and one employment matter. Ever since then, Ravi's family had made unannounced visits with interesting gifts and cuisine, including Chicken Curry, one of Matt's favorites, although it usually stayed with him most of the day, to the dismay of those around him.

"Glad to hear that," Matt said. "Tell everyone I said hello."

"I will, thank you. What can I do for you, Mr. Frazier?"

"First off, Ravi, our system is working down here. Don't know how you did it that quick, but I appreciate it. One more step toward feeling like I'm part of society again."

"Yes, well, we had to work with AT&T first. And then we had security issues with our server..." Ravi went on for several minutes, explaining all of the technical ins and outs about why things worked, then didn't work, then finally worked. This was the one drawback of talking with Ravi. He had to explain everything. Matt let him go on until he seemed to be finished.

"That's amazing, Ravi. I'm glad there's someone in this firm whose highest and best use is being realized."

Ravi didn't pick up Matt's lame attempt at levity. "Are you calling because of problems with the system?"

"No," Matt said. "Something much simpler than that. Mr. McCabe's wife, Cathy, is coming by later today to pick up some of his things, and I am helping her out. He, uh, had saved several documents – wills, family-related documents, things like that – to FileManage, which he designated as personal documents, not firm documents."

"I see, I see," said Ravi. "Yes."

"So, I was wondering if I could get Mr. McCabe's user name and password so I can access those documents."

Ravi was quiet for a second, and Matt wondered if he had pushed the envelope too far. Ravi was very strict on security. "Well, you know, Mr. Frazier, passwords are sensitive, and we have a policy against giving them out."

"I know you do, Ravi, and I wouldn't ask you to do anything if I thought it was a breach of policy or if I thought it would get you into any trouble. But Mr. McCabe is dead, you know. His widow will be here in a few hours, and I need to go over some of these documents with her while she's here. I don't see the need to make her come back to the spot where he killed himself and subject herself to the anguish at another time if I can take care of it today." Matt felt bad not telling Ravi the whole truth, but he justified his actions by telling himself he would indeed look at the estate documents and anything else he thought Cathy may want.

"Sure, I understand," Ravi said. "Actually, I don't know if the password restriction survives someone's death as the files would ultimately have to be accessed by someone anyway, so they can be reviewed and purged if necessary."

"Well can you do it?" Matt asked. He crossed his fingers.

"Yes, yes. I can."

"Thanks, Ravi. I appreciate it."

"Hold on, please. I will find it."

Matt could hear Ravi flying through his keyboard with the occasional intermittent key stroke pause while Ravi presumably waited for a screen to come up. It was taking longer than Matt thought.

"This is very strange," Ravi said, partly to himself. "His password information has been taken offline, and I cannot find it."

What? "*You* can't find it?"

"Yes, I know." Even Ravi appreciated the irony now. Matt could hear Ravi typing as he spoke. "Let me keep searching, and I will call you back once I find his password. His user name should be JMCCABE. Everyone uses their first initial and last name –"

"I tried that."

" – then I do not understand why I cannot locate his password." Matt could hear the tension in Ravi's voice; he was not used to getting technical roadblocks – especially ones of this nature.

"As soon as you get it, then, can you call me?"

"What time will Mrs. McCabe arrive?" Ravi asked.

"Sometime today. Probably late morning, before lunch."

"I will try and have it to you by then," Ravi said.

"Great, Ravi, I appreciate it." Matt thought for a moment. "Even if you find it this afternoon, let me know, okay? I may be able to follow-up with her this evening or tomorrow before she leaves."

"Yes sir," Ravi said. "Thank you, Mr. Frazier."

"Thank you, Ravi." Matt hung up and leaned back in his chair. He picked up the pumpkin and flipped it back and forth through his fingers in his right hand. *Deleted, huh? Talk to me, Jeff. Talk to me . . .*

By the time Cathy arrived a few hours later, Matt had a box filled with keepsakes from Jeff's office waiting for her on the couch. She briefly looked through them, and Matt set them aside to load in her car. She looked better than he thought she would, although Matt could sense her deep sadness by the way she carried herself – slow moving, shoulders slumped, head down. She denied his offer of a cup of coffee as he poured one for himself, nor did she want anything to eat. Matt always thought Cathy carried herself well, but as he spoke to her, he thought she looked old. And extremely tired.

"Did you get everything?" she asked Matt, as he carried the box over to the door.

"I think so," Matt said. "Do you want to go through his office? I can go in there with you, if you'd like."

"I have been thinking about that since I got down here," Cathy said. "I just don't know if I can. Or if I even want to."

"You know it's been cleaned up, so there is nothing... disturbing in there for you to see."

"I know. I just don't think I want to be in that – in that room, you know?"

"Well, you certainly don't have to. Everything I found I thought you might want I put in the box."

"Thank you, Matt. I trust your judgment on this. I think I will pass." He and Cathy reminisced about shared events with Jeff, and she even got to laughing over some of them. Matt asked Cathy about Jeff's will, and she said she had that taken care of. With their having had no children, there wasn't a whole lot to it. He also asked if Jeff had moved anything out of the office to prepare for the storm.

"Not that I know of," Cathy said. "He told me he was going to stay and board some things up at the house, then meet up with me later."

Matt saw the beginning of tears, and he moved over to sit next to her. "There's something else I want to show you," Matt said, "that I found when digging through my house." Matt wiped the cover of the photo album with his shirt and handed it to Cathy. "I tried to clean it up a bit."

Cathy's face lit up with recognition, and she sat down and turned the pages, one by one. Matt watched her go back in time, and she commented on nearly every picture, touching some with her hand, and occasionally, clutching the binder to her chest in a tight embrace. She did cry some, but she also laughed a lot. Matt just sat quietly and nodded and smiled on the few occasions Cathy directed her comments his way or looked at him. She gave him a huge hug as she closed the book.

"Priceless, Matt. This is priceless. What a find."

"I just wish Jeff could have seen it," Matt said. "Maybe it would've helped him with, well, whatever it was he was struggling with."

"Maybe so," Cathy said through a sigh. They sat there for a few minutes, the weight of the memories hanging between them, before Matt spoke up.

"Cathy, was Jeff in any kind of trouble or danger or anything?"

"What do you mean?"

"I mean, did he have any old criminal clients or anyone mad at him who would cause him to feel threatened?"

"No, not that I'm aware of. Why do you ask?"

"I don't know. Just trying to run down all the angles, I guess. I didn't expect he did. I've never known him to be in any hot water. Or have any vices for that matter. And I just can't reconcile what happened with –"

He detected a shift in Cathy when he mentioned vices and stopped talking. She closed the photo album and looked at him with a pained expression. "Well, that may not be totally accurate."

She had his full attention now.

"You know how he got in the door representing casinos, don't you?"

"Well, yes, as I understand it, Jeff developed relationships early on with some of the big players down here, and when they saw what he brought to the table, they started loading him up until the Bing tapped him to be The Majestic's main man."

"That's the glass-half-full telling of the story. The truth of the matter is that Jeff developed these relationships with the casino management because he spent so much time inside the estab-lishments. *Lots of time.* Jeff had a gambling problem, Matt." Cathy looked hurt now; not like she did when she was grieving, but like someone recalling a difficult time.

"Gambling problem?"

"Addicted. Nearly blew every bit of savings we had."

"But how?" This was the first Matt had heard of this, and he was floored. "And how could he have this, this – issue, yet spend the majority of his waking hours representing casinos?"

"I know," Cathy said. "Fox guarding the henhouse. It was a major concern for some time, and we both went through some intensive counseling. I don't think Jeff ever totally got over it, but he found ways to manage it and still do his job."

"Did anyone at the Bing know about this?"

"As far as I know, no. Jeff had it under control long before the firm hired him and long before he started working for The Majestic."

"You don't think that had anything to do with his death, do you?"

"No, no. I don't think so," Cathy said. "This was years ago."

"Yeah, I guess so. What about the gun they found on him? I've always known Jeff to be a peacemaker. Not the type to carry or even own a gun."

"I don't think he ever owned a gun," Cathy said. "Not as long as we've been married that I am aware of."

"Any idea where he got it?"

"No," Cathy said. "I haven't asked the police, and, frankly, I don't want to know." She frowned. "You still seem concerned, Matt. Do you think he was in danger?"

"No." Matt could feel that pang in the back of his neck just under his skull that stung him when he lied. "At least I hope not. He never indicated he had anything going on, and I knew him pretty dang well." Neither said anything for a few minutes. "I don't know, Cathy, I'm just trying to make sense out of something that defies all logic. This is my way to deal with it: try and figure out why. Shelley always says I over-think things, and she is right. My apologies for going down this trail with you."

"I'm sorry you had to find him, Matt. I never even asked how you are coping, and I apologize for that."

"Don't worry about me. You just take care of yourself. I'll be fine."

"Jeff always thought very highly of you – as a lawyer *and* a friend."

"I thought a lot of him too. He was good to me, and I am really going to miss him."

"Me too," Cathy said through a long sniffle. She gazed off into the distance for a few seconds and then her eyes came into focus and she abruptly stood up. "Well, I'd better go. I don't want to take up any more of your time. Did you find anything of yours as good as this?"

"I found a few things here and there," Matt said. "I even found one of our large family portraits, but it is not in near the shape your album is. I kept it anyway."

"Well, you should, Matt. Keep all of it."

"Yeah, I plan to." He turned to Cathy. "Listen, I found a red North Face duffel bag near the spot where I found that photo album. Does that sound like something that may be yours or could have been Jeff's?"

With his coffee to his lips, Matt watched Cathy's eyes over the rim of his cup to see if they flashed any recognition or conceal-ment before she spoke. If she knew of any misbehavior on Jeff's part, the bag reference would certainly be a trigger. "No, Matt, we don't own, or we didn't own, any duffel bags that I am aware of." She looked directly at Matt when she said it, and her expression remained flat.

She's telling the truth. "Just checking," Matt said. "Things from all over the neighborhood washed up in my house."

"I hear everyone's possessions are scattered for miles," Cathy said. She had already forgotten about Matt's inquiry.

"You're right."

"Well, anything else?" she asked, as Matt walked her and the box out to the car.

"Not that I can think of, although I may call you if something comes up." Here goes, Matt thought. "Oh, that does remind me," Matt said. "We're finally online, and I am trying to get the litigation files back in order. Looks like I'll be transitioning to cover Jeff's cases."

"Yes?" Cathy asked.

"I came across a file with a reference that I am not familiar with. Did Jeff ever talk to you about or do any work for a business or bank with the initials 'PBT'?"

"PBT?" Cathy asked. "Or PB&T?"

"PBT, PB&T. Both, I guess," Matt replied, feeling hopeful.

"If it's the same PBT I am thinking of, I call it PB&T. Matt, you know I grew up in Tupelo but my granddaddy's family was from Pontotoc, just a few miles west. After he died, Jeff helped my daddy go through granddaddy's things up there. PB&T is one of only two banks in Pontotoc."

"Really?" Matt said, now quite interested. "So your grandfather banked with PBT – I mean PB&T?"

"No, he didn't," Cathy said, "Granddaddy used the other bank – First Bank of Pontotoc, so I don't know why Jeff would have a PB&T file. PB&T – Pontotoc Bank &Trust – is right outside the Wapegan reservation, just down the road from the Crescent Moon Casino."

Matt's heart thumped.

"The only people I know of that use PB&T are the Indians," Cathy said.

Matt tried to maintain his composure as he helped Cathy in her car. She gave him a big hug, thanked him for everything and waved goodbye. He called Hop as soon as he started back upstairs.

"Hey," Hop said. "You got something for me?"

"Pack your bags, Hop. We're going to Pontotoc."

26

T HE MISSISSIPPI BAND of Wapegan Indians had a remarkably effective lobbying group that made sure any and all critical legislation
that passed through the Mississippi House and Senate would not
do so without the Wapegan weighing in. And if the legislation had
the potential to be adverse to the tribe, the attorneys and palm-
greasers on the Wapegan payroll took whatever steps necessary to
have the tribal interests and demands acknowledged, if not outright
met. Extremely bad press, allegations of civil rights violations and
a royal pain in the ass lay in wait for anyone who dared challenge
their charismatic leader, Chief Warren Osceola. So when the governor signed the bill allowing casinos exclusively on the navigable
waters of the Mississippi Gulf Coast, the Wapegan went to work.
After less than a year of what amounted to a series of closed-door
meetings and pointed news releases, the governor – along with the
full support of Mississippi's legislative leaders – signed the Native
American Regulatory Reform Act, which added an exception to
the waterways-only rule: the Wapegan tribe could build a casino on
Indian-owned land near Pontotoc in the northeast quadrant of the
State. And build it they did.

The Crescent Moon was the first of its kind for Indian casinos.
More than just a standalone cheap metal building surrounded
by a parking lot, the Wapegan took a cue from some of the Las
Vegas properties and built an all-out resort. Not only did they set
up a multi-level gaming area with a world-class third-floor poker
room, but they also incorporated two hotels in the design as well

as a massive waterpark with a lazy river that encircled most of the twenty-eight-and-a-half acres of the designated plat. Restaurant options ranged from five-star steakhouses to a walk up Dog & Burger. The managers and designers wanted people of all ages to gamble, eat, play, and *stay*.

It worked. Families came in droves. Shelley, who was not a gambler, even set aside her puritanical objections and visited with the kids and a girlfriend. She liked it so much, she joined the Crescent Moon players' community just so she could be included on the reduced-ticket and free hotel giveaways that were offered every six months or so. Matt had never joined her. He refused to go on principle alone.

The success of the Crescent Moon had turned the heads of the coast casinos, although no one really worried about it so long as the Moon stayed where it belonged up in North Mississippi. But when rumors started circulating that the Wapegan were considering pursuing a second casino on their holdover land down in Harrison County, people started getting nervous – and with good reason. The Harrison County property wasn't beachfront, like The Majestic's, but it occupied a large tract of land just off I-10 – easier access for travelers passing through and closer to the well-heeled and well-financed New Orleans overnighter crowd.

The Majesticorp Board was not happy and did not intend to sit idly by and watch a good chunk of its Mississippi market share fade away. The corporation had a history of doing anything and everything to maintain its exclusivity, and it, too, had at its disposal a small army of full-time lawyers and lobbyists – much like the Wapegan – to beat back attempts by *any* other gaming houses with the temerity to try to dip their toes into the lucrative Gulfport pool. Once the Wapegan rumors got out, The Majestic mobilized its team, and for years, the fights that ensued between the Majestic and the Wapegan were massive in scale, the battles frequently memorialized in the press and in various law journals throughout the country. Issues ranging from zoning to appropriations to environmental impact were thrown back at the tribe, and even though the Wapegan appeared to make strides each time they came before the Mississippi Gaming Commission, their requests for an additional license thus far had fallen on deaf ears. But word on the street was that the battle lines were changing and that the Wapegan were analyzing different avenues to accomplish their objectives.

So when Cathy potentially linked the bag to one of the casino's banks, Matt's ears perked up. Jeff had been the tip of the spear in much of the litigation involving the Wapegan, and the possibility that the answer to Jeff's death, the money, and the safety deposit box could be found behind enemy lines intrigued Matt, to say the least.

He couldn't get out of Gulfport quickly enough.

———

"Pontotoc?" Hop objected at first, but when Matt filled him in and told him he may have figured out what PBT stood for, Hop told Matt to swing by and pick him up. Matt didn't disclose his thoughts regarding the link to Jeff; he needed more info before opening that door. He told Hop he found some Pontotoc Bank & Trust files on the Bing's system and confirmed the bank's existence with Cathy. It was the first strong lead they had; it warranted follow-up, and he agreed with Hop that a change of scenery might lift their spirits.

"Thirty minutes too soon? If we leave now, we can get there before the bank closes," Matt said.

"Perfect. You got any gas?"

"I do. The Bing folks from Jackson supplied me. Gas, food and clothes."

"Well aren't you special. We spending the night?" Hop asked.

"I don't know. I hope so. I can't see us turning around and driving right back, plus I hate to pass up the opportunity to sleep in a clean hotel bed," Matt said. "And eat real food from a nice restaurant. I'll be there in a few."

Matt grabbed a flash drive out of his desk drawer and put it in the side pocket of his computer bag along with his laptop. He had downloaded the pictures from Hank's camera with the intent to give the device to Shelley when she came down. E-mailing was still spotty, especially large files, and the flash drive was the best option in case she wanted to share the photos with some of her friends. Matt figured the images could provide a less disturbing way to introduce Fin to what he would see when they eventually came back. The flash drive also contained several pre-storm family pictures that he purposefully did not delete in the hope they would put a smile on Shelley's face. Matt didn't tell Hop he intended to make a detour to Meridian on the way back. Had he disclosed it on the front end, Hop might not have agreed to go, and Matt needed a wingman.

He locked his office, put his .38 in the glove compartment, and threw his bags into the back seat before picking Hop up and hitting the road. Their conversations touched on the money and Jeff's death, but they didn't dwell on either. They both found it a lot more enjoyable to discuss high school and college, reminisce about the good times, and try to recall where old friends and girlfriends might be these days. Lance was able to meet them for lunch in Hattiesburg, and he filled them in on what was going on from his perspective. Not as much looting overall as Matt expected but a hell of a lot of people with nowhere to live. When they got halfway to Jackson it dawned on Matt how lush the countryside had turned. He'd become so desensitized by what was left of the brown, dead, salt-water-infused foliage of the coast, he'd forgotten the many hues of greens, yellows, and burgundies thrown off by healthy shrubs and trees.

As expected, Hop fell asleep, and with no one to talk to, Matt wondered if he should touch base with Delia. She'd want to know about The Majestic pumpkins – and she'd damn sure want to know his suspicions about Jeff, especially if Jeff might have been using his firm computer and the Bing's network to do something illegal. At the same time, Matt didn't want to sully Jeff's good name if his friend had been clean, nor did he want to appear paranoid – there was enough of that going around already.

The real reason he didn't want to contact Delia, however, as much as he hated to admit it, was the money. If he filled her in on everything, he would have to disclose, and possibly surrender, the jackpot, and he was not ready for that. Plus, if he called her and she knew he was close, she would want him to come by and see her. Between wanting to get to Pontotoc on the way up and wanting to see Shelley on the way back, Matt just didn't have the inclination for another detour. Once he got to the bottom of this, he said to himself, he would fill Delia in on the details.

Just not yet.

27

"WAKE UP, MAN," Matt said to Hop as they rolled into Pontotoc. "You've been asleep for over an hour now."

"Huh?" Hop said, smacking the dryness out of his lips from sleeping with his mouth open.

"Look for signs for the Crescent Moon or the reservation. If we find them, we should be close to the bank." Hop rubbed his eyes, yawned, and did as he was told. Sure enough, they followed the casino signs and found PB&T in less than five minutes. Matt pulled into the parking lot and left the engine idling for the moment.

"Walk in there like you own the place, bro," Hop said. "I got your back."

Matt took a deep breath, grabbed his computer bag, and he and Hop both went into the bank. As Matt predicted, they asked him for identification when he requested access to box 117. He whipped out his driver's license and slapped it on the desk.

"I'm sorry, but this does not match the authorized signature list," the girl said, handing it back with an all-business smile. Matt thought she looked Indian based on her skin, but he could not tell for sure. She was pretty, and the way Hop looked at her Matt knew he was thinking the same thing.

"Well, is Jeff McCabe on the signature list?" Matt asked.

She glanced at the paper, then back at Matt. "I cannot disclose that, sir. I'm sorry."

Matt did his best to let her know she had set him off. "Ma'am, my name is Matthew Frazier," he began after willing himself to be calm. "I'm from Gulfport. You may have heard of it. Wiped clear off the map by the hurricane a few days ago. Jeff McCabe was my law partner, and I say *was* because Jeff took his life soon after the storm rolled through. He left me this key – for this bank, here in Pontotoc – and I must get in there right now. There are sensitive legal documents that I need to continue to run my law practice." The woman said nothing. The smile was gone now, her face impossible to read. Matt, who was making his case to get into the box on the fly, took a second to get his thoughts together before continuing.

"So I'd sure appreciate your help," he said, now much calmer. "But I'll get a subpoena if I need to, and trust me, you don't want me to get a judge involved. For your sake. So if Jeff's name is on the approved signature list, I suggest you let me access that box. It'll keep you out of a heap of trouble and possibly even jail."

She stared back at him, as did Hop, with some degree of disbelief at Matt's ability to craft this level of bullshit on such short notice. Hop didn't know Matt possessed such a skill.

"I'm sorry, sir, but I can't let you access the box," she said with a slight primness. "You may speak to my manager if you wish."

"I think that's a real good idea –"

"He's right behind you."

Matt turned and saw a tall, thin serious-looking red-skinned man with short dark hair and wearing a bolo tie. "Is there a problem here, Anni?" he said to the receptionist while looking at Matt.

Matt looked at him and weighed his options before replying. "No, sir, there's no problem. Not at the moment. Please excuse me while I make a call." Matt shot a glare at the receptionist and stomped outside, reaching for his phone.

"You want to make a *call?*" Hop asked, hot on his heels and looking back at the faces in the bank door staring at them. "What the hell are you doing, Matt?"

"This is my backup plan."

"Backup plan? Are you really calling someone or is this more smoke and mirrors?"

"No, this is for real. Someone local who may be able to help us out here."

"Local? Who?" Hop asked.

"An old friend and occasional adversary. Ron Tsosie."

———————

Matt first met Ron Tsosie over a cold beer at a gaming law seminar in San Antonio. They had both been sent by their respective employers to meet their annual CLE requirements and hopefully learn something about the latest in casino law. They found out they were close to the same age, and as they talked, they were even more surprised to find they both worked for Mississippi casinos. As it turned out, Ron not only worked as in-house counsel for the Mississippi Band of Wapegan Indians, but he also served as Chief Warren Osceola's number-one advisor. Matt was surprised to find out how engaged Ron was with the tribe, and Ron was shocked find out most of Matt's work involved The Majestic in some form or another.

"The Majestic, huh?" Ron said.

"Yep. Perhaps you have heard of it." They both smiled. Ron had heard of it, all right. "Just surprised I hadn't heard of you."

"Likewise," Matt said, wondering if Ron knew Matt wasn't buying his bullshit. "Where you been hiding out?"

"Chief Osceola likes me to keep a low profile," Ron said. "I'm more of a behind-the-scenes type of guy."

"I bet," Matt said and took another swig, "invisible, even." Ron let out a smirky laugh and ordered another round. That night he and Ron ended up drinking several more cold ones, and as the empties lined up, the two realized they had more in common than not. They ended up grabbing dinner at a Mexican restaurant on the Riverwalk and watched the boats cruise by as they ate. Matt kind of started to like Ron after a few days, and after the conference, Ron and Matt did their best to stay in touch. Ron even stopped by Matt's office one day to visit when he was on the coast for a hearing. Matt wondered how much Ron's friendship was genuine and how much of it was founded on Ron's need to occasionally take The Majestic's pulse. He never quite came to a conclusion one way or another, but he hoped Ron saw Matt as more than a competitor. Either way, Matt was about to see if their friendship – and Ron's influence within the Wapegan family – was legitimate. He sure hoped so. After all, if Ron Tsosie couldn't get him through bank security to access to box 117, no one could.

———

Ron pulled into the parking lot a few minutes after Matt called.

"Matt Frazier! I thought I'd never see you here. At *my* casino," Ron said, giving Matt a handshake and grabbing his arm.

"Hey, Ron," Matt said. "This is my buddy Jason Hopkins."

"Nice to meet you," Ron said. "You two come up here to try and shut us down?"

"Hardly, though while we're up here we may try and take some of your money."

"Good luck," Ron said. "I'll alert security to keep an eye on the both of you. I'll tell 'em we have some card counters in the house. How'd you do in the storm?" Ron asked.

"Not great. House is pretty much gone."

"Really? Damn. Sorry to hear that," Ron said, his tone flattening. "I've been watching the news reports, and we've stayed busy here with evacuees, but I haven't spoken to anyone yet who lost their home altogether. Everyone okay?"

"Shelley and the boys are in Meridian right now, so, yes, we all made it through."

"Good. I heard about The Majestic. Rough shape?"

"Not a total loss," Matt said, bluffing. "But it'll take some time to get back up and running."

"Well, if I can do anything to help, let me know."

"That's actually why I called. Need some assistance with a safety deposit box." He nodded towards the lobby and explained the situation with Jeff. Ron, who knew Jeff through his work with The Majestic, hadn't heard of his passing and looked sick to his stomach. Matt ran through the story as fast as he could and said he was doing a favor for Cathy McCabe, Jeff's widow.

"Okay, but why would they have a box here?" Ron asked.

"I don't know," Matt replied to an obvious question from someone with Indian blood; Cathy had said that Wapegan members were the only ones who banked at PB&T. "She said her grandfather lived here and Jeff did some work for him. Maybe this is the bank he chose."

"Hmm. If you say so. C'mon in."

Anni came out from behind her desk. "Ron!" she said, and gave him a hug and kiss on the cheek. Matt felt that was a good sign. Hop pretended not to watch.

"Matt, I'd like you to meet Anni," Ron said.

Matt bowed and stuck out his hand. "We met before," he said, "and I apologize for my earlier behavior, Miss…?"

"Tsosie," she said in a flat tone. "Ron's my brother." Hop was watching now.

Tsosie. "Please forgive me. My behavior has been inappropriate. Although no explanation will excuse it, this has been a very difficult stretch of days."

"Was *he* treating you bad?" Ron asked his sister while jerking a thumb at Matt. "This guy?"

Hop and Anni both looked at Ron to see if he was being serious.

"Anni, I could tell you stories about Matt Frazier. He's all hot air. Don't listen to a word he said, and if he gives you any more trouble I'll take care of him. Drop kick his ass right out of the bank. Hell, right out of Pontotoc if I have to." Ron chuckled, and they all grinned as the awkwardness lifted.

Matt shook her hand. "My name is Matt Frazier. It's a pleasure to meet you."

"Likewise," Anni said with a smile. She started to say something else, but Hop jumped in.

"And I'm Hop – er – Jason Hopkins, Matt's friend. Most people call me Hop."

"Nice to meet you as well – Hop."

Matt let the two of them talk as he watched Ron speak to the bank manager briefly in an office. Matt could see them through the glass partition. Their conversation began cordially enough, then the thin man turned serious for a minute as, Matt thought, Ron explained the situation. Both occasionally glanced Matt's way. A few minutes later, they came out.

"He's all yours," Ron said.

"Follow me, sir. I owe you an apology as well for the earlier inconvenience."

"Not a problem," Matt said, "the apology is all mine." Matt turned to Ron. "Thanks, Ron. You have no idea how much this helps. Do you have time for dinner?"

"I was about to ask you the same thing," Ron said. "Let's meet in an hour at Tico's, the steakhouse in the main tower. Also, I'll comp a room for you and Mr. Hopkins. Plan on staying with us tonight."

"Ron, you don't need to do that –"

"Not another word. This one's on me."

After thanking Ron again, Matt left him with Hop and Anni in the lobby. The manager escorted Matt into the vault and pointed Matt to box 117, one of the medium-sized drawers. After the manager inserted the guard key, Matt put the key in and held his breath. When the keys turned, Matt tried his best not to show his relief and thanked the manager with as little expression as he could. The manager dismissed himself, and, once Matt was alone in the vault, he opened the door all the way, pulled the long, slender tray out, and lifted up the hinged top.

His eyes grew wide yet again. More money. Just like in the duffel bag, although on a smaller scale and with no pumpkins. Matt counted out 15 sets of banded $100 bills – $150,000 total. Also in the back of the box, Matt found a blue USB flash drive.

"What in the world?" Matt said as he looked around and put the flash drive into his pocket. He picked up the bills and looked under them to see if anything else was in the tray. Finding nothing, he slid the tray back in, but paused before closing the door. His hand felt clammy as he pulled the tray back out, but he did not stop. Matt reached in and took three stacks of hundreds and dropped them into the file folder in his bag. Why not? Matt asked himself as he closed the door to the box and walked back into the lobby.

Why not?

28

R ON HAD ALREADY left by the time Matt returned to Hop and Anni, and the two now seemed to be getting along quite well. Matt stopped by the manager's office on the way out and pointed to his bag.

"Got what I need. I appreciate it, and, again, sorry for being so difficult early on."

"I am glad we could help. Let us know if you need anything else," the manager replied and watched Matt walk out.

"I'll see you at dinner," Hop said to Anni as he left.

Hop turned to look at Matt to get a read, but Matt didn't return his gaze. Neither said anything until they got back in the truck.

"She's a different kind of fine, isn't she?" Hop said, looking over his shoulder. "I asked her to join us for chow if you don't mind."

"Focus, Hop."

"I am – oh, you mean on the safety deposit box. Yes... yes, of course."

Matt cut his eyes at his friend.

"Well?" Hop asked. "Did the key work?"

"Sure did," Matt said.

"Talk to me. What was in there?"

"Close to a hundred-fifty grand in cash and a flash drive."

Hop let out a whistle. "*150k?* And a flash drive you said?"

"Flash drive, thumb drive, whatever you call it.

"Did you grab it?"

"Damn right," Matt said, slapping his pocket.

"What about the money?"

He started to accelerate through a yellow light but thought better of it and braked to a sudden stop. "Do you think I should've grabbed the money?"

"Do I think you should have grabbed the money..." Hop repeated. "Nahh. I guess not. It would have been different if you found it – like the duffel, where no one knows about it. Here, they have a record of you accessing it and if, on the outside chance this happens to be above board, taking money from someone else's box would be flat-out stealing. Probably a felony."

Matt looked at a broken-down car on the shoulder of the other side of the highway and tried to suppress the panic rising in his throat. Hop was exactly right about there being a record of these funds, and Matt knew he'd been stupid to walk out of there with thirty grand. He tried to push it out of his mind as he turned at the light toward the Crescent Moon.

"I guess another buck-fifty puts it well over the two million mark now, huh?" Hop asked.

"Yep," Matt said.

"You brought your laptop, right?"

"Sure did. I can check this flash drive when we get back to the room."

"Have to do that after we eat," Hop said, holding his stomach. "I'm starving. Plus, your buddy Ron already set up the reservations. He said to call when we arrived – he and Anni will meet us at our table."

Matt looked over at him. "Lucky she's even talking to you, the way I acted."

"True, but she said a friend of Ron's is a friend of hers, so all is forgiven. Anyhow, booting up that drive'll have to wait till later."

"I can handle that. I'm pretty hungry too."

Ron remained true to his word. A bellman greeted Matt and Hop by name when they walked through the door. Matt kept his computer bag on him and followed the luggage to the room while

Hop checked in. Once the bellman left, Matt placed the file folder holding the money in the middle slot, right next to his laptop. He thought about bringing the bag down to dinner, but figured it would be weird, so he left it on the desk and made sure he locked the room tight.

When they ordered, Matt thought their eyes were bigger than their stomachs, but by the end of the meal, he and Hop had both cleaned their plates and knocked out most of the sides. They leaned back in their chairs, bloated from their gluttony, but feeling good.

"Did you find everything you were looking for at the bank?" Ron asked.

Matt looked at Ron. Matt thought he held the stare a little too long, but Matt was tired and figured he was becoming a bit too paranoid. "Sure did. Got what we needed. Thanks."

"Good. Glad I could help."

Matt changed the subject. "I really appreciate you putting us up tonight."

"It's the least I could do. You deserve it after all you've been through. I should have checked in on you after the storm hit. What are your plans tomorrow?"

"We're leaving pretty early. Gonna go through Meridian to see Shelley and the boys."

This got Hop's attention. Matt saw him stir but he didn't say anything. Ron invited them to stay as long as they wanted – on the house – and instructed Matt to bring his family back up for a long weekend.

"I may take you up on that. Right now, though, I'm going to hit the sack. It's been a long day."

"You sure you don't want to stay for another drink or two?" Ron asked. "Still early."

"I'm good," Matt said. "Worn out tired. The thought of kicking back on a real bed with air conditioning sounds very good to me right now."

"How 'bout we grab some coffee in the morning before you head out?"

"Will do. Why don't I call you?"

"Fair enough."

Matt looked over at Hop, who was deep in conversation with Anni. "You coming or staying?"

Hop looked at Matt and then turned and mumbled something to Anni, who giggled. "I'll be up in a little while. We're going to grab an after dinner aperitif."

"Don't be fooled by those fancy words, Anni," Matt said. "He's dumb as a rock." Hop overplayed his offense to the comment, and when Anni laughed, Matt noticed she grabbed Hop's hand. Ron walked Matt to the elevator, and they agreed to meet the next morning.

Matt carded open his door, his mind on the money and the flash drive. He wondered if Ron had done any probing with the bank manager after he left. No way Ron knew what was in that safety deposit box, Matt thought. There are rules against that. Matt shrugged his shoulders. He could ponder this all night, but he really wanted to get some sleep.

Matt walked into the room, turned on the lamp and, out of habit, clicked on the TV. He hadn't had the pleasure of watching the television for over a week and was looking forward to some mindless down time. He started to kick his shoes off when his peripheral vision caught the slightest hint of movement in the mirror.

By the time Matt turned to look, a meaty fist struck his left eye.

29

T HE FORCE OF the punch knocked Matt back over the bed. He felt a
sharp pain in his side as another set of knuckles crashed against
his ribs. Matt rolled and flipped his attacker off the mattress and
onto the floor. He tried to get a look, but the blow had clouded
his vision. All Matt could tell was the person striking him was a
tall male, dressed in black pants and wearing a black, long sleeve
t-shirt. The guy had a stocking cap pulled down, and Matt could
only partially see his face where his eyes and mouth were exposed.
He smelled like a three-day drunk. Matt came down on top, and
they rolled around, each trying to get the upper hand. Matt got
some good licks in, but the other guy seemed to be winning until
Matt grabbed the man in a headlock.

The two grunted out curses and insults while Matt struggled
to punch him and hold him down. He wriggled enough to break
Matt's choke hold, and when he scrambled to reposition himself,
Matt kicked him square in the knee, causing him to buckle sideways and yell. Matt scuttled backwards until he reached the corner
and pushed himself up, using the wall as leverage and knocking
a lamp over in the process. He could barely breathe by this time,
and his attacker was also panting and trying to regain his footing. Matt's head felt heavy, and he tasted blood from his lip. He
decided that while he had the high ground, he would deliver one
more blow before calling security.

His cloudy left eye, now closing, betrayed him.

As Matt approached, he didn't see the butt of the pistol that crunched him square on the side of the head after the man wheeled back around and charged. Matt saw stars as he wheeled and fell back on the bed. He tried to reestablish his footing, but the spinning room pulled him down to the mattress.

When Matt looked up, the man knelt over him with one hand on Matt's throat and the other pointing the gun at his forehead.

"Where is it, cocksucker?"

Blood dripped through the mask near his nose and his eye had a cut as well – Matt could see it through the hole. His teeth didn't look right either, and his breath smelled sickly sweet like he had the flu or a sinus infection.

"Answer me," he snarled.

"Where is what?" Matt mumbled.

The attacker's good eye blinked hard twice, and his cheeks puffed out in frustration. "You know what I'm talkin' bout." Matt didn't like the way he waved the gun barrel in a circle around the direction of Matt's head. He tried to peg the guy's accent: not quite North Mississippi, but not the coast, either.

"Look, I just got here a few hours ago. You want my wallet? Fine." Matt fidgeted to reach his pants. "It's in my back pock –"

The barrel of the gun stopped, and Matt felt cold steel on his nose. "Don't you budge one more inch." The man ran his arm across his face, smearing blood on his sleeve before continuing. "You made a withdrawal from the bank earlier, didn't you?"

What? How did he know about the bank? Matt's heart thundered. *Dammit. Hop was right. I never should've taken that cash.* He thought about lying, but he couldn't cognitively put it together at that point in time. Then, briefly, Shelley and the boys flashed to mind, and he knew the money was not worth fighting for, much less dying over. Anything to get this bastard out of the room. Matt motioned to his computer bag on the desk. "It's in that bag over there, Matt said tasting blood again in his mouth. "Th – that computer bag."

The man was back on his feet faster than would seem possible, and Matt thought maybe he hadn't hurt him as badly as he hoped. He reached the desk and set the bag upright with one hand. At first he kept the weapon trained back on Matt, but the bag wasn't cooperating. Some of Matt's vision had returned, and he watched with his right eye.

The man fumbled through Matt's bag, and snorted a little laugh of approval when he found his prize.

The blood trickling out of Matt's nose tickled his sinuses and caused a bloody sneeze that hurt so bad it made Matt nauseated once again. Even worse, it caused the perpetrator to turn back to Matt, and he approached the bed. Matt tried not to look at him, but he could see now that the man was limping. Once again, Matt was staring down a barrel.

"I ought to kill you now," he said, his eye looking wild and tangled. "But apparently someone wants to keep you around." He hocked and spat on the pillow and then wiggled his loose tooth with his tongue before speaking. "Shame you were such a pussy and didn't fight back more. Then I would've had a legitimate reason. Some call it self-defense." Matt didn't say a word. His best chance of survival was to lie still and hope for a quick exit. "Aw, shit, what the hell," the man said and hit Matt hard across the side of his head with the butt of the pistol. Matt could feel the warmth of the blood flowing over his ear and cheek. He didn't say a word, and the man got right in his face. "Consider that a warning, Matt Frazier." He smelled terrible. "One more fuck up and you're dead."

When the latch finally clicked closed, Matt rolled back over onto all fours, struggling to breathe. Once he got his wind back, he eased over to the door and threw the bolt lock. He checked the closet and the bathroom and confirmed he was alone. Satisfied he was in one piece, he went to the bathroom and pressed a hand towel to the side of his head and turned back to the desk. He inventoried the contents of the computer bag.

"Just as I suspected, you stupid bastard," Matt said, trying to ignore the throbbing in his head.

The $30,000 remained in the center pocket, untouched.

The flash drive Matt grabbed from Gulfport on the way out of his office was nowhere to be found. Matt felt the outline of his pants and grinned a bloody grin.

The flash drive from PBT 117 was still there.

30

RON TSOSIE STOOD outside Matt's door, giving someone, presumably from security, the ass-chewing of their life. Ron had rounded up the heads of the casino in a hallway for an impromptu counseling session. Hop, Anni, two security guards, a maid, and a doctor Ron dispatched from the reservation's medical clinic gathered around Matt. The doctor cleaned the cuts on his face while Matt relayed what he could recall to the guards as they filled out an incident report. He sat on the bed in a terry-cloth casino bathrobe with a crescent moon embroidered on the pocket, holding an ice pack to his eye and watching the maid pick up and vacuum the lamp's remnants. He was glad when she finished; his head was throbbing like a Lost Weekend hangover, and the vacuum's whirring reverberated in a most unpleasant way.

"I think he was in the middle of a burglary when I showed up. He must have had just enough time to hide because he came at me from over there, out of the closet," Matt said, pointing. "I thought I had him when I got a good kick in, but then he pistol-whipped me and the next thing I know, I was laid out across the bed with this knot on my head. Then he got me again. I'll tell you, that second one was the one that nearly put me out."

"Did you get a good look at him?" one of the guards asked.

"No, sir," Matt said. "He had a mask or cap-thing pulled down over his face, so I couldn't see much. Black long-sleeve t-shirt, black pants."

"Did he take anything?"

"Not that I'm aware of – ouch! Damn, Doc, warn me when you're about to do that."

The doctor, who'd stepped forward again, was pushing on the bone around Matt's eye socket. "Just checking to see if it's broken. Doesn't appear to be. I'll stitch up your head now."

"Thanks," Matt said, touching the spot the doctor just pressed. Matt pulled his hand away and saw no blood. "Anyway, I don't think he stole anything. We had just set our luggage and stuff down before we ate, and it looked untouched."

The security guards stayed for a few more minutes going through their checklist while the doctor sewed nine stitches in Matt's lacerated head.

"He popped you pretty good here, son," the doctor said.

"You're telling me," Matt said. "Sonofabitch pistol-whipped me twice."

"What did he hit you with?"

"Can't tell you exactly. It was a big son of a bitch, though."

"Any idea what kind?"

"Wasn't a revolver – I remember that. Semi-automatic." Matt looked over at Hop sitting on the other bed with Anni, watching.

Ron marched in, pacing the room with a cell phone in one hand and a two-way radio in the other. "We'll run the tapes to see if we can ID the guy," he said to the older guard before turning to Matt. "You said he was tall and wearing all black? And limping when he left?"

"Yep. I tried to break his damn leg, but couldn't."

Ron shook his head in disbelief. "You're lucky you're alive. Should have just let him take whatever he wanted and get the hell out."

"Not my nature. Although after I lost the first round, that clearly became my primary objective."

"It's also not your nature to get your ass kicked or killed because you tried to fight someone carrying a gun."

Matt just looked at him. He thought about it, and if he had to do it again, he wouldn't have changed much, other than to be ready for the blindsiding. And kick the bastard an extra time or two when he had the chance.

"Look, I'm very sorry about this, and I'm embarrassed that it happened on my watch, at my casino," he said. "He must have ducked out before we could get to him. And I don't have a clue how he got in here. You sure you didn't leave an extra key card out somewhere?"

"Positive," Matt said. "And don't beat yourself up. We occasionally get a robbery at The Majestic. Not your fault."

"Well, I lose sleep over things like this. We have to stay one step ahead of the crooks on technology, and I thought we had, at least as far as room security goes."

Matt readjusted the ice pack. "Like I said, don't worry about it. There are some nuts out there, and with this economy, some of them will do anything for money. Although I don't exactly look like a high roller, so I don't know why they picked me." He smiled but it made his head hurt, so he quit.

"We're going to keep a lookout. Now try and get a good night's sleep, and let's still plan on coffee in the morning. If I find out anything between now and then, I'll call you. I'll have the doc call in some pain meds that we'll have delivered up to the room. You need anything else?"

"No, no. That should do it. Thanks again, Ron."

Anni got up to follow her brother out of the room, and Hop stood as well. "Be right back," he said to Matt.

————

Hop let himself back into their room five minutes later. By then Matt had jammed a stack of pillows behind his back on the bed. Hop plopped down in the chair at the desk and swiveled it to face Matt. "Now tell me what really happened, bro."

"Pretty much how you heard it, except for the theft part." Matt took him through the fight blow-by-blow and explained how the man finally just up and left. Then he told Hop what the man was after.

"He came for that flash drive, Hop."

"But you said you still have the flash drive."

"I do," Matt said, and threw it to Hop. He then remembered he hadn't told Hop about the one he packed. "I put my flash drive from home in the computer bag as we were leaving. It had some family pics on it and a bunch of storm photos that I uploaded from Hank's camera. That's the one he grabbed."

"Why'd you bring it here?"

"Well, my plan was to stop by Shelley's mom's on the way back –"

"You sneaky bastard," Hop said, "I heard you mention that earlier, and despite what you told Ron and Anni, I'm no dumbass. I suspected if we were this close, you'd make a special stop on the way home. Can't say I blame you, either."

"Thanks, but a side trip is out. Can't have the kids see me looking like this."

"You're not kidding. You're even uglier now than you were before. So back to your friend. How'd he know you had that flash drive anyway?"

"That's just it, Hop," Matt said. "He knew we went by the bank. He knew we were staying in this room. I'm guessing he planned to go through our stuff and escape without anyone seeing him, but my early arrival screwed that up. He even knew who I was. Called me by name as he was leaving. Told me if I screw up again I'm a dead man. What the hell does that mean?"

"*No shit?*" Hop said. "Dude, you *are* lucky to be alive."

"Hand me the laptop," Matt said, motioning towards the desk, but Hop didn't move. He looked like he'd seen a ghost. "Are you all right?" Matt asked.

"There's something more to this," Hop said. "Think about it, Matt. For that guy to come after you just for that flash drive, he either had to follow us here, or someone at the bank tipped him off. You didn't see anyone following us, did you?"

"No," Matt said. "But I wasn't looking."

"Doesn't matter. What matters is this: one, he had to have had access to box 117; two, he would've had to have known what had been in the box when you arrived; and three, he must have checked the box out after we left. How else could he have known you took the flash drive?"

Matt shrugged his shoulders.

"He targeted you specifically," Hop said. "He had to get it back."

"And he's going to be sorely disappointed when he realizes he grabbed the wrong one."

"You're missing the bigger picture," Hop said. "This cat knows who you are, and as soon as he plugs in the drive he *does* have he'll see he's being treated to first-hand Gulfport destruction photos and some old photos of the smiling Frazier family. And he'll know you wouldn't have the drive you *have* if you didn't possess the key to box 117…"

Matt didn't see where Hop was going with this. "Okay. So?"

"Damn," said Hop, "that knock on your head must have done some damage. He knows you have the drive, Matt. So he knows you had the key to the box, which means he – or whoever he works for –"

"– knows I have the money."

"Exactly," Hop said. "The mother lode."

"Oh, shit."

"And the pumpkin things."

"Is it still in your office?"

"Sure is." Matt felt dread slice through him and looked at the clock next to his bed. "I need to call Hank."

31

ALTHOUGH EVENING HAD set in many hours before, Hank took the call and filled Matt in on the goings-on in the neighborhood. Hank had not taken *Big D* out again, and he did not expect to for another two weeks. He wanted to wait until American Marine opened back up before he went into the building again. He was afraid Wild Bill might yank his privileges if pushed too far. When Matt finally got to speak, he told Hank he was in North Mississippi taking care of something for the casino, and that he needed a favor while he was gone.

"Absolutely," Hank replied. "What can I do for you?"

"Hank, I was wondering if you could ride by the office and check it out to make sure it's secure."

"Sure. Forget to lock up?"

"No, Hank, I'll give you the details when I get back tomorrow, but the short of it is, someone followed me up here thinking I had something of theirs. When I got to my hotel room, whoever it was attacked me. Let's just say neither one of us escaped unscathed."

"Attacked *you?* Dammit, boy. What do you mean attacked you?" Matt could hear Sarah in the background ask if something was wrong. Hank shushed her, and Matt explained what happened.

"Dammit boy," Hank said again. "Are you okay?"

"I guess. Got a few stitches and a shiner you'd be proud of. The guy didn't get what he wanted, and after threatening me, he got out before anyone could catch him."

"Son of a *bitch*. Stitches, huh? I hope you got a piece of him as well. What was he after?" Hank asked.

"I'll have to tell you later, Hank. It's complicated. Trust me."

"You didn't get sideways with the law, did you?" Hank asked and shushed Sarah one more time.

"No, I didn't. It appears to be business-related, and it may have to do with a former client of Jeff McCabe's who thinks Jeff owed him some money." Matt was making stuff up now, and he shrugged his shoulders when Hop looked at him after he mentioned Jeff.

Hank let that sink in for a moment before responding. "Okay," Hank said. "Whatcha need me to do?"

"I believe that the guy who came after me will likely head down to the coast with the intent to break into my office looking for whatever it is he thinks I may have. I just was wondering if you could ride by a few times tonight and in the morning to make sure no one –"

"Absolutely. I'll set up camp out there."

"No, I don't want you to do that, Hank. I don't have an extra key set out anywhere for you to get in, plus –"

"Oh, I can get in," Hank said.

"What?"

"I can get in. No problem."

"Okay, well, you don't have to do that, and you probably shouldn't do it. This guy had a gun, Hank."

"Even better." Hank said. "Changes the rules of engagement."

"Hank, listen, that's not why I called you. Driving by a few times will be fine."

"No, this mission sounds fun. I'm already thinkin' of a plan for securing the place. Plus," Hank was whispering now, "Sarah has been driving me bat-shit crazy. It would do us both some good for me to have something to do outside of the house. Anything else?"

"No. Just – just be careful, Hank. You sure you want to do this?"

"Does a five-pound bag of Martha White flour make a big biscuit?"

"What?"

"Damn right it does. Of course I want to do this."

"Okay," Matt said, shaking his head, "but only if you insist. Thanks for looking out for me. Hopefully, I'll see you before lunch tomorrow. We intend to head south as soon as we wake up."

"See you then. Get a good night's sleep and take care of your-self. I'll hold things steady down here."

"Well, that takes care of that," Matt said after hanging up. "Hank's apparently going to set up at the office, so unless it's been compromised already, it's secure as Fort Knox tonight with him there."

"Nah, it won't have been touched; not enough time for the dude to get back down to Gulfport," Hop said, checking his watch.

"Yes, unless someone's already down there."

"True." Hop replied.

"I'm sure Hank'll check in if he needs us." Matt pulled out the flash drive. "Now let's see why this thing's so important."

32

M**ATT BOOTED UP** his computer and stuck the drive into the USB
port. When he opened it, a folder with the name RED MOON
popped onscreen. Matt clicked it and a list of Word documents
came up:

RedMoonInstr.docx
18033860DDH.docx
28033862HFR.docx
38034011JLC.docx
48034014RFE.docx
58034100SBW.docx
68034104GPH.docx
78034509PJK.docx

He clicked the first one, which opened after a few seconds. "Check
this out, Hop."

Red Moon Instructions:

1. *Pay the Wolf $50k. Upon confirmation of elimination of the CO,
   leave box key with the Wolf for remainder; NOTE: leave res immediately and destroy device if unsuccessful.*
2. *All remaining docs in folder protected. Use password from doc 117
   info and print out materials for delivery.*
3. *Follow delivery instructions in each document; different for each
   contact.*

4. *E-mail SM confirming delivery of packages. No telephone contact whatsoever.*
5. *If you get any pushback, do not under any circumstances try and contact me. Remind recipients this is a mere down payment. Will disburse the remainder upon completion of deal. If you must follow up, route through SM via e-mail.*
6. *Destroy flash drive once all docs have been printed and delivered.*

Matt tried to run the initials in his head for people he knew or Jeff knew. None of them came to mind. "the Wolf? SM? Any idea who these people are, Hop?"

"No. Not off hand. What about 'the CO'? Do you think 'the CO' is someone's initials? If so, this does not sound good for him. Or her."

Matt again tried to go through the names in his brain. Something told him he could identify who the CO was, but he could not quite put it together. He read the first line again.

"Well, $50,000 from box 117 was apparently meant to go to the Wolf, and the Wolf – whoever the hell that is, was to get the rest upon 'elimination of the CO.'"

"Sure sounds like a person to me," Hop said.

"Let me see what the other files say." Matt clicked on *18033860DDH.docx*. A user name and password prompt came up. Matt hit "Enter" out of habit to see if he could bypass the screen, but got a "user name and password incorrect" message.

"Dammit," Matt said. "We're blocked."

He checked every other document and got the same message

"I bet the guy who attacked you was the person in charge of getting the initial $50,000 to this Wolf person," Hop said. "If so, he's got the password."

"That's why he took my flash drive." Matt returned to the original document and reread it twice, then pushed himself away from his computer and crossed his arms. "If he *is* the one, he was instructed to sit tight until the Wolf does his job, whatever that means. Then it says 'leave res immediately if unsuccessful.'" Matt said it again. "Leave res immediately. Hop, this has to be talking about the reservation. His instructions say to stay here until he gets the word – up or down – from the Wolf."

"I don't like this." Hop said, running his fingers through his hair and starting to sound distressed. "This sounds like a hit. We need to call the cops. Having this money is one thing, but having intel like this – talking about 'elimination' and shit – they will most definitely be back for you. For me. Both of us."

Matt needed a stall. "Let's hold off for the time being. Ron's already looking into this –"

"Hold off? *Hold off?*" Hop's knee started bouncing up and down. "We can't wait, Matt. We'll get killed."

Matt tried to redirect him. "Two million plus is a lot of money, Hop. I could sure use it back home."

Hop froze and stared at him. "That's what this is about? Are you serious? I mean, the money's no good if you're not alive to spend it." Matt pretended like he was looking at his computer screen. "This ain't for me," Hop said, "I'm out, Matt. *You* keep the money; *you* take it, whatever. I don't want it anymore, I want no part of this." Matt was sure anyone who happened to be staying in the next room could hear Hop's rant so he motioned for him to keep it down, but Hop paid him no mind. "You're not following me, Matt – if we don't call the damn cops – and I mean *now* – and tell them what's going on, we may not make it home."

"I get all that. I'm just not sure it's time to bring them in yet."

Hop started pacing. Normally easygoing and quick to joke around, he looked angry and frightened. "You are *not* in the right frame of mind. Someone beat the living shit out of you tonight because they were looking for that damned flash drive. Now look at yourself – take a look! The only reason that dude didn't pop your ass is because he had orders not to. But as soon as he figures out you still have *the* drive – and have had time to look at it – he will use that big-ass cannon he blindsided you with and you'll end up dead just like your partner, who –"

"Wait a minute. What did you just say?"

Hop backtracked for a second. "Sorry, Matt. That was a little out of line. I didn't mean to bring Jeff into this. What I meant to tell you is we are in danger. Serious danger."

Matt nodded his head, slowly at first and then faster. He clapped his hands together and stood up. "No, no. You're exactly right. Don't you see?"

Hop looked confused. "See what?"

Matt turned slowly and stared away, biting the nail of his left ring finger. He gazed out the slit in the curtains for a few seconds before turning back towards Hop. Matt had never fully bought the story that Jeff's death was a suicide, and for the first time since Jeff died, it was clear to him. Hop's reference to Jeff being shot by *that* gun left no doubt in his mind.

"Jeff didn't kill himself, Hop. He was murdered."

Hop frowned and started to protest, but Matt turned back and interrupted him. "And I'm pretty sure the dude who attacked me tonight is the same guy who killed Jeff."

33

"**M**URDERED? JEFF?" HOP raised his voice. "Seriously? Why would you think Jeff – who, you remember, committed suicide – would have anything to do with you getting mugged in the middle of Pon-to-fucking-toc, Mississippi? C'mon, Matt. Now you're just pissing me off."

"Jeff *has* to be involved, Hop." Matt figured now was as good a time as any to fill Hop in on all the details. Otherwise, he'd lose him. Matt walked Hop through how he found the duffel bag next to Jeff and Cathy's photo album. He told him about the unexplained absence of The Majestic files. He explained to Hop how, through dumb luck, he spotted the pumpkin under the credenza in Jeff's office. Matt had it in his bag in the same slot where he had hidden the money. He pulled it out and flipped toward Hop, who jerked out of the way to avoid even touching it. It bounced on the ground, and they both stared at it for a few seconds before Matt picked it up. He told Hop about trying to access Jeff's personal files after finding document 117 on the Bing's system only to realize it was blocked. He told him he found several other untitled documents, all saved under Jeff's name and all designated personal, and each of those documents bore the same edit date as 117. He told him how he played loose with the facts with Cathy to get a lead on PBT, and that it was her discussing Jeff's connection to Pontotoc through her family, not any Bing file, that ultimately made the PBT connection.

Hop sat down and thought it through but did not respond.

"Here's the deal," Matt said. "When you said I may end up like Jeff, it came to me when you mentioned the cannon or gun or whatever you called it. The big damn pistol that caused this?" He pointed to his stitches. "It was a Glock G31. I should know; that bastard pointed it at me at point-blank range tonight. I looked right down the damn barrel."

"I still don't see what –"

"Hop," Matt said calmly. "Jeff, who before this week – at least to my knowledge – never owned a gun, never talked about owning one, never even hunted. Now that I remember it all, the one thing that sticks out – more than anything else when I found Jeff – is that *gun*. As horrible as it was finding him, the thing I can't shake is how out of place that big barrel looked sitting in front of his body. And now that I've had time to think about it," Matt said, rubbing his head wound and pointing to the stitches, "I'm fairly certain the same gun used on Jeff was the one that caused this."

The statement hung in the air, made even more powerful by the total silence that filled the room as the air conditioning cycled off. Hop looked first at the floor, then at his bag, then finally at Matt.

"I've known you for years," he said. "Decades even. And you – you truly believe all this, don't you?"

"Yes. I do."

Hop stood and ran both hands through his hair again. He seemed to be trying to find his words before speaking. "Look," he said, his voice tired. "For argument's sake, let's just say I'm on board. Let's say I agree with every theoretical jump you've made to reach this nutfuck conclusion that, one, Jeff was involved in some bad shit paying off some Injuns to do who the hell knows what. Two, that the same guy who jumped you 350 miles from where Jeff 'allegedly' killed himself also killed Jeff." His voice got louder with every sentence. "Three – and here's the good part – the gun used by Jeff; *excuse me*, to *kill* Jeff, magically made its way out of police custody, hitched a ride up here – perhaps to engage in some slot play or video poker – ended up back in the killer's hands and was used to assault you." Hop was fuming. "Are you listening?"

"I'm listening."

"Do you now hear how ludicrous this sounds?" he screamed.

"Sounds plausible to me, Hop," Matt said quietly.

"Whatever. This is ridiculous. My point being, even if it is true, there is no reason we should not call the police or the federal marshals, or the sheriff – it doesn't matter who it is, so long as *some* law enforcement agency is on board. They're better equipped to get to the bottom of this, and, of greater importance, they can provide protection for *us*, Matt." Hop finally sat back down on his bed. "This is for *our* best interest. Come *on*, bro."

Matt could hear the desperation in Hop's voice. "I understand your concern, Hop, and I'm alarmed as well. Hell, just look at me. *I'm* the one who took the beating, and if something else goes down, it will be me who will take the bullet – not you. Trust me, I *know* I can figure this out myself, and if I can do that on the front end and *then* get the cops involved, hopefully, I'll be better positioned to argue we should be able to keep the money, and –"

"The money?" Hop yelled again. "Again, the money. I'm out of here, dude. I'm calling the cops, and then I'm leaving. You can either come with me, or I'll rent a car and drive back to Gulfport. And you just flat won't see me again, Frazier. This money is showing me a side of you I never thought I'd see."

Matt stood in front of his old friend. "Hop, I need you to hear me out. From a business perspective, I also need to get a jump on this because if Jeff *is* involved, and if his involvement – no matter how remote – can be linked somehow to the Bing, then my firm has a potentially huge problem." Hop shook his head, and Matt knew he wasn't buying it.

"I don't give a flying fuck about your business."

Think. Matt rubbed his face with his hands, hoping for something. Then it came to him. "I tell you what, Hop. Give me a day – *one day* – to work this out, and if I can't do it by then, we'll call the cops – hell, I'll go see them myself. That will give me time to see if I can open up these other documents somehow, and it'll let me speak with my partners at the Bing to let them know what's coming down the pike."

Hop shook his head. "Nope."

Dammit. "C'mon, Hop. Until tomorrow. Twenty-four hours."

"Unh-uh."

Set the hook. "Look, if we leave now, you're going to leave Anni hanging."

Hop looked up at him.

Reel. "No telling when you'll see her again," Matt said, sitting back down on the bed.

Hop said nothing.

"Just o*ne day,* Hop."

Hop closed his eyes before speaking. "A day?"

Got him. "Yep."

Hop stared at Matt for a few seconds. Then, satisfied with Matt's proposal, he agreed. "I can do that. Twenty-four hours. No more." Hop put his bag down, swung his legs on the bed, and turned the TV on.

"Keep the volume down for a few minutes," Matt said with a smile Hop didn't see, "I need to call Ron."

34

MATT STEPPED IN the bathroom so he could hear better and dialed Ron up. He answered almost immediately.

"Hello?"

"Ron, it's Matt. Listen, I –"

"Everything okay, Matt?"

"Yeah, yeah. Everything's fine. I wanted to run something by you, though," Matt said.

"What's up?"

"Ron, I think I know why I got jumped tonight."

Matt struggled with what to say next. He was potentially breaching client confidence and exposing the Bing if he got into too many details about Jeff and The Majestic. Matt knew he couldn't tell Ron everything, but he decided he could tell him enough to at least give Ron a picture of the events leading up to the attack, especially since it appeared to involve the reservation. He told Ron Jeff may have been involved in some criminal activity and that the safety deposit box key was found under suspicious circumstances after the storm. Matt didn't tell him about the duffel bag, and he didn't go into too much detail as to what exactly he thought Jeff may have done, despite Ron's pushing. Matt told him he retrieved a flash drive from the box at the bank and the guy who attacked him was after the flash drive – not money. He stayed away from The Majestic chips.

"A *flash* drive?" Ron asked. "Why a flash drive – and how did he know you even had this flash drive?"

"That's one of the reasons I'm calling you. He either followed me to the bank or someone on the inside tipped him off. After he knocked me on the bed with that pistol, he went through my computer bag and went straight for it. He didn't know it at the time, but he took the wrong one. The drive from the bank was still in my pocket."

"Still in your pocket?"

"Yep."

"You still have it?" Ron asked.

"Still do."

"I don't understand why he thought you may have had it in the first place," Ron said. "Let me call Anni to see if she knows of anything or anyone unusual coming in the bank after you left."

"Didn't she leave and come to dinner right about that time?" Matt asked.

"Yes, you're right; she wouldn't have been there." Ron paused for a second. "I'll call Charlie Wallo; he's the guy I spoke to – the bank manager," Ron said.

"Can he pull the signature card or log sheet or whatever they call it?" Matt said. "I'd be curious to know who else may have accessed that box after I did."

"Good point. Hold on, let me get a pen," Ron said. "What was the box number again?"

"117."

"Got it."

"There's something else, Ron. I checked to see what was on the flash drive after everyone cleared out of my room. There were several documents on there that I could not open – they were all password protected. There was one file, however, I could access and, believe it or not, it contained what appears to be a bizarre instruction dealing with a potential hit here on the reservation."

"A hit? As in 'kill somebody' hit? *Here?*"

"I know it sounds bizarre, but yes, a hit. Let me grab my computer, and I'll read it to you." Matt carried his laptop in the bathroom and set it on the counter. "Here's what the note said, word for word: 'Pay the Wolf fifty thousand dollars.' Oh yeah, I forgot to mention, in addition to the flash drive, the box was – is – full of money."

"No kidding?" Ron asked. "How much?"

Lots. "Lots. Now here's the part that concerns me: 'Upon confirmation of elimination of the CO, give box key to the Wolf for remainder of money.' And check out the next line: 'NOTE: leave res immediately and destroy device if unsuccessful.'"

"Read that again, Matt."

Matt read it again, and Ron repeated it out loud to himself as he wrote it down. "Does that sound to you like an order to take someone down?" Matt asked.

"Hard to tell," Ron said. "I wouldn't say it's an order. It's more of a follow-up to a prior agreement of sorts. 'elimination of the CO' sounds like someone's on the block, though, and it says 'leave res.' I just don't know what it means. If you hadn't told me the back story I wouldn't be so concerned, but the fact that this guy went straight for that flash drive – and nothing else – gives me some heartburn."

"Any idea who the Wolf or the CO could be?" Matt asked. "Assuming those are initials?"

"Let me think . . ."

"I'm not from around here, Ron. The only people I know up here are you, Anni, and Chief Osceola."

"Yeah, no one comes to mind right –"

"That's it!" Matt said. "Ron, that's it!" Matt heard Hop mute the TV.

"What's it?"

"*Chief Osceola.* 'The CO' is Chief Osceola."

"No way," Ron said. "No way."

"Who else could it be, Ron? Especially with the mention of the reservation?"

Ron repeated the initials and the name to Matt. "Matt, if you're right… I have to go, right now. I need to check on the chief and brief him on this. I will call you if something comes up. You still planning on taking off tomorrow?"

"Yep."

"Okay. Let's do this. Unless you hear otherwise, let's meet at, let's say nine-thirty tomorrow morning at Crescent Coffee on the first floor next to the gift shop. That will give me time to run all this down."

"See you then, Ron."

"And Matt, thanks for the heads up."

35

MATT SLEPT BETTER than he thought he would. He had to lie on one side, because if he rolled over to his left, his puffy eye and stitched-up head hit the pillow and woke him up. He groaned when he looked in the mirror the next morning. The area around his eye had turned purple, and although it wasn't closed, there was a lot of swelling. He had a bruise on his cheek; his lip poked out, and his hair stuck up around the sutured area of his scalp.

"Beautiful," Hop said through a mouth full of toothpaste. "Try not to scare too many women or children on the way downstairs."

They reached the coffee shop a few minutes early and ordered breakfast. The place was about a third full, and they were served quickly. Matt sipped his coffee the best he could with his fat lip and read the local newspaper while Hop checked his phone for messages. They both looked up when they heard voices at the front of the shop, and Matt saw people standing to greet the approaching entourage. Ron was first, flanked by four men. Matt was surprised to see Chief Osceola himself in the group; trailing him was a giant of a man of obvious Indian descent, who Matt estimated stood at least six foot eight and carried himself like an NFL linebacker. They came over to Matt's table. Hop looked for Anni, but to his disappointment, she wasn't there.

Although he had seen Chief Osceola on television before, Matt had never met him in person and didn't know the proper protocol for greeting him. Matt knew the chief's status demanded more than just keeping his seat, so he watched the others in the room to see what they did. It was hard to see through the cluster of people, though, and Matt felt flustered. Should he bow? Should he wait for the chief to speak? Before he could decide, the chief walked right up, grabbed Matt's hand with a firm grip, and spoke.

"Nice to meet you, Matt Frazier. I'm Warren Osceola."

Matt was flabbergasted. "Believe me, I know who you are, sir. It's an honor to meet you," he said quietly. The big Indian behind the chief didn't say a word, but he stared when Matt and the chief shook hands. Chief Osceola was a lean man with clear, determined eyes and a flawless white smile. Although he had to be in his sixties, he looked much younger. Matt gave him a quick half-bow, which he immediately regretted – it didn't seem appropriate after the handshake. But he felt even more embarrassed at his t-shirt and shorts. "Had I known you were going to be here, sir, I'd have cleaned up a little better."

"You're fine," Chief Osceola said. He mumbled something that Matt couldn't make out and put his hand to the welt on Matt's face, which surprised Matt and made him flinch. "Ron told me what happened. I apologize for our – lapse in security." Chief Osceola shot a glance at Ron, who looked unmoved. The other staff members shifted their weight. "Are you feeling okay?"

"It looks worse than it is," Matt said. "Just glad I don't have a first date tonight."

The Chief didn't laugh. "I'm also sorry to hear about your home. I trust your family is okay."

"Thank you, sir. It was quite a shock, but I can't complain too much. I didn't lose anyone. My wife and sons are safe and secure for the time being. In fact, they're not too far from here. They're in Meridian with her mother."

The chief nodded, introduced himself to Hop, and invited them to join him at a corner table. Matt couldn't stand it any longer and stuck out his hand to the big Indian standing beside the chief. He had dark red skin, a prominent nose, and jet-black hair pulled into a tight braid in the back. He could be straight out of central casting for a Western if he wore the right outfit. "Matt Frazier. Nice to meet you." When the big Indian finally took his hand, Matt felt like he was trying on a baseball glove.

Chief Osceola, Ron, Matt, and Hop sat at one table. A waitress appeared at the chief's elbow in the blink of an eye with a cup of hot tea and offered to refill Matt's coffee cup. The entourage took two adjoining tables, shielding the chief from well-wishers or anyone else who wanted to say hello. The big Indian sat next to the chief and without a word to anyone watched the room. Matt suspected the big Indian packed some heat, although it looked like he could clear the place with his fists and some well-placed kicks if need be without so much as breaking a sweat.

"I know you weren't expecting me," Chief Osceola began, holding Matt's eyes. "But I wanted to come here personally for two reasons. One, to check on you and apologize again for what happened last night in your room. And, two, to thank you for the friendship you forged with Ron long ago."

The comments, while polite, struck Matt as odd. He hid a frown as best he could, sneaked a quick glance at Ron, and looked back at the chief.

"I realize and respect the fact that you – and the Bingham firm – take the representation of your clients seriously," the chief continued. "I also realize your superiors may not have appreciated a young lawyer breaking bread with someone on the Wapegan side."

"Well, sometimes you have to separate life from work, Chief Osceola," Matt said as J.W. and Fin popped into his head. "It's not always easy, but there has to be a balance."

"Yes. Balance," the chief said, looking off into the distance before continuing. "If you had not befriended Ron long ago, we would not be sitting here today, and you would not have been able to warn of a potentially dangerous situation for me and my people."

"Thank you, sir," Matt said. "I, too, am glad we are able to speak. I just wish we were meeting under different circumstances."

The chief motioned to the waitress for some more tea. "I understand you had to reveal to Ron facts and information that you believe could be detrimental to the late Mr. McCabe and possibly your firm."

Matt took a sip of his coffee.

"I give you my word as Chief of the Mississippi Band of Wapegan Indians that your disclosures will remain confidential," Osceola replied. His eye contact was impressive, and he sounded completely sincere. "No reputation will suffer – not yours, not Mr. McCabe's, and not Bingham Samson's – based on the information you shared or what we're discussing now."

"Thank you, sir," Matt said. "I appreciate it. Hop and I had a similar conversation last night about all this and its potential impact. That's why I wanted to dig a little more before we turn this over to the police to see if I can address this on the front end."

"Understood," the Chief said. "What you told Ron was helpful. We are making some progress, but as it now stands, many questions remain unanswered."

Both Matt and Hop looked up at the chief and then back to Ron. The chief nodded to Ron, who cleared his throat.

"I met Charlie Wallo at the bank this morning to review the signature card," Ron said. "Are you familiar with a man named 'Griff Murphy?'"

Matt searched for a second and shook his head. "I know some Murphys, but no Griff Murphy. Hop?"

"None here," Hop mumbled through a mouthful of muffin, shaking his head.

"Well, his identity remains a mystery, although we think he is probably the one who assaulted you last night," Ron said.

"Why do you say that?" Matt asked, leaning forward.

"Mr. Wallo informed me that shortly after you left the bank yesterday, a man came in, accessed box 117 -"

Matt jerked up in his seat. "But how did he get into the box?"

"Well, he signed the card with one of the names on the signatory list. 'Griff Murphy.' I saw the card myself."

"Really?"

"I also looked at the bank surveillance video this morning. I had planned on comparing it with the surveillance here from last night, but for some as yet unexplained reason, the hotel cameras appeared to have malfunctioned." Matt saw the big Indian glower at the security officers standing around the table. They were really tensing up now. "We did, however, get some video of a man matching the description you gave us exiting near the poker room on the casino floor. The man entering and leaving your room and the man in the bank appear to be the same person."

"Same one, huh?" Matt said, looking over at Hop. He licked the bump on his lip. "Knowing what we know now, that makes sense." Matt thought about this new information for a minute, but something didn't add up. "But – well, I wonder if Griff Murphy is the Wolf because–" Matt looked over at the chief. "I hate to even say it in front of you, sir, but whoever the Wolf is was apparently tasked to be your, uh, assailant." Glancing over, Matt could see the big Indian scowling.

"That's where our trail runs cold," Ron said. "No one knows who he is, but we are taking precautions to ensure the chief remains safe." Ron turned to the big Indian. "Matt, this is Philip Kotori." Matt looked over to him, but the big Indian just stared straight ahead.

"Yes, we met earlier," Matt said. Kotori did not flinch.

"Quite the chatterbox," Hop mumbled into his coffee cup, a little too loud. When heads turned toward him, he pretended like he was slurping the remnants out the bottom.

Ron continued. "Mr. Kotori is the head of security here on the reservation and at the Crescent Moon. He was working the gaming floor last night, and has been fully briefed on the events surrounding the breach in your hotel room and is interviewing those on duty one by one. He is well trained in martial arts and marksmanship. Also, he formerly achieved Golden Glove status in the boxing ring. He had a shot at the Olympics at one time."

"Very impressive," Matt said.

"He will serve as the head of Chief Osceola's personal security detail until we determine the level of the threat."

"So what's the plan?" Hop asked.

"Mr. Kotori is reviewing every single security tape to try and piece together this Murphy fellow's movements while he was here. We think there is likely more than we have found so far – even without the tape from the hotel. If he met with someone on the resort property – anywhere on the property - we should know it. Hopefully, if we can figure out who he is working with, we can apprehend him."

"I hope you do – and soon," Matt said. "Find him, we find Murphy. And the Wolf."

When they finished their coffee, the chief stood and again thanked Matt, and, to Matt's surprise, his staff members did the same. The big Indian acknowledged Matt with yet another nod but didn't shake this time, and stood fast by the chief's side.

––––––––

Matt and Hop gathered their bags and checked out. Ron met them at the valet stand, and Anni showed up to see them off. She and Hop huddled around their iPhones, exchanging contact information and taking pictures of each other like teenagers.

"How's the chief taking all of this, Ron?" Matt asked.

"As good as can be expected, I guess. He tends to internalize things and can't figure out why someone would target him, especially someone here on the reservation."

"That's one big dude you have protecting him," Matt said.

Ron laughed. "Yeah, Philip Kotori is something else. Since he joined us a few years ago we have had very little problem keeping the peace around here. He's not too pleased about last night's events."

"I can see that," Matt said. "What's the story on the Olympics?"

Ron frowned and shook his head. "Like I said, he had a chance back in the day, but the opportunity passed. He had the same problem so many of the Wapegan have had in the past. The bottle got the best of him, and he couldn't qualify."

"Sorry to hear that," Matt said. "That's a shame. Behind him now?"

"I think so. He fell off the wagon about a year ago, but I haven't heard of any problems since."

"Well, here's my truck," Matt said, tipping the driver as he got out. Hop embraced Anni for longer than either Matt or Ron expected before climbing in the passenger side. "If anything changes, I'll call," Matt said to Ron. "Hop's really after me to get the police involved, and he agreed to give me until the end of the day to try and figure out Jeff's role and to what degree, if any, the Bing is involved."

"Please do," Ron said, "and I'll do the same if I hear anything. If there's something we can do on this end, let me know."

"I will. This has been quite the trip, hasn't it?" Matt asked.

"Never a dull moment." Ron shook his hand. "Good seeing you. When this blows over, we'll do it again."

"We will. Except next time, I'll try to keep from getting my ass kicked," Matt said and started to leave. Before he made it out from under the canopy, he remembered he wanted to ask Ron one more question about the surveillance video.

Matt hung his head out of the window, but didn't see Ron at first. When he finally located him, he waved, but by this time, Ron was in the valet booth, chasing the attendant out. Ron shut the door and pulled out his phone.

Matt kept his hand out for a minute, but Ron never looked up and eventually turned his back to the window. From the way Ron was gesturing, the call appeared to be important. It can wait, Matt thought.

He put his truck in gear and eased out onto the frontage road.

36

MATT TRIED TO make sense out of the last twenty-four hours as he and Hop motored toward Gulfport, but found it difficult to concentrate because Hop wouldn't stop talking about Anni. Matt hoped he would lighten up after they ate in Jackson, but Hop started up again as soon as they pulled back onto Highway 49. Matt engaged him for a while, and eventually the discussion wound down, and Hop changed the subject.

"So how many pictures were on that flash drive that dude took?" Hop asked.

"What, my pictures or Hank's?"

"Hank's. You know, storm pictures."

"Probably over a hundred," Matt said. "There's some wild shit in some of them. You know Hank stayed, right?"

"No, but I'm not surprised."

"He was taking the pictures the whole time. I looked at them. Our street looked like an overflowing ditch. All you could see were tops of houses during the thick of it. Bizarre."

"I'd like to see them. Did you save any of them on your computer?"

"Yeah, I saved all of 'em on my hard drive. Once you boot it up, look in the C: drive for "Hank's Hurricane pics.'"

Hop reached in the back seat and grabbed the computer bag. Something told Matt he should get the computer himself and hand it over to Hop, and as Hop unzipped it, Matt felt a wave of panic shoot up his back. He reached over to snatch the bag from Hop, but he was too late. Hop's mouth was open, dumbfounded. He pulled his hands out of the bag then slowly turned towards Matt with a pained expression on his face. He had the pumpkin in one hand. The other held three stacks of hundred dollar bills.

37

MATT AND HOP spoke at the same time, but Hop won out on volume so Matt let him go ahead.

"Talk to me, man. What the hell is this?"

"Look," Matt said, "I can explain. When I was in that vault, the first thing I grabbed was that flash drive."

"The *first* thing? "

"The first thing. And then as I started to close it, I saw all that money – there's $30,000 there Hop - and thought, well, who is it going to hurt, you know? This is dirty money, too, so…"

"Are you serious?"

"I was going to tell you, Hop; I just didn't know when. We can split it, no problem."

Hop shook his head and closed his eyes. "This hurts, man. Hurts."

"I know. I'm sorry I didn't include you on this. I should have told you straight up."

"That's not it."

"What?"

Hop looked at Matt. "You've changed," Hop said.

"Changed?"

Hop allowed a few barely perceptible nods to himself before answering. "Do you know how long I've looked up to you, Matt? Ever since high school, you were the one that didn't screw up like the rest of us."

"Hop –"

"No. Shut up and listen. You made good grades. You got a scholarship to Southern Miss. You didn't drive drunk. You found a pretty girl – and stuck with her. You went to law school, for Pete's sake. You went to church – regularly, even. All the shit I didn't have the stones or resolve or brains or will power or whatever to do, you did."

"You make it sound like I was some sort of angel."

"Compared to the rest of us slapdicks, you were. You were the moral compass for our group, Matt. That's why I'm having a hard time with this. Not because you didn't bring me in on it. Not because you wanted to keep the money to yourself. But because you did it in the first place. I already told you, I don't want any of this money, and I want out of this more now than the last time we talked about it. I just don't get it. What happened, bro?"

"What do you mean 'what happened?'"

"Is it the cash that's corrupted you? Is that what it is? Or did it start when Shelley walked out?"

Matt didn't know what to say. Hop hit it square on the head. He had felt dirty since that night in Vegas, and no matter how hard he tried to scrub it, the lingering tinge of deceit seemed to color everything he did. He couldn't figure out how to shake it. When he first found the money, he thought he had the solution – to his financial future, to his reconciliation with Shelley, and further to his self-image. It even served as a misplaced means to get past the impact of Jeff's death. But hearing it now from Hop, he realized the money just pulled him deeper into the mire. The list just went on: he had entertained thoughts about how to screw Hop out of his share, how to hide it from the authorities, how to put off telling Shelley and, to make things worse, he had taken *more* money out of someone else's safety deposit box. It had to end.

"You're right. I don't know what happened Hop, and I'm truly sorry. Sorry for the way I've treated you, hell, everyone. I want to go back, Hop. Do it over. Everything. Starting with Shelley, then the bag, the bank, everything. I feel lost, and I don't even know where to start."

Hop looked at him and smiled. "You know, bro. You know. You just said it."

"Said what?"

"You start with Shelley."

———

She answered on the first ring and sounded halfway glad to hear from him, although she was startled by the tone of the call. "Hop's with me," Matt said. His heart was beating fast again, and he felt sweaty all over. But this had to be done and, like Hop said, done now. "We're on our way back from Pontotoc."

"Pontotoc? Why-"

"I'll get to why in a minute. But a lot of things have happened since the storm – a lot of things I'm not proud of – and I need to come clean about them with you."

"I thought we already had this conversation..."

"Stay with me, Shelley. That was only half of it." He took a deep breath and started from the beginning, telling her everything he could think of. If he forgot a detail, Hop got him back on track, and by the time he finished nearly an hour later, Shelley knew about the duffel bag with the money, The Majestic's chips, Matt's suspicion about Jeff's death, the finding of the deposit box key, the trip to Pontotoc and meeting up with Ron. Shelley had heard Matt speak of Ron in the past but had never met him. When Matt explained why Ron got involved, the conversation detoured as he described finding the flash drive and taking the $30,000. She, like Hop, could not understand what would possess Matt to do such a thing. She chastised him for it but wanted to hear more. She continued to interrupt him as he relayed the assault in the hotel room and his description of Griff Murphy and his purported motives. Matt was glad to hear most of her concerns were about his health. He explained what he found on the flash drive, the threat to Chief Osceola, and his breakfast meeting. Finally, Matt told her about

Hank watching the office back home and the possibility that he may get a visitor.

"Well, you've managed to get yourself in quite a pickle, haven't you?"

Matt couldn't make heads or tails of her tone, but he hoped for the best and assumed she was trying to be somewhat supportive. At least she hadn't told him to go to hell.

"Guess so, Shelley. Took Hop to help me realize it," he said. "But I've made a mess of trying to fix this whole thing. Now, I suppose, I have to figure out what to do next."

Shelley was good at problem solving. She helped her girlfriends through difficult situations with husbands or children, and people gravitated toward to her for her kindness and her ability to determine the best path to resolution. She didn't sugarcoat an issue when asked for assistance, though, and she was all business when she responded.

"Well, obviously, you need to let Delia know," she said. "If everything you told me about Jeff is true, Delia should be in the loop. Don't worry about whether you'll end up with the money or whether you'll be out of a job. You're way past that now."

"Agreed."

"As for calling the police, that's tricky, considering you basically robbed a bank. I would reach out to Lance. He's not GPD, but he can give you some measured advice on the criminal front that someone else may not. And he's not likely to arrest you."

"Okay. I'll call him when I get back. Need to speak to Hank first." Matt blew out a sigh. "One more thing, Shelley. Will you be okay?"

"Of course. Why?"

"Scared me to death when he knew who I was, and I just worry about something happening to y'all."

Shelley paused. "Don't. Seriously. He has no idea where I am, and I have no plans to show my face anywhere near Gulfport until this is resolved."

"Just keep your eyes open, okay? If anything seems even a little bit weird, will you call me?"

"Of course, but it's you I'm worried about. This guy wants to kill you, Matt."

"Yeah, I'd be worried, too, but for the fact that, one, Hank is involved; and two, Murphy's not going to do anything before tomorrow morning. He needs the flash drive and the money, and if I'm dead, he'll never get it. By then, between Lance and Hank, I'll have back-up. "

"Hank certainly helps. You're right, I can't see anyone getting past him."

"Thanks so much, Shelley. I really look forward to seeing you sometime soon."

"You too, Matt. I miss you. Bye."

Matt set the phone down and stared out the window after she hung up.

He didn't expect that.

38

MATT RAN SHELLEY's suggestions by Hop, and he agreed with the plan of action. From a timing standpoint, Matt thought it best to get back to the office and try to open the flash drive files – if he could – to put it all in context. Plus, whatever was on the drive could provide better footing to counter his taking the money from the bank. He would call Delia and Lance after that.

Matt dropped Hop off on the way in. Hop offered him his couch, but Matt declined. "Let me know what's on that drive," Hop said as he got out of the truck.

"Will do. Now go call Anni." Hop waved his phone over his head as he sprinted upstairs to his loft.

When Matt parked in front of his office, he found Hank reclining in a folding chair out front on the sidewalk. A book rested on his lap, and a black molded plastic box leaned up against his chair. Instead of greeting Matt with his usual gregarious overture, Hank looked dark when Matt stepped out of the truck.

"Dammit, boy."

"You all right, Hank? What's wrong?"

Hank walked over to Matt and stared at his face.

"Cocksucker did get you pretty good, that son of a bitch."

Matt now understood. His black eye, busted lip, and scratches on his face set Hank back a bit.

"Oh," Matt said, touching his temple. "That he did. You should see the other guy."

Hank didn't smile. "You want to tell me what this is all about now?" Hank asked.

"Sure," Matt said. "Let's go upstairs. What's with the box?"

"Gun case. I was sitting out here with my AR-15, but the cops made me put it up. They said I couldn't have it out in public. Go figure. So I got Gimpy here in the box."

"Gimpy?"

".44 Magnum. Game changer, this one. Real game changer."

"I bet," Matt said.

"Before you go to the office," Hank said, "I need to show you what I've done. Follow me."

About halfway up the stairs, Hank pointed out a thin metal wire that ran from the stair baseboard into a small box mounted on the outside of one of the balusters. Matt would not have noticed it if Hank hadn't pointed it out.

"What is that?" Matt asked.

"Trip wire. If someone comes up to your office and don't see it, they'll clip it. You see this box over here?"

"Yep."

"The wire is attached to this ring, here. You see that?"

"I do," Matt said.

"That ring is connected to a flash-bang grenade pin. Someone hits the wire, the pin comes out and 'boom.'"

"Did you say grenade, Hank?"

"Flash-bang grenade. Magnesium-based, creates a blinding flare and has one hell of a report. Not designed to kill any-one, although if you get close enough to it, I guess it could. Anyway, there's not a much better warning system out there. If anyone sets it off, you and probably everyone else on the block will know it. Son of a bitch who trips it will for sure. Should dis-orient the hell out of him. May even deafen him a bit until his ears recover."

Matt could see Hank took pride in his work.

"That's why I slept so good last night," Hank said. "Once I got here I rigged this up, then I put an extra slide lock on your office door before hitting the rack. Between the trip wire, the lock, Gimpy, and your couch, I slept like a baby. And I didn't have to hear Sarah drone on and on. Amen to that, I say. Amen."

Once they got upstairs Matt looked around the office, and it appeared to be just as he left it. The ottoman had not moved.

"Now, tell me, what in the hell have you gotten yourself into?" Hank asked as he plopped down on the couch.

After his conversation with Shelley, Matt thought about what version of the story he should tell Hank, and he weighed all of his options. He ultimately decided to speak freely with Hank as well. He trusted him and valued their friendship, and if Hank found out down the road that Matt had not been entirely truthful with him, it could break that bond. Hank listened to everything and for once did not offer much by way of comment, although he did let out a whistle when Matt raised the ottoman cover to show him the money. Eventually, Matt wrapped up. "So this evening I'm going to try and find anything else that may help. Then I'm going to make a few phone calls. And that's where it stands now."

Hank stared at Matt for a few seconds. "I think I should stay here with you."

"What?"

"I don't understand this computer thing, but it sounds important. I got a nose for danger, and something smells like a doberman's asshole. I don't like this one bit. Not a bit."

"Well there's a pleasant analogy. Don't be so dramatic, Hank. Frankly, I feel more comfortable now that I'm here. And with your SEAL engineering, I think I'll sleep fine, too. Plus, I've got my own mini-Gimpy I keep with me – in case of such an emergency. So I'm good."

"I still don't like it. Don't like it at all. But you're a hard-headed bastard like me. You still got the radio I gave you a few weeks ago?"

"It's in my truck – under the seat, I think."

"You bring it up here, and I'll leave you alone. Just keep it handy, and if you need to call me, I can be here in five minutes. Under five minutes, actually."

"Thanks, Hank, for all of your help and for watching over my place. If you could just keep this under wraps for a little while longer, I would appreciate it."

"I give you my word, Matt."

"Thank you."

"You good for chow tonight?"

"Yep. We picked up some Subway in Wiggins on the way in for dinner. I have the remnants of a foot-long and some chips waiting on me," Matt said.

"Good enough, then."

Matt walked Hank out, and Hank made sure Matt retrieved the radio before he left. Matt waved goodbye, unloaded the rest of his truck and scanned the street after Hank pulled out of sight. Nothing unusual as far as he could tell. He wondered exactly what he was going to do when he got back to his office. He was no computer hack, and he did not know where to begin with the flash drive. Matt made sure to be careful negotiating the trip wire on the way in, bolted the door, and checked out the new lock. Matt didn't think a battering ram could get through his door with all the steel Hank had strapped onto it.

He started unpacking and noticed the message light on his office phone was blinking. He put it on speaker. A familiar East Indian voice spoke up.

"Mr. Frazier, this is Ravi. Please call me. I have Mr. McCabe's user name and password for you. My cell phone number is…"

Matt put down his clothes and reached for a legal pad.

39

RAVI APOLOGIZED FOR taking so long to get back to Matt. He said while the Bing was set up to close out personal information and files when someone quits or retires, there were no protocols in place for when someone dies suddenly or commits suicide. Ravi said the last two words under his breath. He assumed someone took Jeff's log-in information offline because of the special circumstances surrounding Jeff's death. He could not explain why he was not informed of the deletion. Ravi then launched into a monologue explaining the process he went through to backtrack the network to find Jeff's log-in data. Matt tried to sound interested when Ravi made points that Ravi deemed important, but Matt was lost for much of the conversation.

"Mr. McCabe changed his password five weeks prior to his death, which was sooner than the mandated password change date."

That got his attention. Matt wrote *McCabe password change – 5 weeks before death???* on a legal pad. "Well, some people do that, I guess," Matt said.

"Anyway, his user name is the same – JMCCABE, and his password is 'Cathy&Me40.' It is case sensitive, so the "C" in Cathy and the "M" are capitalized. Also, that's an ampersand between 'Cathy' and 'Me.'"

Matt wrote it down. "Got it, Ravi. Thanks."

"No spaces."

"No spaces. Noted."

"Is there anything else I can do for you, sir?" Ravi asked.

"No, you have been very helpful."

"Very well. Goodbye, Mr. Frazier. Have a very nice evening."

"You too, Ravi," Matt said. Matt looked at the password. Cathy&Me40? Matt couldn't find anything in the password that had any meaning relative to the money. Even Matt's password was a combination of his kids' names and ages, so this didn't seem too far off the mark.

Matt swiveled around in his chair and booted up his computer. He typed in Jeff's username and entered the password. "Here we go," said Matt, looking back and forth between his legal pad and the screen to make sure he got it right. He tapped "enter" and waited. Jeff's desktop programs came up.

"Good work, Ravi," Matt said to the screen, leaning forward and clicking to the FileManage home screen. Matt ran a query of Jeff's personal files, and they came up just as they had a few days prior. The program arranged them chronologically, and Matt scrolled down. He slowed when he got to document 117, and, just as before, the seven or so documents following document 117 contained no titles. Matt looked at the document numbers and wrote them down on his pad. He then returned to 117 and clicked on it. The computer took a few seconds to open Microsoft Word, and Matt breathed an anxious sigh as the document began to come up.

Matt looked at the screen and frowned.

It was blank.

"What the hell –?" Matt scrolled down through the document. No text anywhere. He glanced at the screen and double-checked the title to make sure he had the right document. It was open, but there was nothing on the screen.

"You've got to be kidding me." Matt closed and reopened it to try again. Still blank. He then went back to the query screen and clicked on the next seven untitled documents. All of them were blank as well.

"Son of a *bitch*," Matt said. He backtracked to some of Jeff's other personal documents and tried them. The documents containing his will and insurance information opened, and all were populated. Matt started opening other documents at random, and they all came up as expected. The only documents in Jeff's personal files Matt could find that came up blank were the first set he checked.

"Why are these documents empty?" Matt whispered. He scrolled through them again to see if there was any kind of code or words on them that would lead him somewhere. Nothing.

Then Matt clicked document 117's history, and his jaw dropped. It had been accessed and edited that morning.

40

THE TIME STAMP on the history note put the edit at around the time Matt and Hop had coffee at the Crescent Moon with Ron and Chief Osceola. He checked the histories on the other seven. They had been accessed and edited that morning as well.

He gazed across his office and interlaced his fingers behind his head. Matt looked back down at the FileManage document numbers he wrote on his legal pad:

8033860
8033862
8034011
8034014
8034100
8034104
8034509

They looked familiar to him, but he couldn't put them together. He stared at them for a few minutes. "Seven numbers," he said out loud. "What does that mean?"

He got up and started pacing the room. He thought about the money in the deposit box. Nothing there. He thought about the money in the ottoman. Six bundles of cash. That doesn't fit.

Then the safety deposit box key came to mind. Matt pulled open his desk drawer and found the envelope which originally held the key. He looked at the number written on the front.

Seven.

Matt fished the flash drive out of his pocket, plugged it in and pulled up the documents one more time. Seven numbered documents came up again:

RedMoonInstr.docx
18033860DDH.docx
28033862HFR.docx
38034011JLC.docx
48034014RFE.docx
58034100SBW.docx
68034104GPH.docx
78034509PJK.docx

Aha! He held his notebook up next to the computer monitor.

18033860DDH.docx	*8033860*
28033862HFR.docx	*8033862*
38034011JLC.docx	*8034011*
48034014RFE.docx	*8034014*
58034100SBW.docx	*8034100*
68034104GPH.docx	*8034104*
78034509PJK.docx	*8034509*

He took away the initials and the sequential first number in each document on the flash drive, and every document matched exactly. He clicked on the first number, and a username/password prompt came up. Matt entered *JMCCABE*, tabbed down and entered *Cathy&Me40*.

"And here we go," Matt said, beginning to smile.

Another error prompt: *Access Denied. Invalid User Name and Password. Please Try Again.*

What? Matt tried Jeff's user name and password again, this time typing more slowly. He noticed his fingers were shaking a bit. Same message.

He thought about calling Ravi to see if he could get into the documents but decided against it. As cautious as Ravi was, he would not go through with such a request, especially since he just turned the system inside out looking for Jeff's password. Plus, it was too late in the evening for another call. Matt clicked on *RedMoonInstr. docx*. It had been the only document on the flash drive that opened for Matt, and he hoped he could possibly find a clue he had missed before. He read through each line slowly and realized, in his prior review, he had indeed overlooked line 2:

2. *All remaining docs in folder protected. Use password from doc 117 info and print out materials for delivery.*

He mumbled it to himself three times, stopping on the second sentence. "Use password from doc 117." *Use password from doc 117.* He turned back to Jeff's FileManage documents and clicked on *117* again. Again, the document came up blank.

Matt clicked to Jeff's e-mail page and scrolled through the *Sent Items* folder to see if document 117 had been attached to any outgoing document. "Surely Jeff would not be so stupid to have e-mailed this out," Matt said as his eyes followed the line of e-mails going up his screen. Jeff's *Sent Items* folder had a 30-day history, but Matt could find nothing out of the ordinary. He was actually surprised Jeff's e-mail account was still open. Matt clicked back to the document. He returned to the FileManage screen. He checked the history and did numerous searches to see if any prior drafts existed that may not have been edited. Dead end. Matt reached for the remains of his Subway and took a bite. He got up to stretch and turn on the lamp and resumed his pacing, glancing at the monitor between nibbles, hoping to find inspiration somewhere.

The history of document 117 showed Jeff accessing it on more than one occasion before he finally left it alone. Matt wondered if Jeff had ever saved it offline on a hard drive. Matt often saved working copies of documents to his local drive if he was traveling and needed to pull them up on a plane or somewhere where he may not have an internet connection…

Matt stopped in his tracks and put his sandwich down. He sprinted to his computer, wiping mayonnaise on his shorts to degrease his fingers. He clicked open his C: drive and scrolled through his documents.

"Yes!" When Matt had searched FileManage the first day the system was back up and couldn't open document 117, he saved it to his hard drive to see if he could bypass the password if the document was not on the Bing's system. It didn't work, because even on his hard drive Matt needed Jeff's Bing password. Matt wondered if, now that he was logged in as Jeff, it would work. He found *117*, clicked on it, and drummed his fingers on his desk as his computer hummed.

It opened.

And it was not blank.

"Finally, a break," Matt said as he read the text.

-Key – Pontotoc B&T 117
-Instructions on flash drive in box
-roulette/CrescentWaning1911
-Contact the Wolf after you access box; see instructions.

Matt said it again, but wrote it down this time. This had to be for Murphy, Matt thought. It provided the location of the safety deposit and gave him an idea of what to do once he got to the box.

"There is our friend again," Matt said to the screen. He circled the third line on his legal pad.

Matt returned to the documents he had pulled up on the flash drive. He clicked on the first one, *18033860DDH.docx*. He entered *roulette* in the user name box and *CrescentWaning1911* in the password box.

He did not get an "access denied" message.

He did not get a blank document.

What he did get made him step back. He looked at it again and then pulled out his gun and set it next to his monitor, along with Hank's extra box of shells.

Donald D. Hood - BUNDLE 1 - $700,000.00.

Donald Hood was the sitting Governor of the State of Mississippi.

41

A LARGE MAJORITY OF voters had elected Governor Hood to his second term less than a year before the storm. Depending on one's political persuasions, Governor Hood was either one of the best governors or one of the worst governors in the Magnolia State's recent past. Whenever he did something, he did it big, and he had a reputation for driving his agenda through with no holds barred. His successes during his first term earned him recognition on a national scale, and word on the street was that he was on the short list of those being considered as the next Vice President of the United States. It did not hurt that prior to his decision to run for governor, Donald Hood managed one of the most prolific lobbying firms inside the Beltway. He maintained those relationships after he took the governor's oath of office, and his insider status served him – and the State of Mississippi – well when he needed something done. Moreover, he was an important client of the Bing's governmental affairs group, and he often called on the Bing to help ensure crucial pieces of legislation deftly and successfully maneuvered through the minefields of the Mississippi Senate and House floors before landing on his desk for signature.

Matt scrolled down and read the rest of the document. The first section contained detailed directions for where, when, how, and to whom the *initial* payment of $700,000 would be delivered. A timeline of events was laid out on the next page, and the trigger for it all, apparently, was the untimely death of Chief Warren Osceola. Matt felt the pressure in his chest ease for the moment.

He had been right; a hit *had* been put out on the Wapegan chief. He made a note to call Ron to let him know.

Instructions for the governor followed.

Upon the death of Chief Osceola, The Governor will introduce the Native American Regulatory Reform Accountability Addendum. Draft legislation and comments follow. The Governor will make every effort to ensure its passage.

He read on. Several pages of what appeared to be proposed legislation pertaining to casino gaming in Mississippi followed. The legislation was drafted, in effect, to put back-door limitations on the original Native American Regulatory Reform Act, and to make the state's decision in 1995 to allow Indian casinos in Mississippi conditional upon future applicants meeting certain standards and requirements in the name of equity.

At first, Matt didn't see anything sinister in the drafts, nor could he identify any of the players involved. After all, every casino seeking approval to operate in Mississippi had to jump through a number of regulatory, legal, and legislative hurdles before opening their doors. Even the Crescent Moon hadn't been exempt from all of them. Once he got into the details, though, he realized the new standards made it all but impossible for any proposed *Indian* casino to go forward. For starters, truly draconian environmental regulations were slated to go on the books. Matt had done environmental impact-type work for non-casino clients on the energy side, and he knew the green initiatives in this new legislation would be so cost-prohibitive that meeting even the minimum standards would put most operations – including Indian casinos – deep in the red.

The new legislation also eliminated every last one of the tax incentives the Wapegan tribe currently enjoyed with the Crescent Moon, citing the current economic climate as well as the lack of a constitutional basis for what was essentially an unfair business advantage over the non-Native American gaming sites. Additionally, the legislation discussed an increased need for raising the impact fees associated with a new casino to pay for the "anticipated and unanticipated" costs of the newly-burdened infrastructure. These "costs" included payment for increased utilities, sewer, and water usage, not to mention necessary additions to the fire and police departments.

What Matt truly found ludicrous, though, was the "cultural impact" clause. Instead of respecting the Native American culture, as Matt had expected, this clause allowed any city in Mississippi where Native Americans were considering building a casino to place limitations on the casino's development — so long as the city had an underlying interest in preserving the "cultural climate" of the municipality and surrounding areas.

Under the banner of cultural impact, a city could place restrictions on casino signage, the size of the casino gaming floor, the number of slot machines, the number of table games, the number of hotel rooms and restaurants, the height and footprint of buildings, and the design of the hotel and related structures. In short, the legislation would essentially shut down any proposed development before it even got off the ground.

"This will never pass," Matt mumbled. He felt his blood boil as he continued reading the document – next were suggestions and instructions for Governor Hood.

The demise of Chief Osceola will greatly reduce any resistance (public or private) from the Wapegan nation to this legislation. A new Chief will be appointed, who will be more receptive to the Governor's and the state's directives.

Matt scribbled a note on his pad: *New Chief: Ron???*

The Governor should spin the new environmental regulations for the Wapegan into his green campaign and relate it back to the Indians' tradition of environmental respect to give it credence.

"What a load of shit," Matt said.

The Governor will hold numerous press events, stressing the dire state of the economy and the impact of a new Native American casino with an unfair economic advantage over casinos that traditionally employ non-Native American citizens of the state of Mississippi

*The Governor will launch a "Return to Nostalgia" campaign focus-
ing on family values, responsibility, and a renewal of roots. Inherent in
this campaign will be a focus on the unique characteristics of Mississippi's
towns and cities and the need to maintain those characteristics for future
generations. The Governor will merge this campaign into the gaming legislation, pushing the need for towns and cities to make their own decisions
on how they should grow, while maintaining their heritage and unique
personalities.*

*The Governor should capitalize on the current "get the government out
of our affairs" mentality and bring it down to the state level, proposing that
the state of Mississippi get out of the business of regulating its municipali-
ties. This positioning, more than anything else, will provide a viable basis
for arguing that cities should be allowed to impose local limitations on new
gaming establishments.*

Two follow-up drafts of the legislation followed. All three said
essentially the same thing, but some contained softer language
than others. The instructions asked Hood to review the three and
determine which he believed had the best chance of success. The
document also instructed Hood to work with various impression-
able senators and staff on proposed modifications to the legislation, should they be necessary, while keeping the ultimate goals
in mind.

The next page contained press-release-type material on The
Majestic: its economic impact, the jobs it had created, its effect on
tourism, and the revenue The Majestic had generated for Gulfport
and the state of Mississippi since it opened. The document even
identified, by initials only, a contact from The Majestic for the governor as well as a secure phone line for discussion.

The contact: SM.

"*SM?*" Matt said, dumbfounded. Then he scribbled again on
his legal pad: *Was Jeff involved? What did he know? Who drafted the
legislation?* He cocked his head to the side and wrote: *Was Jeff 'SM'?*
Matt thumped his pencil on the pad and wrote several more question marks at the end of the sentence as he pondered that last

question. He then wrote *Jeff = SM*, and closed his eyes and thought through what he knew so far. When he opened them, he drew a line through it.

It didn't make sense. Jeff's files had been accessed *that morning*, so he was not the kingpin. But, Matt thought, he *did* have possession of the flash drive at the outset. After a few minutes of staring at the pad, he wrote *SM/Jeff/Bing?* near the bottom of the page and underlined it three times. Under that, *Call Delia ASAP*. He circled this instruction and would do it soon. But he continued reading – he knew she'd want to hear absolutely all of this. He also began saving each document to his local drive as he opened them, in case he somehow lost any or could no longer find them – he'd learned that lesson once already. He could only imagine how Delia would distance the Bing from Governor Hood and the inevitable shit-storm that would follow, and he hoped that if the Bing was involved, the connection would hang on Tripp and not Delia.

But that was for later.

Although the legislation piqued his interest, Matt was most disturbed by the next grouping of pages in the governor's files. They contained a list of all legislators and their anticipated vote on the proposed legislation. The first set was identified as the "yes" votes and included not much more than the legislators' names, their respective districts, and contact information. The next two classifications – the "maybes" and the "nos" – however, included quite a bit more data. Each page contained detailed profiles on the various "on-the-fence" and "no" votes. Because most of the legislators also had full-time jobs, the dossiers included their work addresses, their work supervisors and subordinates, e-mail addresses, phone numbers, and annual projected salaries. Matt thought that inclusion of the supervisors, subordinates, and salaries was a bit much, but it did not prepare him for what followed next. The files also listed information on their families, including their spouses' or significant others' names, places of employment (if applicable), the names of children, stepchildren, grandchildren, and where each went to school. Matt's eyes were drawn, however, to the last heading in each legislator's respective sub-file entitled, *Angles of Approach.*

"Someone has certainly done their homework," Matt said, shaking his head as he scanned the monitor.

Almost every senator or representative had something in this category, and the entries ranged from mildly embarrassing to somewhat sensitive, to downright career and/or family ending. The notes detailed the legislators' various indiscretions, and most were not pretty – long histories of infidelity were backed up with contacts for the various paramours, and some files even included photos. Other legislators had gambling issues, the sidenotes pointing out how much money would be needed to influence their decision making. More than Matt expected had an affinity for pornography – not all of it legal – and their search histories, as well as their files, had been catalogued. Some had a history of bribes, some petty, some large, and their respective payout histories were laid out in great detail, bullet-point style. Some were closet homosexuals, some liked the whiskey, and most doctored their expense reports. For those who had no nefarious history, the document suggested various ways to call their credibility into question or, if necessary, orchestrate smear campaigns as a means to get their attention.

No stone remained unturned in the efforts to line up votes to get the addendum passed. Governor Hood would now have, at his fingertips, the information necessary to influence anyone who might think about voting against him.

"Wow," was all Matt could say. He scanned through the pages again, not so much interested in the lurid details, but amazed at the scope of the research that had gone into the preparation. What else you got? Matt wondered.

Matt clicked on the next document, *28033862HFR.docx*, provided the requisite password and it, too, opened.

Holden F. Reed – BUNDLE 2 - $500,000.00

This wasn't a complete surprise. Senator Holden Reed had served as the state senator from Matt's own district for two terms and was joined with Hood at the hip. Like the prior document, Senator Reed's packet also contained drop-off instructions for his bribe. The remainder of the file, though essentially copying Governor Hood's package, tasked Reed to reach out to his fellow legislators in whatever way he deemed to be most effective. That included a state-wide initiative tour to drum up public support for the bill's passage.

Matt went through the rest of the documents and found similarly-themed instructions, all designed to influence the passage of the act and/or to minimize the presence of the Wapegan in Gulfport. All contained detailed drop and contact instructions, and all contained an identical projected timeline of events. The specific instructions, while collectively accomplishing the same goal, varied greatly.

Document *38034011JLC.docx* provided for the delivery of $500,000 to Jack L. Cassady, Mississippi's gaming commissioner. Commissioner Cassady's directive was to table or defer any requests by the Wapegan that could move the plans for a coast casino forward. He would also receive a copy of the legislation, although the commissioner would not have the pleasure of reviewing the salacious backgrounds of the various legislators. Commissioner Cassady's document did, however, provide an explanation of the governor's plan to spin the legislation and encouraged him to take a similar tack when addressing colleagues or the public.

Document *48034014RFE.docx* contained instructions for Bundle 4 – in the amount of $125,000 – to be delivered to Rush Enoch, president of Gulfport's zoning board. His instructions were simple: allow no zoning or property variances that would set the stage for a preliminary build out of a Wapegan casino on the Coast.

The mayor of Gulfport, Brandon Wilkes, would receive $100,000 in exchange for engaging in what amounted to a not-so-subtle show of support for all things Majestic, according to document *58034100SBW.docx*. This included Wilkes' throwing his full support behind any proposals involving The Majestic, appearing at all social events sponsored by The Majestic, talking up the budget, and gently reminding the public what The Majestic provided for the city's tax rolls. Likewise, Wilkes would downplay any positive impact an Indian casino would have on Gulfport and coast residents – he would insist that it would actually *cost* the city money under the current tax-exempt structure. Finally, Wilkes would refuse to engage in meaningful discussions with any Wapegan representatives, either formally or informally, as a show of solidarity for The Majestic.

The next document caused Matt to lean back in his chair and shake his head. "Now it makes sense, you two-faced bastard," Matt said as he stared at the name that came up when he clicked on *68034104GPH.docx.*

George Halliday.

Gulfport's chief of police stood to receive $75,000 to "undertake any directives at his discretion to discourage a Wapegan presence" on the coast. He would also "provide Mayor Wilkes with support" for any directives the mayor designed to accomplish the same goal. Halliday's orders even suggested that Wapegan guests and dignitaries should be profiled so they'd know they weren't welcome on the coast. There was even a directive to "handle any remaining money issues" related to the Wapegan initiative, and noted that there would likewise be extra compensation involved for him.

Of all the people involved so far, Matt was most disappointed in this last one. "No wonder you were so willing to take the lead investigating Jeff's death," Matt mumbled, turning to the final document on the drive. He was getting tired and didn't think it could get any worse until he clicked on *78034509PJK.docx.* A name he would not have recognized just two days prior appeared at the top of the page: "Phillip J. Kotori."

Matt frowned at the screen for a second, but as soon as he read more, he grabbed his phone and tried to dial and continue scrolling at the same time.

42

PHILLIP KOTORI, ACCORDING to the plan, would not receive his initial payment from one of the numbered cash bundles. Instead, he was set to receive his remuneration in two separate, conditional installments of $50,000 and $100,000 – money from the same safety deposit box Matt had his hands in the day before.

The document identified the big Indian as the contact responsible for "eliminating Chief Warren Osceola." He would get $50K before the hit and an additional $100K once he completed the job. He could pull in additional cash if he successfully facilitated the appointment of a new Wapegan chief, although the amount wasn't specified and seemed to depend on how pleased Governor Hood was about everything. Matt stared at the screen. It disturbed him that the hulk of a man assigned to protect the chief had planned to kill him. Worse, this was the final document of the bunch, and Matt still didn't know who the Wolf was. One thing was for sure: Matt had to call Ron Tsosie.

A sleepy voice answered after several rings. "Hello?"

"Ron, it's Matt Frazier. I know how late it is, and I'm sorry to be calling you again at a strange hour, but this is urgent."

"Matt? What's up?"

"Listen: remember how I told you the flash drive I got from that safety deposit box up there had several other documents I couldn't open?"

It took Ron a second, and Matt wondered if Ron had yet realized the emergent nature of the situation. "Yeah," he said. Now he sounded a little more like himself. "He got the wrong one. Murphy, I'm talking about."

"Right. Do you remember me telling you that the other one had a number of documents on it that I couldn't open because I didn't have the password?"

"Kind of," Ron said, "I guess."

"Well I got the password. Where is Chief Osceola right now?"

"Should be at home, Matt. Why?"

"Is Kotori with him?"

"No, he's not," Ron said carefully, and not without some suspicion. "The chief's other detail is guarding his home at the moment. After you took off this morning, Phillip said he wanted to go back and try and fill in the holes in the security films. Haven't heard from him since. Do I need to get him over there?"

"No, I'd keep him far away. According to what I just pulled up, Phillip Kotori is the hit man."

"*Phillip?*" Ron Tsosie was wide awake now. "Not a chance. Are you sure?"

"Positive. It says here he got fifty grand up front and gets another hundred upon completion."

"Matt, he's the chief's right-hand security man."

"So you say," Matt said, "I don't know the man. I can give you some background details later, but the important thing is first to make sure he *cannot* access the chief, and, second, lock him down until we get to the bottom of this."

"Hold on. I want to know exactly what was on that flash drive."

"I can read it to you," Matt said.

"Please do," Ron said. "I want to hear this for myself." Matt recited the big Indian's file verbatim to so Ron could scratch down the details.

"What did the other documents say?" Ron asked.

Matt paused before answering. "They dealt with some under-the-table political payoffs and things." Matt stopped there. No need to share the details. "This is big, Ron. I can brief you on it when we have more time. What is important is that you get out there and secure the chief. If I'm right, the sooner the better."

Ron let out a low whistle. "This explains the security breaches. He would've had access to the tapes and to the 'Moon's hotel keys, and he may very well have been the one who helped Murphy get in your room."

"Very possible," Matt said. "But I still don't know who the Wolf is. Is Kotori a middleman, you think, and he got someone else to do this?"

Ron sighed hard. "I know who he is, and I don't see how I missed it before. I told you Kotori was a Golden Gloves boxer –"

"Yep."

"Well, as the story goes, his real name didn't exactly strike fear in opponents' hearts. And since he fits the mold of a stereotypical American Indian, as you saw yesterday, he decided to change his boxing name to something with a little more flair. Even grew a ponytail that he braided to play up the Indian theme. Care to guess what the name was?"

"No idea."

"Fighting Wolf."

"Really?" Matt said. "That's the best he could do?"

"I never said he was a smart man," Ron said. "Just goes to show you, Matt."

"What's that?"

"Sometimes, you never know who to trust."

43

M ATT ASKED RON to call him back once Chief Osceola was secure, and for a report on how well the big Indian held up under Ron's questioning. He thought about calling Hop to update him, but the midnight hour had already passed. He went back through his e-mails in search of clues that linked Jeff, The Majestic, and the Wapegan tribe. Nothing relevant jumped out at him, but one particular e-mail caught his attention; he'd opened it earlier, and now he put it on his list to discuss with Delia.

It was from Tripp Massey, and the e-mail, which went to all the attorneys, was entitled "*Future of Coast Office.*" When Matt opened it, the e-mail detailed the condition of the coast office, Jeff's death, and the status of The Majestic post-hurricane. He didn't say it straight up, but despite Delia's prior reassurances, Tripp gave the indication that the Bing should fully consider closing the coast office since its primary revenue source may no longer be a viable option.

Tripp didn't call Matt by name or discuss his future, which was probably by design. Tripp knew Matt and Delia were tight, and he probably sent the e-mail suggesting the office close to spite Delia more than him. Then Matt noticed Tripp's new title in bold typeface below his e-mail signature: Firm Chairman. He figured this *had* to be a slap at Delia – one more way Tripp could remind Delia who'd come out on top at the most recent partnership election. What an asshole.

Matt read a few more e-mails, but sleep tugged at him, and he wanted at least a few hours of shuteye before sunrise. He had a big day ahead. He would call Delia and Lance at the crack of dawn, get them up to speed, and lay out the facts just like he'd done with Shelley and Hank. Now that he knew Chief Halliday's hands were dirty, he didn't feel quite as awful about swiping the thirty grand from the safety deposit box – at least Lance would listen to the whole story without jumping to conclusions. Or so he hoped, anyway. He double-checked to make sure he'd transferred and copied the flash drive files. Then he printed copies of all the documents before boxing and storing them in the ottoman with the duffel. He had learned he couldn't be *too* careful, and in that vein he made sure the door was locked, his gun loaded, and Hank's radio nearby. He stretched out on the couch and fell asleep.

———

Older buildings have a way of speaking a language that their occupants grow to appreciate over time. The tongue-and-groove subflooring - usually oak, pine, or pecan - moves, twists, and creaks in a way that provides a fairly reliable means to triangulate the location of a person walking from room to room, traveling up or down stairs, opening or closing a door, or, in some cases, even standing up or sitting down. Matt's office, which had been built sometime around 1912, was no exception. On occasion Matt complained of its draftiness and the loud, outdated plumbing, but he wouldn't trade the big, imperfect old windows, tin tiles, high ceilings and plaster molding for anything. He found comfort in the patinaed floors and their noisy boards.

This acquired familiarity awakened his subconscious and told him, even in sleep, that someone was inside. At first, it was simply a faint acknowledgment – an awareness of a pressure or weight shift within the building, but it grew quickly, and in the back of Matt's stirring mind, he felt someone walking up the stairs. Slowly... slowly....

Before he could pinpoint it, an explosion rocked him so hard he rolled off his couch onto the floor. For a split second, Matt thought someone shot him. His ears rang, but not so much that he couldn't hear anything else. He ran toward the sound of someone falling backwards down the stairwell and reached for his gun. Matt pulled the slide on Hank's lock, flung the door open, and fired several shots into the dark below. The muzzle flashes blasted out strobes of light, illuminating the scene, and through the smoky haze, Matt saw a figure huddled at the bottom of the landing, legs kicking and flailing.

Matt threw on the light switch and recognized him immediately.

"Murphy! Griff Murphy!" he yelled, and a tall redhead briefly turned and looked at Matt, his face aghast and confused. A trickle of blood dripped from one of his ears, and one of his eyes had a purplish bruise.

Matt aimed and fired a few more rounds, but Murphy regained his wits just enough to duck outside. Matt clambered down after him, careful not to trip on the baluster now leaning over the stair treads from the detonation. He reached the bottom, cut through the smoke, and bolted through the front door in time to see Murphy pull himself up into the passenger seat of a black Suburban. Matt again raised his weapon, but this time a bullet – fired by the driver through Murphy's open door, zinged past his head, and he felt a sting on the back of his neck from brick shrapnel that caromed off the building where the slug hit.

He backed out of the way and couldn't get another round off before the Suburban sped away. As Murphy pulled the door closed, though, the dome light inside the vehicle gave Matt a look at the man behind the wheel. His unmistakable large frame was enough of a giveaway, but the dark-braided ponytail draping over the headrest cinched it.

The Wolf had made it down to Gulfport after all.

44

MATT WALKED BACK to inspect the damage once the vehicle pulled out of view. Other than the broken baluster and a few burn marks where the grenade went off, the stairwell and wall held up remarkably well. He squatted down to inspect the railing and, out of the corner of his eye, noticed something on the floor below. He hurried down the stairs, and lying next to a push broom and some cleaning supplies was a pistol.

It was a Glock G31.

"Well, hello, stranger," he said. He looked back up the stairs, then down at the spot where he'd found the gun – it most definitely wasn't there before Murphy made his grand entrance. Matt hit the Glock's release, and a full magazine dropped out; when he pulled back the slide, a round popped into the air. He caught it and examined the bullet before placing the gun under his arm. Sure enough, it was a .357.

Matt checked around for a few minutes to see if anything else looked unusual and, finding nothing, blocked the front door to the best he could with whatever furniture he could locate. Satisfied, Matt went upstairs and bolted himself back in his office. He thought the police might show up since the grenade went off and shots had been fired, and decided to watch for them from his office window upstairs.

Matt cut the lights and pulled up a chair at an angle that allowed him to peek down at the road through his blinds without being seen. He stayed there for nearly an hour. When he looked at his watch, it read 3:46 a.m. and still no sign of the cops. Apparently, no one had reported the commotion, and the police never showed. Or perhaps the police had been notified but they had orders to stand down. That was fine with him. He didn't feel like dealing with the law anyway, and he wouldn't know what he would do if Chief Halliday knocked on his door. Between the fight at the hotel, the flash-bang effects, and the tumble down the stairs, Matt didn't expect Murphy to return, although he wondered if Kotori would make another go at it.

The thought of the him being in Gulfport prompted Matt to call Ron yet again. The phone rang a few times and went to voice mail. Matt tried again and got the same thing, which he found unusual, considering the events of the prior few hours. "Ron, this is Matt. Got news for you. Call me when you get this message."

Matt set the phone down on the windowsill and looked out over the street. It was still empty. Due to the adrenaline rush from Hank's booby trap going off, there would be no more sleep, so he grabbed a Diet Coke and popped the top. As he was taking his first sip, his phone rang. *Ron.* Matt hoped the chief was okay. When he got close enough to read the caller name on the screen, he stopped and debated whether he should answer.

It read "Unknown." He picked it up anyway. "This is Matt," he said.

The caller on the other end spoke rapidly and sounded like he was out of breath. "No more games. I will not –"

"Who is this?" Matt asked.

The caller could barely speak he was breathing so hard. "I done told you once to back away from this, yet you didn't pay no attention. I'll give you one more chance, and if you don't do what I say, it's over. Now you walk out your office right now and head through the back alley to the beach until you reach the harbor. In your office, you will leave –"

"Kiss my ass."

"– don't interrupt me again, boy. I've about had it. One more push and you and your family are done for, you hear me? You *will* leave your office and walk without looking back until you reach the harbor. You *will* leave behind your computer, your phone, my flash drive, and all the money. If I suspect anything even remotely out of place, the deal is off, and I'll kill you on the spot."

Matt snorted at this and sat back down on the couch. "First, don't you ever talk about my family. Do you understand? Second, there is no deal, asshole."

"Oh, no, boy, this is the deal. You are lucky to even have options. I spared you once; I won't again –"

"Listen, you want a piece of me, come get me. And this time, try not to blow yourself up, okay?"

"I done told you what has to be done. If you don't do it and somehow happen to live, there won't be a day that goes by where you ain't thinkin' of me."

"And why might that be?"

"I'm sending out some buddies of mine from up near the reservation. And there ain't nothin' about their instructions that's good for you."

"Oh yeah?" Matt said. "And where might I find this posse?" Matt asked, enjoying the rapport. "Outside my door, yet again perhaps?"

Now Murphy was laughing. "Oh no, not in Gulfport."

"Please enlighten me," Matt said. "Where, then?"

"Meridian," Murphy said, and hung up.

45

MATT'S REPLY DIED in his throat.

They *were* going after his family now. He fought back a wave of panic. He had to call Shelley right away. Before he could complete the thought, his phone lit up. When he saw the number on caller ID, he didn't know whether to feel relieved or confused.

"Shelley!" Matt said. "You okay?"

"Oh, Matt, thank God you picked up!"

"What is it?"

Her voice was shaking and Matt could tell she was crying. "Matt, someone's here."

46

MATT WAS TOTALLY confused. "What do you mean, *someone's here*?" Matt sat straight up. He'd *just* got off the phone with Murphy. There was no way – *no way* – anyone could or should be in Meridian looking for Shelley. Didn't Murphy say he *was sending* someone? Not that he *had sent* them already? His hysteria rose with every question. "Who is it? Did they break in? Where are the boys?"

"We're okay," she whispered. "But you told me to call if anything weird happened –"

Matt heard a loud banging in the background over the phone and what sounded like his mother-in-law's voice.

"Shelley, listen to me," Matt said. "I need to know everything that's happening *right now.*"

"Let me go in the kitchen –" A couple of seconds passed. Matt felt his heart thumping and he let a tight breath out when she got back on the line. "Okay, so, a few minutes ago there was a knock – well, more like pounding – on the door. I mean, it's four in the morning, right, so who'd be at the door this early? Anyway, Mom went to the living room window and looked out, and there were two cars parked in the street. She looked through the peephole and saw two men standing there. Wait… Mom's saying something…"

Matt went to his own window and looked out. He half expected to see guns trained on him, but it looked just as quiet up and down his block as it did minutes before.

"Mom says they're policemen."

Matt tried to visualize this, but something didn't add up. "Meridian or Highway Patrol?"

"No, not Meridian police, but they're in uniform." Matt heard his mother-in-law whispering. "One of the cars that pulled up is a cruiser," Shelley continued. "Has a siren on top – wait, who are they, Mom?"

Matt waited for what seemed like forever for Shelley's mom to explain.

"Oh, that's weird. That explains the uniforms. These aren't local cops."

"What do you mean?" Matt asked.

"They're from the Crescent Moon."

47

*O*H SHIT. "THEY'RE from the *Crescent Moon?*"

"The casino, yeah. That's what they told Mom. Casino security,"
Shelley said. "Why on earth would they be here?"

Matt swallowed hard. "Listen, I don't know how they got your
mom's address, but the guy who attacked me in Pontotoc last night
tried again here at the office in Gulfport."

"Oh, God, Matt! When?"

"Hour and a half ago, maybe. Hank had booby-trapped the
stairs with –"

The wrong thing to say, Matt realized too late. Now Shelley was
getting upset.

"– Shelley, calm down and listen to me! The same guy just
called again, Shelley, not two minutes ago. He knows you are in
Meridian. Do you hear me? *He knows you are in Meridian.* You and
the boys must get the hell out of there right now. And I mean *right
now!*"

"But how...?"

"Doesn't matter. Load up and leave. Go straight to Poplarville.
I'll let Mom and Dad know you're on the way."

"I can't just walk out the door, Matt. You just said –"

"Is your Yukon in the garage?"

"Yes."

This might work, Matt thought. Shelley's mother lived in a
garden community where the homes and neighborhood were

designed for curb appeal. To maintain the streetscape, residents entered their homes from alleys running behind the main streets.

"Keep your lights off till you clear the garage and alley," he said. "Once you get on the road, get *moving* – I mean it, Shelley. Haul ass. Stop for no one. And call me when you get to the interstate."

"I'm scared, Matt."

"Me too. Now go. Get the boys up and go. Let me speak to your mom and help her buy a little time. They won't be expecting y'all to leave that way, okay?"

His mother-in-law picked up the phone and seemed like she was listening to him for a change. He told her not to open the front door but to keep talking to the men and do her best to keep them occupied until Shelley had had time to escape.

"Give them my cell number," he said. "Whoever's in charge should call me immediately. Keep them out there another couple of minutes – long as you can – and as soon as you're off the phone you call the Meridian police, okay?"

She said she'd do it and hung up. Matt paced and looked out the window. He glanced at his phone, then at the clock. He imagined Shelley and the boys leaving her mom's neighborhood. Fin and J.W. were young enough to be lifted right out bed, put in their car seats, and stay sound asleep – he hoped. "Get out of there, Shelley," he said to himself as he paced. "*Get out of there.*"

The phone rang five long minutes later. If this was Shelley, she'd sure reached the interstate fast. He didn't recognize the number, but a 662 area code was on the screen, which meant North Mississippi. He dispensed with the niceties.

"Who's this?" he barked into the phone

"Matt? Is that you?" the voice asked. "Where's Shelley? Where is she?"

Matt wasn't about to respond. "Who is this?"

"Settle down, Matt. Settle down. It's Ron."

48

MATT WAS FURIOUS. "Settle down? Where is Shelley? Where am I? Why, I'm in Gulfport, Ron, like I was hours ago. Where the hell are *you*? A hit has been put out on Chief Osceola, remember?"

"I'm in Meridian. I – "

"Meridian?" Matt yelled.

"– I called as soon as I got your number from this lady, who I understand is Shelley's mother –"

"You already *had* my number," Matt said through clenched teeth, "and you didn't need to get it from my mother-in-law. You've got about one second to explain what the hell you're doing there, or I swear I'll –"

"Whoa, Matt. Why are you so upset? I'm trying to help."

"Why am I upset? Why am I *upset*? I'll tell you why I'm upset. I just got my ass nearly shot off; it's the middle of the damn night; I've been trying to reach you, and by all appearances, you're traipsing all over the state stalking my wife for reasons which are still not entirely clear. That's why I'm upset. Do you even have a clue where Kotori is right now?" Matt asked.

"Don't know. That's one reason why we're here. Have you spoken to Shelley? Is she okay?"

"She's down here on the Coast." It was the first thing Matt could think of to provide a cover, and he wondered if it was the best option. If Ron had been conning him all along, this could put a wrinkle in Ron's plans if he believed Shelley was in Gulfport.

"Thank goodness," Ron said. "It appears Kotori thought she was in Meridian, which is why I got here as soon as I could. I was worried about her." Ron explained that after he verified the chief was okay, he tried to run Kotori down and began by searching his office. He had obviously left in a hurry, Ron noted, because Kotori left without shutting down his computer.

"Okay, but why would he think Shelley's in Meridian, let alone even know who she is?" Matt asked, his pulse finally lowering.

Ron explained that when he got to Kotori's office, he noticed Kotori had accessed the Crescent Moon's internal program used to track its Players' Club participants. This in and of itself was not so unusual. It was the account he had pulled up that got Ron's attention. When Ron saw Shelley's patron page on the screen, he immediately ran a query on Kotori's history, and it revealed that Kotori had accessed Shelley's Crescent Moon player's account.

"That doesn't make sense, Ron. How did he even know who Shelley was? And which account to access?"

"That's where it gets interesting. The first thing he did was Google your name and 'Gulfport" and both your and Shelley's name came up with your address."

"Okay."

"Then he cross-referenced your name in our system."

"*My name?* I don't have a player's account with you. Never will. Not as long as I represent The Majestic."

"You're absolutely right. You don't. Wouldn't expect you to. But your wife does."

"So?"

"So, when she signed up, she had to provide an alternate contact number –"

"Me. Dammit."

"Yep."

"Okay. But Meridian?"

"Meridian took a little bit more thinking. I actually had to lay out the pieces myself before I figured out how he did it. Do you recall meeting Kotori and the chief the other day?"

"How could I forget."

"During the conversation, the chief asked how your family was doing. Do you remember what you said?"

Matt thought about it for a second. "Told him they were okay."

"What you actually said, as I recall, is that they were in Meridian with your wife's mother."

"Shit," Matt said, "I guess I did. Murphy alluded earlier that he thought Shelley was in Meridian –"

"Murphy? You spoke with Murphy?" Ron asked.

"Yes. I'll fill you in on the details later. So the big Indian must have told him. Still no way he could get her mother's address, though."

"'Big Indian'?" Ron asked.

"Kotori. Wolf. Whatever. Who the hell else could I be talking about?" Matt asked. "Plus, I thought you said this guy wasn't too bright. How the hell'd he figure out this by himself?"

"My guess is someone else is involved – nothing would surprise me at this point. But you're right, Kotori had to be the one to tell Murphy."

"No doubt about it. They're together. I saw them in the wee hours this morning. I'll tell you about it in a minute, but first let me know how he got her address."

"This morning? What the hell are you talking about?" Ron asked. "Where?"

"Here in Gulfport. Now go on."

"You know how the casino incentive programs work," Ron said. "Set up primarily to get bodies in the door. And the best way, as you know, is word of mouth. Referrals, I'm talking about, like The Majestic. You refer us to new potential players who also sign up for the Players Club, you get a free hotel or slot credit or whatever."

"Right, right. Get 'em in the door."

"So who do you think Shelley listed as a potential prospect?"

"No clue. Get to the point, Ron."

"Her mother."

Matt sighed. "Her mother. And her address?"

"Standard operating procedure. Right on the form. I printed a copy of what Kotori looked at and have it in front of me."

Matt thought of Shelley again and prayed she and the boys were leaving Meridian safely. If she'd gotten out as planned, he would hear from her soon. "I get all that, Ron, but why are you just telling me now? Shouldn't you have called me earlier?"

"My first responsibility is to Chief Osceola," he said without hesitation. "After we talked and you said he might be in danger, I checked with him to make sure he was okay. Then, when I realized Kotori had potentially tracked down your wife, I radioed the chief again and explained everything and asked how he wanted it handled. He said to drop everything and get to Meridian immediately. When the chief says move, you don't wait around. So I went straight to dispatch and commandeered a cruiser and two deputies. Once I was on the road and had things settled I reached for my phone to call you – and realized I didn't have it."

Matt still didn't totally buy it. "And no one else had a phone...?"

"They all did, but I don't have your number memorized. I tried Shelley's mother several times en route – at the number from the printout – but the calls wouldn't go through."

"What's the number?" Matt asked and Ron read it to him.

"Land line," Matt said. "She hasn't had that number for a few years now."

"Then that's why I didn't get her. I'm on one of the deputies' phones now. And look, man, I'm sorry about scaring y'all," Ron said. "But tell me this: you said Kotori and Murphy are together... and on the Coast? You're sure of that?"

Matt explained that Murphy made another grab at the flash drive, and this time, shots were fired from both sides, although no one got hurt. He told Ron Kotori was one of the trigger men.

"He took a shot at me, and I looked straight at him before they pulled off. It's hard to mistake that dude for someone else."

"Well, if Shelley's safe and Kotori's down there, I'm going to send everyone back home. Unless you'd prefer we do something else."

"You may want to hang around." Matt told Ron about Murphy's ultimatum and his threat to come after Shelley in Meridian if Matt didn't cooperate.

"I'll stay as long as I need to if it will help me round up all of these traitorous bastards," Ron said. "We're going to lay low here until you tell me otherwise. I'll keep this phone. Call me if you need anything or if anything transpires."

"Will do."

"You sure you're okay down there?"

"They can't touch me here. Secure, armed and ready."

"What are you going to do?"

"I have a plan in mind," Matt said. "It's time to end this once and for all."

49

SHELLEY CALLED SECONDS after Matt hung up with Ron. She was now on the road and headed toward Poplarville, the boys fast asleep. She wasn't being followed as best she could tell. Matt said he'd check on her soon and called his parents next, waking his mother. He explained that although this was no life-or-death emergency, Shelley and the grandkids were on their way. His mother was glad to hear that, and although she and Matt's dad would have a slew of questions when everyone arrived in pajamas and without suitcases. He'd worry about that later.

He still didn't know if he could trust Ron, but there was little he could do about it at this point. Matt had accomplished his immediate goal, and Shelley was out of harm's way. If Ron had bad intentions, at least he couldn't carry them out against Matt's family. Ron believed Shelley was on the Coast, and Matt didn't intend to tell him otherwise. He planned to ask Lance to send some of Mississippi's finest to Meridian, Gulfport, and Poplarville to cover the bases. If Ron was clean, great. If not, knowing Lance, there would be hell to pay.

Speaking of which, Matt needed to go ahead and give Lance and Delia a call. According to his phone, it was getting close to 5:00, and Matt sat down at his desk so he could spread out his notes. He'd identified a vast and complicated conspiracy to commit murder – there were definite plans to eliminate Wapegan Chief Warren Osceola – and Matt figured it wouldn't hurt to refresh his memory on all the players and their roles. Once he had all the facts understood and covered, he'd call Delia and Lance, then let Hank know about the evening's encounter with Griff Murphy. Hank would likely try to mobilize for an all-out assault next, while relishing the fact that his trip wire and flash-bang grenade worked to perfection. Matt would link Lance up with Hank to keep Hank out of trouble. Between the two of them, justice would be served.

Or so Matt hoped.

Matt reread everything and was again amazed at both the sheer number and the stature of those involved. Some bright people had worked long and hard on this, and while Jeff's fingerprints seemed to be all over it, Matt just couldn't fathom his being the *architect*. Whether Jeff planned it or not, Matt couldn't say; regardless, Jeff definitely appeared to be one of the principals, and with that in mind, Matt turned to the Bing.

For starters, someone had drafted the new Indian Regulatory Reform Act legislation. And based upon the citations, language used, and complexity of the proposed bill, it was written by a lawyer with some experience in gaming and governmental affairs. Matt couldn't find anything tying the draft legislation to anyone specific at the Bing, but he wondered if anybody at the firm played a role in writing the original law several decades before, and if so, if he could link it, somehow, to this draft. Jeff was the only Bing lawyer Matt could connect by name, and that breakthrough wouldn't have been possible without the flash drive. Yet the documents in Jeff's personal account were deleted after his death, so someone on the inside *had* to know about them.

Matt yawned, then sat completely still when a car went past. Every single sound had him on edge now. He peered back at the computer and stared at the figures in front of him. *If not Jeff,* he almost said aloud, *then who?* He tried to think things through one final time, but when he found himself reading the same lines of text again and again he started saving and closing the windows layered on his screen. One by one he clicked them until the *RedMoonInstr.docx* was the sole remaining open document. Matt was about to close it, too, when something caught his eye. He cracked his back, sat up straight, and reread instructions four and five:

4) *E-mail SM confirming delivery of packages. No telephone contact whatsoever.*

5) *If you get any pushback, do not under any circumstances try and contact me. Remind recipients this is a mere down payment. Will disburse the remainder upon completion of deal. If you must follow up, route through SM via e-mail.*

"How could I forget? *SM.* Who is SM?" Matt reopened and searched the flash drive. He read it aloud.

"*E-mail SM confirming delivery of packages . . . route through SM via e-mail.*"

"Here we go again," Matt said as he searched the Bing's database for "SM," initially throwing a wide net and then winnowing it down to Jeff's personal folders. Again, for what seemed like the hundredth time, Matt hit a dead end.

"Dammit!" He looked at the instructions one more time.
E-mail SM confirming delivery of packages.
Route through SM via e-mail.

"E-mail," Matt said, leaning back into the headrest. "*E-mail.*"

He clicked over to Jeff's inbox and scanned the messages again. Everything looked normal. Matt went back over the e-mails Jeff had sent – nothing stood out there, either. He pushed his chair up on its back legs and stared at the screen as his frustration mounted. He eased the chair back down, and clicked back to his own inbox out of habit, hoping he'd find something of value. He breezed through them quickly, as most dealt, as they had before, with the status of the firm post-hurricane. There were several well-wishers and many typical firm update-type e-mails from Tripp Massey, who couldn't remind everyone often enough he was the new firm chair.

And there was that stupid e-mail that read *Future of Coast Office – Follow-Up* in the subject line. Matt clicked it open and got pissed off all over again at the fancy signature. But this time something grabbed his attention:

Stephen Andrew Massey III
FIRM CHAIRMAN
Bingham, Samson & Toflin

Matt frowned and looked at it again, focusing on the first line.

Stephen Andrew Massey III

Matt let a weary exhale escape and rubbed his eyes in disbelief. "I should have caught this by now," he grunted, rubbing his eyes. "Unbelievable."

50

STEPHEN MASSEY. SM.

That bastard.

Makes sense, though. After all, he would love to see Delia fall, and he would move mountains if he thought it would give him a leg up on one of her most lucrative clients. He had tried to hamstring her in the past, and he *was* a son of a bitch. Even so, this was a bit much. Did he concoct this elaborate scheme to keep the Wapegan out of Gulfport by cutting a deal with the Majestic decision-makers in exchange for shutting Delia out? Even if he was out to get her, he had his own clients – lots of them. Why would he risk everything – *everything* – just to one-up Delia?

And why this? Why now? Matt reread the documents containing the instructions and wrote down the players on his pad, beginning with Governor Hood at the top and going down from there. What tied them together? Hate for the Wapegan? No, prejudice didn't seem to be driving this. The money? It helped, although it was not likely the primary catalyst, even though the cash in the bag appeared to be seed money with the promise of larger payments later. Every one of the individuals mentioned in the file was the biggest fish in their respective ponds, and all wielded, proportionately, significant power in their jobs.

Matt started drawing arrows and making scribbles, trying to identify any links, no matter how remote. Some had mutual friends; some had worked together in the past; many had gone to the same college. After a few minutes, Matt set the pad down and looked at his work. Suddenly, it became clear. Nearly all of the arrows eventually pointed up. From Hood on down, everyone appeared to have higher aspirations in mind. Hood wanted to go to Washington; Reed would follow him. Matt knew the Gulfport mayor wanted to run for secretary of state, and the list went on and on. Matt realized the contents of the flash drive told only half the story. For those in this chain, success meant promotion.

A bigger pond.

All of them except Tripp Massey. After all, he had just been elected the Bing chairman and seemed to be settling in and making it his own. What could he possibly want with this? The only possible explanation is that someone hung a carrot out there that he couldn't resist. Matt wrote Tripp Massey's name at the bottom and drew a long arrow connecting him back to the governor. Next to it he wrote "political?" and chewed on the tip of his pen. It was feasible, Matt thought. Tripp and his wife, Jeannie, had hosted a huge fundraiser for Governor Hood at their house in Eastover during the last election cycle. Matt remembered it because those in the firm who opposed Hood were not comfortable having the Bing's name linked to such an event, but Massey, as usual, went ahead and did what he wanted. Matt wrote Tripp's name at the top of the page and circled it and then drew a line from it to the other name at the top of the page.

"Ahhh," Matt said, looking back and forth at the two names, then circling the other name so it overlapped with Tripp's in a Venn diagram. "*Governor*," Matt said. "You sneaky son of a bitch." Matt chewed on the pen some more and then drew a "VP" through Hood, leaving Tripp's name the only one at the top.

This was certainly going to be an eye-opener for Delia and the rest of the Bing. He drummed his fingers on the table and rested his chin in his hand. He stared at the e-mail again and looked over at the menu to the left. "I wonder…" he whispered as he clicked back to Jeff's *Sent Items* folder. He wanted to see if there were any recent e-mails to Tripp Massey.

There weren't any, so Matt clicked on Jeff's contact list and scrolled down, not expecting to find anything important, and stopped when he reached T. He didn't see Tripp's name there either, so he backed up to S.

And there was SM.

Whoa.

He clicked on *Properties.* It, too, was blank, with no identifying information, not even an e-mail address. So this was how they kept everything under the radar... or was it?

Well, well, Matt thought. Now, what to do? Is this the infamous 'SM'? He leaned back and chewed some more on his pen, feeling giddy that he might have found the final piece of the puzzle. "Only one way to find out," he said, exhaling. Matt returned to Jeff's inbox, clicked *New* and when the *To* box came up, Matt clicked on Jeff's address book, scrolled down to *SM*, and clicked it.

Matt's head spun and he ran his hands through his hair, stopping to finger the stitches on his head, which had begun to itch. He could not tell if it was fatigue or nerves – or both, but he could not think straight. "Okay, Matt," he said to himself, "if this is the 'SM' you think it is, and you were Murphy, what would the e-mail say?"

Matt waited several minutes before typing a message with shaky hands, then deleted it and typed it again. He got up, walked around his office to clear his mind, sat back down, re-edited the text, shook his head to clear out the cobwebs and read his message one more time.

Had trouble but returned to Gulfport office. Logged onto JM's computer and the subject files have been erased as planned. Now have money, envelope, flash drive; able to get duffel without contact with Matt before he got back. Awaiting further instructions.

Matt read it, puffed out his cheeks, and clicked *Send.*

He fell back into his chair and rubbed his face with his hands, being careful not to put too much pressure on his eye. He didn't expect to get a response, but toggled the volume up just in case. He stood up, stretched, and walked stiff-legged over to the food box on top of his refrigerator to grab a Pop-Tart.

Before he could get halfway across the room, the computer pinged.

Matt wheeled around. An e-mail had arrived.

"Aha," Matt said. "The little bastard must be getting antsy."

Matt hurried back, clicked open the response, and hunched down over the console to read it.

On my way. Take Matt Frazier out.

Matt swallowed hard, and his throat felt terribly dry all of a sudden. He looked up at the screen and physically felt his heart skip a hard beat. His hands started shaking even worse now, but not because of what the message said. He was now staring at the e-mail address of the person who sent the message, and he mouthed the words silently as he read it again.

steelmagnolia@msnetwork.com

51

STEEL MAGNOLIA? "No, Delia," Matt whispered. "Not you. Please, not you."

Matt felt like his knees would buckle, and he slunk down in his chair. He grabbed his phone and started to call Delia but thought better of it. He set the phone down, walked to his window, and stared out. The sun was just beginning to rise on what would have been a very nice day.

"Think," he said to the room. "Think, Matt."

There was no way Delia could be behind this. Delia, the bastion of integrity, Delia the true figurehead of the firm, Delia the friend. She would be horrified if she thought Matt even considered her as a possibility. He ran through all of the circumstances in his head – just like he had done when he initially began to suspect Jeff – and like Jeff, none implicated Delia in this scheme. Yet Jeff clearly played some role in this. How deep Matt did not yet know. Why not Delia, too?

"Please be wrong, please be wrong," Matt said to himself. He returned to the e-mail again, trying to separate Delia from Jeff, but he couldn't.

Who else could this be? He got back on the system and ran another search of FileManage, this time hunting for documents she authored. The massive number of hits made it impossible to delve into them in any sort of detail, and the more he thought about Delia being mixed up in this, the sicker he became. He felt his mind spin out of control and now wondered if he truly was, in fact, a conspiracy theorist – as Hop had alluded to in Pontotoc (which suddenly seemed like weeks ago). After all, he'd convinced himself Tripp Massey was the maestro not two minutes prior and had Tripp gunning for governor, for Pete's sake.

Matt leaned back and took a deep breath. He closed his eyes and continued running the scenarios. When he looked back at the screen, he concluded that Delia was not – *could not* be – involved. In fact, he would call her and tell her what he knew – leaving out the Steel Magnolia part – and see how she reacted. If he even remotely got a weird vibe, he would just hang up and go to Hank's until he could get in touch with Lance.

He second-guessed himself and dialed Hop first. Matt knew it was early, but the sun had been rising for half an hour now, so he thought he had a decent chance of Hop picking up. Despite Hop's prior criticisms of Matt's state of mind, Matt really wanted to bounce his thoughts about Delia off him to see what he had to say, and braced himself for another speech.

The call went to voice mail. Matt hung up and dialed him again.

"C'mon, you lazy bastard," Matt whispered, walking back to his couch. Hop didn't answer the second time, either. "Hop, wake up," Matt said to Hop's voice mail. "Call me ASAP. I want to run something by you." Matt hung up and went back to his computer. Calling Hop reminded Matt he also needed to backup his files.

He logged out as Jeff, logged back in as himself, and drafted an e-mail. He did indeed have a plan, and this e-mail was central to its success. When he was finished he attached copies of all the flash drive documents – everything he'd eyeballed in recent days was included. He typed *Backup Documents* in the subject line and explained them in the body of the e-mail. He also included a set of time-sensitive instructions, and he even sent the e-mail through his Gmail account instead of the Bing network in case someone was tracking him. Finally, he confirmed its delivery to the intended recipient. "Covering my ass," he said before shutting his computer down.

Then he flipped to a new page on the legal pad and jotted down a brief timeline of the events because he knew Delia would want to know everything. He even grabbed the box of documents from the ottoman and arranged them by document number across his desk so he could get his hands on them right away if necessary. Matt then picked up his phone, lifted a brief prayer to the ceiling, and pushed Delia's contact number. He could hear himself exhaling into the receiver as the phone rang.

"Hello," Delia said on the other end. *Breathe*, he told himself. *Try not to sound too alarmed.*

"Morning, Delia," Matt said. "Sorry to be calling before working hours." His hands were sweating again.

"No problem, darling. Actually on my way in. Got an early start and am walking out of the parking garage to the office right now."

Thank goodness.

"Where are you?" Delia asked.

"Still down here in Gulfport," Matt said.

"Everything okay? You sound a little… edgy."

Dammit. "Yes – well, actually, no, Delia – everything isn't all right."

"What do you mean? Talk to me, Matt."

Here we go. He looked at the outline on his desk. "It's about Jeff. And the Bing," he said. "And The Majestic…"

"Slow down, Matt," Delia said calmly. "Settle down and tell me wha-"

The resounding drone of a train horn blared, interrupting Delia mid-sentence. Instinctively, Matt looked at his watch.

It was 7:00.

When the train quit blowing, Matt pulled the phone back and looked at the screen, confirming Delia was still on the line, although she had quit talking. Matt cocked his head and frowned. He walked to his window and pulled the string to adjust the shades. The train sounded again.

And this time Matt heard it through *her* phone.

Then Delia hung up.

Matt looked out the window and, sure enough, the train was flying down the tracks right on time. Matt didn't pay it much attention, however. Standing right there on the sidewalk, just two blocks down and in front of Triplett-Day, was Delia. Chief Halliday stood next to her, and Matt could tell by the way Delia was pacing she was upset.

A black Suburban zoomed up to the curb right then, and he watched as Delia hurried over to it and – after pointing to her watch – reached in and throttled the passenger. She was yelling so loud that people on the sidewalk had stopped and were now staring at her. Someone in the SUV must have said something, because Delia seemed to freeze. Then, slowly, she turned, adjusted her blouse, and looked up and over her shoulder at Matt's office window.

Matt jumped and pressed his back flat against the wall. He didn't think she saw him, but he wasn't sure. He was breathing fast now and inventoried in his mind what he would need to grab in the event of a hasty retreat. He needed to check one more time to see where they were. He waited a few seconds and then carefully peeked around the corner.

Delia and Chief Halliday were now walking down the sidewalk with some new additions. Kotori flanked Halliday's right side. Taking up the rear, with a noticeable limp and a bandage on his left ear, was a tall, red-headed fellow.

They were all heading Matt's way.

52

MATT JERKED BACK from the window again, then peeked through one more time to confirm what he had seen. Sure enough, all four of them were a few blocks down, and they appeared to be walking faster with every step, although Murphy impeded their pace. Waves of panic coursed through his body, and for a split second, he felt he would throw up. He turned, surveyed his office, told himself to calm down, and took action.

Matt ran to his computer and held the power button until it shut down. With his free hand, he pulled out the flash drive and shoved it and his truck keys into his pocket. He took all of the copies of the documents stacked on his desk and hid them in the ottoman. He decided the Glock and his legal pad should join them, and he dropped them in before closing the cover and shoving the ottoman out of the middle of the room. He grabbed his phone and headed for the door. Before he got there, he spun back around to his computer and picked up his gun.

He cursed as he flew down the stairs and saw the furniture he had stacked up in front of the door. He did his best to yank it all aside, and when he had cleared enough to squeeze through, he cracked the front door and looked outside, praying they weren't already upon him.

At first he didn't see anyone, and he thought they were waiting on him just around the corner out of his line of sight. He looked farther down and saw them a block away, just about to cross over to his side of the street. His truck chirped when he hit the keyless entry remote one time too many, and when he heard it, Matt burst out onto the sidewalk in an all-out, full run.

If the truck beeping didn't grab their attention, his sudden appearance sure did. Matt saw Delia look up first and point as Chief Halliday broke into a sprint. Murphy reached for his pocket, but Halliday yelled something over his shoulder, and Murphy released his grip. Matt realized then they would not shoot. At least not there, not in broad daylight.

As Matt turned in front of his hood toward the driver door, he saw Halliday and Kotori gaining, but Delia and Murphy had turned and were now running – and hobbling – the other way. Kotori stopped as well, and he looked confused, as if he didn't know where to go. In as fluid a movement Matt could hope for, he slid into his seat, cranked the truck, and closed the door all in less than two seconds. Chief Halliday was about ten paces away when Matt jerked the big Ford in reverse and backed out. Halliday got close enough to bang once on the tailgate before Matt pulled away. He checked his rear view to see if Halliday had drawn his gun. He had not, but Matt saw him pull out his radio as he, too, turned to follow Delia and the others.

Matt clicked on his hazards and fled, all of a sudden realizing he didn't know where to go. A hasty retreat was *not* part of the plan. The only thing he could come up with was to get out of town as fast as his wheels could take him. If he could cover the few miles to I-10 he could haul ass towards Alabama.

He made it to Cowan Road and turned north without incident. He kept the pedal down and thought he was in the clear, but he soon saw blue lights in his rearview mirror. By the looks of it, Matt counted three Crown Vics heading his way, and although they still had a lot of ground to cover, they were gaining.

Matt kept driving, trying to keep his thoughts ahead of his truck. He realized after a few minutes there was no way he would make it to the cloverleaf before they caught up to him. Besides, even if Matt pulled off a miracle and reached the exit, Halliday would be radioing ahead to have law enforcement all up and down I-10 waiting on him. Matt had blundered into a murder plot and corruption scandal that reached all the way to the governor and perhaps far beyond; Halliday would do whatever he needed to keep Matt buttoned-up.

Matt was about to give in to sheer panic as he reached the light at Seaway Road when something dawned on him. He swerved to his left at the last second and started down the straightaway as fast as the truck would go.

He was less than a mile from American Marine.

53

H E REACHED DOWN below his seat to grab the radio to give Hank a quick heads up. Matt felt along the floorboard and when he couldn't find it he realized in his haste to flee, he left it at the office. "Dammit!" Matt said, banging the steering wheel. He picked up his .38 off the seat and flung the chamber open. He had not reloaded after he fired at Murphy in the stairwell. He had no rounds left, and Hank's box of ammunition was still sitting next to his computer. He set the gun down, trying to remain calm and wondered what else he had neglected to consider.

He picked up his phone and tried to call Hop but got his voicemail again. "Shit!" Matt said, and decided a message was better than nothing at all. Hop had to get up soon. "Hurry up, dammit," he said as Hop's recorded greeting droned on.

"Hop, it's Matt!" he yelled, once he heard the beep. "Listen, they're after me. Murphy, my boss, Chief Halliday, Philip Kotori – are all of 'em are in on it, and all of 'em have guns. No shit. I'm in my truck driving down Seaway toward American Marine. If I can make it, I intend to grab a boat and hide out at Smugglers until I figure this out. Call Lance and let him know what's going on. Do not, *I repeat*, do not call Gulfport P.D."

Matt fishtailed through the gravel parking lot to the door and slammed the truck to a stop. The sirens sounded twice as loud when he climbed out, and he looked back only to find the cops had already crested the hill. He dashed to the keypad and put his hands to his head. "What's your number, Hank?" he said under his breath. "Come on, Matt. Think!"

The blaring interrupted his concentration. Matt glanced over his shoulder and saw the blue and whites making the turn off the asphalt. He had only a few seconds. He punched in HM and knew this was correct – Hank used his initials – but what was the number code? Matt could feel the hair stand up on his neck as he stared at the numbers.

"Think, boy. Come on, come on." Matt replayed his conversations with Hank and thought about all Hank had told him. Then he remembered. The advent of the Navy SEALs. Hank drilled that date into him on more occasions than he could count and often cited it as a precursor to his military tales. Matt punched in 1961 as the rocks and oyster shells twisted and crunched under the weight of the sedans.

"I sure hope y'all cut the power back on," Matt said, hitting the last number and grabbing the handle.

The door buzzed just as the cops poured out of their cars, guns drawn, and started his way. Matt slid in and slammed the door, and within seconds he heard them banging on the exterior, telling Matt he was under arrest for murder – murder! – and demanding he come out or they would shoot. To Matt's relief, *Big D* remained moored where he and Hank had left it after their excursion the week before. He heard more cars pulling in as he sprinted up the stairs towards Wild Bill's office to get the key. Matt immediately recognized the big orange fob with the SEAL Trident emblazoned on the side, grabbed it, ran back down the stairs and started throwing the lines off the pier to free up the boat.

Matt hopped in and cranked the big diesel engine, and it fired up on the first try. "Thank you, thank you, thank you," he said as the boat roared to life. The *D* had just over half a tank of fuel left – plenty for the mission. Matt jumped back out and hit the button to roll up the marina door. It paused a second and then squealed as the cog engaged the metal wheels, which began pulling the aluminum panels up the track.

Matt unwound the last rope from the cleat and pushed off, positioning the boat so he could get out. The door creaked up a few inches at a time, and Matt wondered if the police would use this lull to try to block his only remaining avenue of escape. He could no longer hear anything over the metal screeching, and as the exit gap grew wider and the bay came into view, he saw shadows dancing across the reeds on the opposite bank, indicating the cops were taking up positions toward the back of the building by the dock.

Matt could no longer stand the door's dawdling progress, so he slightly elevated the throttle, trolling the boat toward the exit. Once he thought he could make it, he braced himself, squatted low in the seat and pushed forward. A swirl of water splashed and bubbled up behind him as the prop engaged and a large cloud of blue smoke enveloped him, causing his eyes to burn. As the boat left the building, Matt jumped as a series of unfamiliar sounds peppered his ears, and he ducked down even lower than he had earlier when he stooped to clear the overhead door.

Loud pings – some throwing sparks – echoed off the hull and windshield, and for the second time in the same day, Matt was under fire.

54

MATT THANKED HANK Mallette, the United States Navy, and American Marine for the engineering that went into the *Big D*. Whatever top secret, clandestine, and classified materials they used to coat and reinforce the hull provided enough protection to keep the bullets from penetrating, and the windshield likewise deflected the incoming shots. Matt raised his head just enough to see when he needed to turn, and when *Big D* straightened out in the channel, he pushed the throttle higher, and soon the building disappeared behind him.

Matt leaned back a bit, but wouldn't allow himself to sit all the way up. He was still shaken from the surprise at the dock and did not want to be exposed in case of an ambush. He clicked the radio on to see if he could pick up any chatter from the Coast Guard or anyone else that might relate to his exodus, but found nothing.

He remembered the debris he and Hank encountered on their last outing and tried to stay in the middle of the strait as much as possible. From the looks of it, much had been cleared out, but odd, misplaced things still jutted above the waterline, especially around bends and in shallow areas. Matt throttled down. Better to be safe than sorry; if he got hung up, he'd never get through. Even so, he needed to put as much space between him and anyone inclined to give chase, so he tried to make up some time whenever he came across patches of open water, but it still felt painfully slow.

Matt crossed under the Cowan Road bridge and turned south. Within minutes he arrived at the mouth of the Gulf and bore west toward the ship channel, riding parallel to the beach. Now in the ocean, he accelerated, although the swells hampered his efforts. It had taken him about a half hour to finally get in open water, and he felt the need to speed up. Ahead, he could see the Gulfport small craft harbor and the outline of The Majestic Hotel. He scanned the skies for a police helicopter and relaxed when he spotted a lone Blackhawk flying its daily route.

Matt turned on the GPS to enter his destination, but it was already pulled up from the last excursion. Matt pushed "Enter" to confirm.

The new plan of action was taking shape. According to the monitor, Matt would reach Cat Island in less than one hour.

55

A S HE NEARED the deep waters of the ship channel, Matt looked around again. As far as he could tell, he hadn't been followed. He noticed one boat up ahead near the harbor, but since it wasn't moving, Matt didn't pay it much attention. The chop made driving the boat difficult, so Matt shifted more of his weight to the chair to gain some leverage. He adjusted his speed again, and when he glanced up, he saw that the boat in front of him was now turning in his direction. Matt shaded his eyes with his phone and squinted to see if he recognized it. A peculiar feeling twisted his stomach. He stood up and leaned over the windshield to get a better look and to place its silhouette.

The *Queen* was coming about in front of him, and when Matt saw who was in the crow's nest, his gut clenched up again. Chief Halliday had the wheel.

Matt straightened in his seat as the *Queen* revved and started closing. As it neared, Matt turned and bore due south. Halliday copied him. By Matt's estimate, if he kept the same course at the same speed, the two boats would run right into each other. Veering to starboard was not an option because if Halliday cut the *Queen* that way, it would close Matt off, and he would soon run out of water. If, on the other hand, Matt cut any harder to the port side, he could tail out, slow down, or take too long to make the arc. He hadn't logged enough time driving the *D* to know how it would react.

He decided he would give it everything it had and go full throttle straight ahead. "C'mon baby," Matt said and pushed the knob as hard as he could all the way up. He leaned over the console and gripped tight to the steering wheel.

The engine screamed, and the boat planed out of the water. As the *Big D* took off, Matt saw Halliday yell something down below, and within seconds, Kotori lumbered out of the cabin with a rifle in hand. He tried to steady himself and take aim, but the rising and falling of the swells kept him from drawing an accurate bead. Matt cursed and ducked down below the top of the glass. Although he saw muzzle flashes, Matt did not hear the report of the rifle over the revving motor, nor did he note any pings ricocheting off the boat like he did when he left American Marine.

Matt passed in front of the *Queen* with plenty of time to spare and then angled harder out into the Gulf. The *Queen* had to maneuver to come back behind the *Big D*, and by the time it came around, barely a wake trail remained for it to follow. Matt kept going full bore, but instead of heading toward Cat Island, while still in Halliday's line of sight, he veered back southeast toward Ship Island. Halliday took the bait and followed. Matt let off just enough to make him think he was on the trail and crisscrossed then sped up again out of sight of the *Queen*. Once he got far enough ahead, Matt turned back west, and resumed his trek to Cat Island.

He picked up his phone in the hope he still had reception, but by now he was too far out. He turned the radio back up to see if there was any additional chatter. It, too, was quiet, and Matt sped on for another half hour, to further throw Halliday off course in the event he was somehow tracking him. After seeing no one anywhere around him after several more miles of running, Matt turned toward his destination. When Cat Island's familiar landscape came into view, Matt steered *Big D* around the natural quay into the sheltered water nearest to him. Matt finally felt his muscles relax once he turned into the light waters leading up to the entrance to Smuggler's Cove.

He throttled down to a drift and, for the first time that day, breathed a little easier. With the pressure of the chase off, he went over everything that had happened since midnight and shuddered at how close he had come to being caught or shot. He checked his watch, reached down below the seat into a cooler, and grabbed a bottled water. It wasn't cold, but Matt didn't care. He drank some of it anyway. He suddenly felt famished and rummaged around in some of the storage compartments, trying to remember where Hank kept his MREs. He started to pour the remaining water from the bottle on his face to wash off the salt, but a sudden noise caused him to stop and stand straight up.

Matt killed the engine and shut off the radio, then blinked the water out of his eyes and tilted his head to the side, one hand still grasping the wheel. He scanned the shore and tried to look through the trees.

He heard the wheezy cough of an outboard engine cranking up.

It came from Smuggler's.

56

MATT STARED STRAIGHT ahead, his body frozen but for his chest rising and falling. He hoped he was wrong, but when the second motor cranked, he saw the long, slender bow of a fishing boat creep out near the entrance. The forward movement of the boat revealed the word *King* on its side, followed by a purple, gold, and green crown in the center of a poker chip over The Majestic logo. The rumble of the twins revved higher as they pushed the craft around the corner.

Matt recognized the driver – despite the fact that he wore a baseball cap pulled down low, covering his hair. The look on his face was one that Matt knew too well. Full of hate, rage, and tinged with a bit of fear, Griff Murphy reminded Matt of some of the criminal defendants he'd seen in court – angry and defiant, yet wide-eyed with uneasy anticipation about what the future held for them. Murphy's female passenger exhibited a similar countenance. *Shit.* He should never have taken Delia to Smuggler's in the first place. She turned to him and pointed.

Matt had little time to react. He revved the Big D back up, dropping the throttle down hard in reverse. The engine gurgled and spat as the prop sped up, and Matt backed and turned as fast as he could.

Murphy had no intention of stopping or slowing, and Matt thought for sure he wouldn't have time to get out of the way. The *Big D* jerked low in the water when Matt rammed the gear back up. It took a few seconds for the boat to regain forward momentum, but the *Big D* kicked in just fast enough to keep from being hit.

By the time Matt made his way back out of the inlet, he was up to about half speed. Murphy and Delia were closing, but Matt kept his distance and thought he could widen the gap once he got back into open water and maxed out. He knew he didn't have enough fuel for a chase any farther south through the Gulf of Mexico out towards Chandeleur, so Matt decided to go the long way around Cat and head north back towards Gulfport. If he could indeed keep some space between *Big D* and the *King*, he would have time to call for some help on the radio.

A slight tide stirred the surf, but Matt barely noticed. He didn't have a rearview mirror, so he had to alternate between looking ahead to drive and checking behind him to see what Murphy and Delia were doing. The pine trees to Matt's right flew by as he circled the island. He kept the depth finder on so he wouldn't bottom out and tried his best to follow it. He had been a guest on the *King* once before on one of The Majestic's boondoggle weekends, and, although it was fast, it drew more water than the *Big D*, which allowed Matt a little more flexibility in choosing his route.

Matt rounded the western bend and started his turn back north when he came across a small finger of land jutting out several hundred yards near the birdcage, an old iron structure that used to serve as a foundation for a lighthouse. Along the isthmus, the scrub dropped off into water, creating what appeared to be passable gaps. Matt picked an opening too small for the *King* but wide enough for the *Big D* and headed in that direction. No matter how bad he wanted to get him, Matt could not see Murphy risk losing the chase and possibly bottoming out or wrecking the *King* in the process.

Once he made up his mind to go through the pass, Matt checked behind him again to see if Murphy would follow. As he suspected, Murphy and Delia, who was hanging onto the struts, had already pulled back and had begun taking the longer trek around the cape. Matt saw Murphy speaking into the marine receiver and wondered if Halliday was on the other end.

This reminded Matt to turn the *D's* radio back on. He reached up to turn the knob, but his hand never made it past the steering console.

The boat shuddered and groaned for a millisecond as the impact from the wreck slammed Matt into the windshield, catching his ribs and causing him to heave a loud grunt as the wind left him.

The stern ripping in two was the last thing Matt saw before he went airborne.

———

The *Lady Kathryn* was a medium-sized shrimp boat owned by a second-generation family of fishermen from Gulfport. Named after their mother, the three brothers renovated the boat after their dad passed away, and it became the flagship of the family business. Before the storm, they kept her moored near the old piers behind The Majestic, where most of the Gulfport shrimp boats docked. While several of their colleagues moved their boats to the Back Bay for shelter after the hurricane warning, the brothers felt the *Lady Kathryn* would be fine in her slip, so long as they set the spring lines properly. So that's where they left her, along with a dozen or so other shrimp boats whose owners followed suit.

Keeping the boat moored at the dock turned out to be a bad decision. The only parts of the dock that remained after the storm were the pilings, and not one shrimper who left his boat in the pier found it. During the storm, the *Lady Kathryn* broke free of her restraints early on and drifted out to sea. Many of the other boats sunk or broke apart during the journey, but the *Lady Kathryn* managed to make it all the way to Cat Island. Unlike the majority of the debris and other boats, the *Lady Kathryn* floated all the way around the island before she finally took on too much water and began to fall apart and sink.

The boat ultimately broke in half, and the front section disintegrated into floating pieces of wood and fiberglass. The back section stayed intact and eventually drifted up near the island, entrenching itself in the sand several feet underwater. It ended up with the stern's port corner poking up toward the surface, just below the lapping of the waves – virtually invisible.

————

Matt never saw it, and when the *Big D* hit it going thirty-five knots, the last remaining section of the *Lady Kathryn* held fast, bringing the *Big D* to a complete stop in the water before tearing it apart. Matt flipped over the glass, and his thigh hit the steel gun post on the bow, snapping his femur and spinning him sideways into the water where he skidded to a stop near the island.

The pain blinded him, and he thought he would pass out. He tried to yell, but when he opened his mouth, it filled with salt water. Matt convulsed, thrashed and started to sink. He lost his bearing until he felt the bottom, and, once he righted himself, ground his fingers in the sand and pulled himself forward up the slope leading to shore. He could feel air on top of his head, and, with each panic-driven effort, he cleared the water a little more, eventually moving in far enough to get his gaping mouth above the surface.

He coughed, gagged, and tried to pull himself farther up, but he couldn't move his leg. He spat and saw blood droplets in the water. He thought a tooth was loose and put his hand to his face.

By the time he got his head and body half way up and out onto the beach, he had no energy left, he could barely breathe, and he did not have much luck trying to rise up on his elbows. His whole torso writhed as he wretched and vomited, his head hovering inches above the sand.

He could hear *Big D's* motor sputtering to its untimely death behind him, and, now finally taking oxygen in, pushed himself to crawl just a little further inland. As Murphy and Delia pulled up behind him and cut the *King's* engines, Matt tried to look up, but his vision blurred. He dropped his head to the sand, and his eyes rolled back into the darkness.

57

MATT FELT SOMETHING tugging at his shoulder. He must have resisted because after a few seconds, someone yanked him so hard, he flipped over onto his back. The move caused his fractured leg to jut out at a grotesque angle, and the white streaks shooting across his eyes made him think he was hallucinating. The shock caused him to throw up again, and the purging brought him back to reality. It felt to Matt like his head weighed fifty pounds when he tilted it up to look around.

Matt didn't know how long he had been out, but it had to have been for more than just a few minutes. For one, his hair and the top of his shirt had dried, and, from his perspective, he saw several sets of legs standing on the beach that weren't there when he crashed. The sun was high in the sky, and he was terribly thirsty. It took a minute to get his bearings, and then things slowly came back to him. He tried to look up, but had to wait while his eyes adjusted to the sunlight. Through the glare, he could tell someone was coming his way, but he couldn't make out who it was.

"You're going to be okay, Matt." He recognized the voice instantly.

"Delia?" Matt replied. His mouth hurt like hell. He must have banged it on something and started to bring his hand to his face, but she caught it.

"You've been through a lot, honey, and I'm sure you are very confused right now. I'm here to help."

Matt's eyes finally focused, and he looked her right in the face as she held his hand. She had that same look of compassion and concern he had seen so many times before. What was happening?

"I *am* confused, Delia," Matt breathed. "None of this makes sense."

"I can explain it, Matt, but first we should do a couple of things. One, we need to get you to a hospital. Before we do that, though, I need to know where you're keeping that flash drive and any files that you may have downloaded. I'll be glad to pick them up and then run through them with you when you feel better. That way I can put everything in proper context."

I'm lying here half dead and she's asking about files? Her requests rang with a slight hint of desperation, which Matt found odd. He looked up at Delia and saw her shoot a glance at the person directly above him. He craned his neck and could now see the rest of the cast of characters. Kotori stood on Matt's right side. Delia squatted down to his left, and Chief Halliday stood over her shoulder. It took him a second to place the person Delia looked at because the sun hit him directly in the eyes, but when the man shifted, and Matt saw him favor his knee, he knew: Griff Murphy.

Son of a *bitch.*

Murphy gave a subtle nod back to Delia, and she looked down at Matt with a delicate smile.

Matt let the exchange he witnessed between Delia and Murphy sink in for a second. They – most definitely Murphy – still wanted him dead. But they weren't going to shoot him or drown him or hack him into little pieces until the flash drive was in their hands. That being the case, he wondered if he could flip this exchange to his advantage. And at least buy some time until they *did* try to kill him.

"Flash drive?" he asked.

"Yes, Matt," Delia said patiently.

"Files? What files?"

He watched Delia carefully. Her expression didn't change, but from the corner of his eye Matt saw Murphy shift his weight. "*The* files. You remember them, don't you?"

Matt felt everyone staring at him. "I'm sorry... must've hit my head..."

Delia moved closer. Now her face was inches from his. He could smell a hint of perfume, mixed with her perspiration and the salt from the air. "The files you found. On the flash drive from the bank."

Matt feigned confusion then raised his eyebrows. "Oh, the *files*," Matt said and looked her straight in the eye. "Why didn't you say so, Delia?" Matt paused for effect. "Or, would you prefer that I call you *Steel Magnolia*?" He let that hang for a second then smacked his lips, even though it hurt his broken tooth. "You know, to, as you say, *put everything in proper context.*'"

Her grip tightened on Matt's hand for a fleeting instant, but it was truly her eyes that gave away the game. He'd seen her in action for years and couldn't ever recall Delia's ever letting her guard down – not in court, not in a deposition, and not in the office. Matt had never seen her waver. Until now. When Matt said *Steel Magnolia* her eyes widened the tiniest bit. The calm mask was back on in a nanosecond, but he'd spotted anger and contempt – and *fear.*

"You know, my leg appears to be torn all to pieces, I probably lost a couple of teeth, and I can hardly breathe – broken ribs," Matt said, touching his side. It hurt to even talk, but a part of him was going to enjoy this moment. "And I'm trying like hell to remember files and a flash drive. But I'm afraid I'm coming up slap empty, Delia. I wish I could help you."

A sandy shoe clipped Matt's ear. "Now you listen here, you little shit." Murphy spoke, squatting down awkwardly with his banged-up knee over Matt's face and spitting when he talked. Oddly enough, all Matt could think of was that he looked even uglier than before. "You know damn well what she's talking about, and I suggest –"

"Griff –" Delia said.

"– you tell us right now before I personally kick –"

"Griff!" Delia roared, and this time he shut up. Delia turned back to Matt. The mask was still in place; the woman's self-control was impressive. "I know you have accessed some sensitive files. Let's make this easier on everyone. Tell me where they are, and then we'll get you to a hospital." She leaned close to him. "I need to know *now*."

Matt struggled to sit, but he could only prop himself halfway up on one elbow. He leaned in to Delia, stopping inches from her face as she glanced around before looking back at Matt.

"Delia, since day one, you preached to me the importance of integrity, reputation, and truth, and I have –" A jolt of paint caused him to shiver and he paused to catch his breath before continuing. "– and I have tried my best to follow and work by those principles. But now – now I see it's all been a ruse. You are a fraud, Delia. You have betrayed me and you have betrayed the firm. The saddest thing, though, Delia? You have betrayed yourself."

Delia didn't respond, but her expression changed again. This time Matt saw hurt.

"How dare you, Delia. How dare you," Matt said.

Then he saw anger.

"How dare you?" she said in a voice so spooky it chilled him, even as he lay there half dead and knowing the end was near. Delia craned in so close to Matt that their noses almost touched. Her head was slightly shaking, and her teeth clenched so tight she could barely speak. Her eyes looked black they were so dark, and a muscle twitched at the corner of her mouth as she began.

"Let me tell you something, Matt Frazier. Don't you *ever* judge me. You have no idea what I have gone through for the past thirty years. I have given my *life* for this firm, only to have my efforts, time and time again, rebuffed, ignored, discounted, and laughed at by Tripp Massey and others."

And there it is.

"I have never been appreciated for my efforts, certainly not by my partners who called me their friend, and not by greedy, young, egotistical associates like yourself. I finally had a plan together that would get me out of here and recognize me for what I'm worth –"

Matt couldn't help himself. "Congratulations. You must be proud of your –"

"Don't you mock me, you little shit," she yelled. "Do you realize, Matt, that I will be the Attorney General of the United States? No, of course you don't, because you've spent the last three years with your head three feet up Jeff McCabe's ass and don't have a clue what I'm about or what I've had to put up with –"

"Kiss my ass, Delia."

She slapped him so hard he dropped back onto the sand. Then she grabbed him by the shirt and pulled him back up. It hurt like hell, but Matt wouldn't give her the pleasure of seeing him wince so he turned his head the other way.

"Look at me when I'm talking to you, dammit," she continued in a low growl. "This job will finally elevate me from the shit stain under Tripp Massey's shoe to someone he will finally *have* to respect. And you – *look at me, you bastard* – you, who have no clue what I've been through all my life have the temerity to address me in a condescending manner. *How dare you, Delia?* No, Matt, how dare *you.*"

Matt tongued the inside of his cheek where it throbbed, but said nothing. He had no idea Delia would ever let Massey cloud her judgment to this degree of irrationality, but apparently, he underestimated the impact of Tripp's overtures. Delia gave him a little shake and started back in.

"Now, I have done too much and gone too far to have this messed up at the end by the likes of you," she said. "So you tell me what you did with those files *right now.* This is your last chance."

He took his time answering her, partly because he was still smarting from the slap and partly because he relished seeing Delia on edge and in a position to have to threaten him. When he looked at her he saw that the expression on her face had progressed from anger to downright pleading. She must have seen his reaction, too, because she leaned in and pitched her voice so low Matt knew the others couldn't hear her.

"I can get you out of here," she said urgently. "Back home. Alive. No questions asked. Just tell me where they are."

In that moment, Matt felt more tired than he'd ever been in his life. But he also felt a resigned sense of relaxation. He stared at her, and with the wind twisting her hair and her face taking on a feral expression, she looked like a crazed homeless person. He thought of coming back with a retort, but knew it would get him nowhere. He looked her straight in the eyes, slowly shook his head, mouthed a silent "No" and lay back down on the beach. Delia let go of him and stood up. She looked over at Murphy, which must have been his cue.

"If you don't tell us where all that shit – and the money – is right now, we will leave you here," Murphy said. "Then, we'll go back and tear your office and every last thing you own to pieces until we find them."

Matt, while making a point of ignoring Murphy, noticed Kotori stiffen at the mention of the loot. Murphy put his hands on his knees and looked down at Matt.

"And you will die."

Matt turned his head away and stared out toward the sea. Then Murphy kneeled down next to him, his bad leg kicked out sideways.

"Hold on, here," Murphy said. "Hold on. I know what I can do. Yes indeed, yes in-deed!" He grinned and squatted closer and Matt could smell his raspy, sickly breath. "Your pretty wife, Shelley, will know something. I bet I can make her talk. You should know by now that I can be *very* influential –"

Murphy sneered, and when he did, Matt grabbed him in a headlock and bit his ear as hard as he could. Murphy started flailing, but Matt didn't let go until Kotori kicked him in the ribs. It stunned Matt, but he felt satisfied when Murphy fell back away, squealing and crying as blood streamed out between the fingers covering his ear.

Matt spit a quarter size piece of cartilage onto the sand and spoke through bloody lips. "How many times do I have to say it? Don't ever talk about my family." He saw Murphy regain his footing and get ready to charge – there wasn't much Matt could do about it at this point – but Halliday yelled, and Kotori grabbed him before he could attack.

"You're a dead man!" Murphy shouted. "You hear me? Dead!"

Matt looked up at him. "Whether I die or not, it's too late for you. All of y'all for that matter." He tried his best to find Delia, wanting to look her in the eye one more time as he dropped this latest bit of news. "Before I left this morning, I e-mailed those files you want so bad to a friend of mine with some very pointed instructions in case I turn up missing. And as we speak, those files are being handed over to the authorities." He looked over to Halliday. "*Proper* authorities, Chief Halliday. Game over."

But Halliday broke into a smile. "A friend, you say?"

Murphy started guffawing, but what really surprised Matt was Kotori's little giggly laugh. It was the first thing he'd ever heard out of the man, and it belied his size and stature.

"Jason Hopkins, maybe?" Halliday said. His grin widened. Mr. 'Hop'? Yeah, we know who your friend is, all right. Let's get him out here."

58

PHILIP KOTORI DISAPPEARED from sight before emerging a few seconds later with his arms around Hop, half carrying him and half dragging him. Duct tape bound Hop's mouth, hands and feet, and fresh bruises mottled his face. Hop's hair was crimson slick on one side where the blood had dried it flat. He shot wide-eyed looks from one person to another, but could only grunt in fear. Halliday cleared his throat, ready to assume control again. The smug bastard was enjoying this, and Matt hated him for it.

"Being the good citizen and friend that he is," Halliday began in his drawl, "Mr. Hopkins here took it upon himself to call the police early this morning to let us know about the trouble you had gotten yourself into, Mr. Frazier. About the time we showed up, you called and left a most interesting message. Thanks to your foresight, we knew right where to find you."

Halliday ripped the tape off his mouth, and Hop spit on the ground. "But what we didn't know – and what Mr. Hopkins here didn't tell us, however, is that you had also sent him an e-mail detailing your exploits. This is indeed news to us. Thanks for the second heads-up. We will stop at his place first when we get back."

Chief Halliday nudged Hop forward and threw him down onto the sand next to Matt. The air whooshed out of him as he landed, and it took him a second to get his wind after he rolled over.

"Sorry, bro," he mumbled. "Looks like I jumped the gun."

Matt gave Hop what he hoped was a reassuring smile, wanting it to convey the appreciation he felt for his best friend. Hop had been there for him all these years, and he'd provided a real gift by getting Matt and Shelley back on the road to reconciliation, albeit cut short by this turn of events. Matt took in as deep a breath as his lungs would hold, held it there for an instant, and let it go slowly. He savored the salty air before looking back up at his group of tormentors, knowing these breaths might be his last. Murphy and Kotori, of course, were no more than guns hired to do bad things to people. Halliday was a civil servant gone bad – Matt was disappointed in what he'd become, but he had no emotional investment in the man's future. Delia, though, was another story. All things considered, he felt pity for her. He looked at all three as they stood there, staring at him with bated breath, and then the strangest thing happened.

"Hop?" Matt said to Halliday, his eyes flashing. "Hop?" Then Matt felt it begin deep down in his belly. His diaphragm started convulsing, filling his lungs with air before they, too broke into spasms, pushing the noise past his trachea out his mouth until it burst through as deep, rolling laughter. He laughed through the pain of broken ribs, a broken leg, and a broken body and stopped only to catch his breath to laugh some more.

The fact that he was laughing surprised Matt nearly as much as the others. He had laughed hard only one other time since the storm – after Hank tried to shoot at him the first day back. Now, here, literally in the jaws of death, he couldn't stop snickering. Someone looking down would have concluded he had absolutely lost his mind. He was lying in the sand, missing teeth, leg broken, shirt torn, face beat up, and blood covering his chin, cheek, and mouth from snacking on Murphy's ear, yet he was cracking up with hilarity – so much so he could feel the warm wetness of tears trickle down near his sideburns. "You –" he said between breaths, "you – you think I sent it to *Hop*?" Matt screeched with glee and threw his head back into the sand. Hop stared over at Matt, confused and dumb-looking.

By now, everyone was watching him, waiting for whatever overtook him to leave so that he would speak coherently again. When Matt's amusement finally dialed down to mere chuckles, he addressed his captive audience.

"All of you, so sad," Matt said, with as much compassion as he could muster. "So sad." His voice was still pitched a little higher from laughing, but his expression began to return to normal again, and he cleared his throat. He could feel Hop still staring at him, but Matt couldn't worry himself with what Hop thought at this point. Plus, Hop hadn't figured it out yet. Regardless of whether Matt gave them the flash drive and the files, he and Hop would not be making the trip back. They were still alive only because Matt had not yet told them anything.

Delia tried one more time. "Matt, did the files go to Hop? Work with me. I can be your lifeline here. I can – "

Matt cleared his throat. "Shut up, Delia," Matt said. "Just shut the hell up. It's over." This absolutely stunned his former mentor – no one spoke to Delia Farrell like that – but Matt ignored her and addressed the group, serious again, although his eyes were still watery. "When I said I sent those files to a friend, it wasn't Hop, although he is as loyal a friend as any man could ask for." Matt looked over at Hop, and he was crying now. Maybe Hop had realized their fate after all. "And when Hop didn't answer his phone this morning, I knew something was wrong."

Matt turned back to Delia. "No, Delia, I didn't send them to Hop. But I did send them to my lifeline, all right. I sent them to Shelley." Murphy, without being aware of it, put his hand to his raw ear with the mention of her name. "And I left her specific instructions as to what to do with them if she didn't hear back from me by a certain time. Right about now, she should be meeting with another good friend of mine. Lieutenant Lance Glenn. Mississippi Highway Patrol. With documents in tow."

Delia gasped as pure terror filled her eyes, and Halliday took her by the arm a few feet away. They began speaking in hushed tones, and after a minute, they called the Kotori and Murphy over to join the conference. Matt lay there, smiling at the satisfaction he felt in letting them know it was over. At least he got that before he died. He tried to hear what they were saying, but could not pick up anything, although he had a good idea where the conversation was going. Shortly thereafter, Murphy returned and announced that Delia and Halliday would leave right away.

Delia walked over to Matt, and when Matt looked at her, she opened her mouth as if to say something, but then she stopped, jutted out her chin, turned, and walked away. Halliday cranked the boat, and Matt heard him shift the engine into gear and start to back up. The only ones left on the beach were Matt, Hop, Murphy, and Kotori.

Murphy smiled, and Matt saw he had a pistol in his hand.

"I get this one," he said, pointing at Matt. "I earnt it." Kotori backed away as Murphy swaggered up to Matt, positioning himself just over Matt's shoulders.

Strangely enough, Matt didn't feel scared. He felt sad for his family and returned to the routine he had observed for years. He said a prayer, and, this time, he rested his head on the sand and looked straight up into the heavens, peacefully resigned to his fate.

Matt heard the slide click, and then Murphy spoke the last words Matt would ever hear him say.

"I shoulda' done this the first time I had the chance."

59

A .50 CALIBER BULLET is one-half-inch wide and just over two inches long. If the shell dimensions are added, its total length exceeds five and a half inches. The .50 caliber bullet has a number of applications, including use as an armor-piercing device, incendiary device, and as the weapon of choice of the A10 Warthog. While it has been a valuable tool to stop machinery or shoot down aircraft, the lethality of a .50 caliber bullet is best demonstrated when used on flesh-and-blood targets. When fired from a machine gun or a long-range sniper rifle, the slug travels at over 2,800 feet per second. When it hits a human, the effects are immediate, catastrophic, and graphic. Shots to the middle of the body cut a person clean in half, and a head shot usually leaves nothing from the chest up. The bullet travels so fast the target is eliminated before the report of the weapon reaches the victim. Many of those killed by .50 caliber rounds die before they even hear a shot.

Which explained Matt's surprise when, just after Griff Murphy cocked his pistol, Murphy's arm, shoulder, and half of his left side disappeared in a puff of red mist. Murphy's remains hit the ground before Matt heard the .50 cal's unmistakable signature echo through the air. Kotori wheeled toward the sound and, having seen what was left of Murphy, threw his hands in the air and sunk to his knees.

Matt heard yelling and screaming from the others, and he raised his head to see where the shot came from. He did a double take when he thought he saw the *Big D* banking around the bend at a high rate of speed. It took Matt a second to realize it was not the *Big D*, but rather one of the prototypes Hank showed him back at American Marine. There was Hank on the bow, legs spread wide, swiveling the .50 cal on its mount, looking for another target. Matt couldn't identify the driver or the crew.

"What's going on?" Hop asked.

"Keep your head down, Hop," Matt said. "Stay low."

Delia yelled something at Halliday, and Halliday jerked the *Queen* forward as Delia crouched down. Halliday pulled his service revolver and aimed it at Hank. At about the same time, Matt saw something he had heard of, but had never witnessed before. The *Queen* started vibrating so violently it literally appeared to hop out of the surf, creating hundreds of staccato-splashes of water all around it. When small hunks and pieces of the *Queen* started flying off, Matt realized that Hank had turned the big gun on the boat and was laying steel into it at ten rounds per second, causing it to dance in the water. Just as Matt figured it out, Hank's barrage reached the fuel tank, and the boat exploded, sending a fireball and a black plume of smoke high in the air. The boat's remnants continued to burn as it took on water and started to sink.

There was no sign of Halliday or Delia, and for a split-second Matt felt a pang of deep sorrow. But Delia had made her choices, and she lived – and died – by them. Matt turned back to Kotori. Hank's boat came around, and the driver cut the engine as it approached. Hank hopped out and ran up to him, gun drawn.

"Anyone else, you big red bastard?" Hank yelled, and for the first time, Matt heard Kotori speak.

"No, sir," he said.

"He tellin' the truth, Matt?" Hank yelled, never taking his eyes off the man.

"Think so, Hank. Far as I can tell."

Hank put his gun to the back of Kotori's head and bound his hands behind him with zip-tie restraints. "If anyone else pops up, you're a dead sonofabitch," Hank said. "You hear me Tonto? Dead sonofabitch." He kicked him over on his side.

"Don't worry, son. We got help coming." Hank looked over at Murphy's remains. "Though looks like we got it under control. I never seen Wild Bill drive a boat so fast. Never seen it." Hank waved to the boat, giving the "all clear" signal.

Matt looked up at Hank and smiled the best he could. "Not bad, old man."

"Well, you look like shit. Both y'all do."

"Feel like shit, Hank."

"You better make it, son. That's all I got to say."

"So that's Wild Bill, huh?" Matt asked. "He don't look too bad, Hank."

"That's him, all right," Hank said. "Mean as a snake with a toothache."

"Hank, how did you know to come out here? I mean –"

Hank smiled, told Matt to hold on a sec and turned back to the boat. "I done gave you the signal for 'all clear'," he yelled. "That means y'all can come ashore. Bring her out here, Bill."

Matt, mustering all the strength he had, lifted a hand to shield his eyes from the glare and peered at the boat. A second later Wild Bill helped someone up from the cabin and into view.

It was Shelley.

60

SHELLEY THREW HER leg over the gunwale and ran to him through the surf. She flung herself onto her hands and knees and kissed Matt's forehead, then moved to a sitting position and cradled his head on her lap. She was crying softly, and even Hank wiped away a tear.

"She's how I knew to come here, son," he said. "She's how I knew."

Hank explained that when Matt used his passcode to get into the boat shop, an alert was sent to Wild Bill, who called Hank to find out why he was going in so early on a day the shop was closed.

"Only other person who knows my code is you, Matt," he said. "I figured you were still secure downtown, so I cursed at Wild Bill and called him the senile old bastard he is and hung up. But about then I got a call from Shelley. She was half an hour outside Gulfport with your Highway Patrol buddy and explained about the e-mail you sent her and thought you were in trouble because she couldn't reach you."

Matt took Shelley's hand and squeezed. She squeezed back.

"I went straight to your office and found the grenade detonated and what looked like the remnants of one hell of a firefight," Hank continued. "When I saw your truck was gone, I remembered the call from Wild Bill and figured you'd gone to hide at the shop – which wasn't a bad damn idea, boy. Not a bad idea at all."

Hank spat on the ground and saw Kotori looking over at them. Hank yelled at him to turn around before he let a round off in self-defense. When he looked one more time, Hank took a shot that hit the sand in front of his crotch. "I done told you, kemosabe. Eyes front. Consider that a warning. Balls'll be the last thing you're worried about once I let the next one off."

Kotori didn't look any more.

"Anyhow, I called Shelley and told her to meet me there. I hauled ass to the shop, met up with Wild Bill, and saw *Big D* was missing –"

Big D. "Hank," Matt said, "I'm so sorry about your boat. I shouldn't have –"

"Sorry?" Hank asked. "Shit, boy, you was thinking. Proud of you for that command decision you made. No need to apologize. No need at all."

"But Hank, *Big D* is – is gone."

"I know. But you ain't. And that's what matters," Hank said.

"I still don't see how y'all got *here*, though," Matt said.

"Well, if you'd hush up and let me finish, I'll tell you," Hank said. Shelley grinned and Wild Bill just nodded, as if he'd heard that line before. "Most people don't know this, but I put a GPS tracker in *Big D*. Sarah likes to use it when I'm out front by myself so she can keep tabs on me. I had Wild Bill pull it up, and when I saw the *Big D* was bearing towards Cat, we were on the water in two shakes of a dog's tail. And let me tell you something about this woman –" Hank said, resting his hand on Shelley's shoulder. "– she's as stubborn as a shoulder-deep deer tick. She insisted she come along, and even tried to tell me and Will Bill a thing or two about boatin' when she thought we weren't movin' fast enough."

Shelley grabbed Hank's hand. "Aren't you glad I came, Hank? I know you enjoyed the company," Shelley asked, smiling up to him.

"I guess so," Hank said, leaning in for a hug. "Truth be told, we wouldn't have put it all together if she hadn't made the call in the first place."

"I don't know what to say," Matt said. "You risked a lot coming out here."

"Don't tell anybody," Hank said, "but me and Wild Bill haven't done anything like this for quite a while. Haven't had this much fun since I wore the uniform. Like old times," Hank said. "Like old times." Wild Bill gave a confirmatory thumbs-up. The radio crackled, and Hank stood up, checking his watch. "Right on time. We got company."

A larger craft came into view, and Matt recognized the red and white U.S. Coast Guard markings. The officers pulled up next to the *King* and, after a brief discussion with Wild Bill, hopped on and made sure it was clear. When the Coast Guard boat pulled closer to the shore, an officer and two enlisted men jumped out and waded up onto the sand. They promptly arrested Philip Kotori and turned their attention to Matt and Hop.

"You guys are a sight for sore eyes," Matt said when the captain knelt down next to him.

"We came soon as she called."

"She?"

"Your wife," the captain said with a big grin on his face. "Took charge of the whole operation, ordering us around on the radio like she was some kind of admiral or something."

Hank laughed. "Oh, yeah. I forgot to tell you. On the way in she done that, too."

Matt looked at her. "You did all this?"

"I guess so," Shelley said.

"I love you, babe." Matt said.

"I love you, too." Shelley responded as she leaned down to kiss him on the cheek. "Always have."

Matt laid back and let the corpsman attend to his wounds. As the morphine started to kick in, he looked straight up at the sky and watched the frigate birds make wide circles high up in the air. The sun felt warm on his face, and for the first time that day, Matt became aware of the gentle sounds of the surf lapping up on the beach. He turned his head to look out across the sound. To his surprise, the choppiness had dissipated. Matt smiled.

The water was rough no more.

EPILOGUE

MATT SAT ON the back porch swing, watching the boys play hide-and-go-seek in the yard. He couldn't believe how much they had grown. He already felt nostalgic for their youth, and he wished he could bottle up the moment and save it for a later date.

The rebuilding process took longer than expected, but they eventually moved back in, nearly two years to the date of the storm. Matt blamed part of the delay on his extensive rehabilitation and his general lack of mobility at the beginning. Once he progressed past the cane, however, life got much easier and somewhat back to normal. Now, he rarely even walked with a limp, and that occurred only when the temperature uncharacteristically dipped below thirty.

Most of the Bing principals remained, although they changed the firm's name after the story broke detailing the firm's involvement in the bribery scandal. For damage control, as much as anything else, the Bing set up a recovery fund for storm victims with the bribe money, and Tripp Massey held a press conference at the Gulfport harbor when he cut the first check. While on the coast, he offered Matt a share in the partnership. Matt politely declined but had the good sense to take advantage of Tripp's largesse and negotiated a worthy severance package. Matt explained that several weeks in the hospital gave him time to do some soul-searching, and he decided it best for him to try to make a go of it on his own. That way, he could more or less set his schedule and, of greater importance, could stay closer to home.

Matt did not go without work, however. While in the hospital, Ron Tsosie, Chief Osceola and several tribal elders visited him. As it turned out, Ron's story was legitimate and, as Ron explained, they captured and arrested two more individuals from Pontotoc when they arrived at Shelley's mother's. One of them happened to be John Wallo, who had ratted Matt out at the bank the day he accessed the safety deposit box. By the time Ron and the chief left the hospital, Matt had accepted an offer to serve as the chief counsel for the Wapegan's Southern Gaming Division. His new job consisted of overseeing the construction of, and acting as in-house counsel for The Rising Sun, Gulfport's newest casino resort and hotel. Billed as "The New Crown Jewel of the Coast," it had all the bells and whistles expected of a five-star resort, including a massive hybrid water/amusement park that J.W. and Fin might as well have called their summer home. Plus, The Rising Sun was able to capitalize on Majesticorp's decision to altogether pull out of gaming in Mississippi.

Matt even hired his own associate, who now occupied Jeff's old office. During the repainting, Matt dug out the slug that had lodged in the crown molding above Jeff's chair. The forensics experts used it in Philip Kotori's prosecution. When presented with ballistics that matched the Glock Matt found, he plead out to conspiracy to commit murder, admitting Griff Murphy, with the assistance of Chief Halliday, killed Jeff after Jeff lost the duffel bag. As to the identity of the Bing insider, Ravi was called in to investigate the Bing network, and after a long weekend, he tied all of the e-traffic back to Delia.

The explanation for Jeff's involvement was not so simple. As it turns out, Jeff's frequent trips to The Majestic's gaming floor involved much more than mere business development. Soon after the Bing hired Jeff to represent The Majestic on the coast, Delia found out, quite unexpectedly, about Jeff's inability to keep his gambling in check. The Majestic staff and management, who tracked the wins and losses of the high rollers, alerted Delia, and she quietly kept tabs on Jeff's dalliance. While Jeff's propensity to gamble in and of itself was not a problem, the means he used to finance it had severe – and permanent – implications. Delia discovered Jeff was accessing client trust fund money to finance his addiction. When Delia called him on the carpet for it and informed Jeff that he would lose his job, his license and – of greatest importance – his reputation, he caved and asked what, if anything, he could do to rectify the situation. His quandary provided the missing link Delia needed, and she blackmailed him into being the mule for her bribery scheme. As long as he executed the plan and kept Delia's fingerprints off it, life could go on, and nothing would ever be publicly disclosed about his transgressions.

After the storm, the rebirth of the neighborhood remained slow but steady. It took nearly a year to clear out the debris, clean the lots, and resurface the roads. Homes in various stages of construction dotted the street, and many of the new homes – including Matt's – retained some of the pre-storm architectural character. Hank made it a habit to visit Matt at least once a week, and his recounting of Operation Cat & the Matt, as he called it, became a permanent thread in Hank's tapestry of war stories. He never rebuilt *Big D*, but Wild Bill agreed to let him take the gunboat prototype out (sans .50 cal) whenever he pleased.

Trinity continued its mission, although now the crowds it fed no longer consisted of hungry Gulfport residents with nowhere to eat. Instead, Trinity housed and provided food for the multitude of church groups from around the country who rotated in for days or weeks at a time to assist the needy in their rebuilding efforts. In a featured report during the one-year anniversary, the Sun-Herald estimated that Trinity served over 50,000 meals since the storm. The newspaper even quoted the Reverend R.J. Curtis, who praised those who helped, "from the youngest hands in the serving line, to the generosity of the anonymous donor who mailed in an envelope containing $30,000 in cash, the Lord continues to bless us more and more each day."

Matt checked his watch and figured he should start getting the burgers ready, but the sea breeze wafting through made him not want to move. Matt invited the Glenns and Tsosies to come with kids in tow, and Hop and Anni also planned to join them.

Matt still had to set up the Slip and Slide and get the projector ready for the outdoor movie they planned to watch later that evening. J.W. picked *Toy Story 3*, but Matt heard Fin trying to negotiate a more current flick. Matt grinned when he heard the back and forth between the two, and he felt confident Fin would end up getting his little brother to adopt his position.

Shelley walked out onto the porch, and Matt patted the seat next to him. She looked beautiful as she walked over and sat down. Matt put his hand on her leg and then moved it up and rested it on her belly.

"Has he kicked any this morning?" Matt asked.

Shelley put her hand on his. "Oh, yeah. Try here." She moved it lower, and after a second, Matt felt a ripple. It never ceased to amaze him.

"Won't be long now, will it?"

"No," she said and rubbed Matt's arm. "Three boys. Can you believe it?"

Matt kissed Shelley on the cheek and looked her in the eyes. "No, I can't believe it. Life is good, honey." He looked out over the back yard and saw the light dancing on the water in the distance. The swing creaked as the two of them swayed with the breeze, and they laughed as Fin chased J.W. around the yard with the water hose.

Out front, someone had spray painted a white line on the power pole, marking the high water mark as a remembrance of the storm. Above Matt's front door hung the old beat-up "2005" address marker he had salvaged from their old house. Matt thought about repainting it so it would better match the new exterior color, but he liked the way that it, too, reminded him of those things that really mattered.

He left it alone.

ACKNOWLEDGMENTS

As I sit here in my home in Gulfport, some ten years after Hurricane Katrina came through and absolutely obliterated our city, I find myself at a loss for words as to who I should thank for getting this book from a mere concept rattling around in my head to the printed page. It's not that I'm having trouble finding someone to thank, it's just that there are so many who have contributed in so many ways, I don't know how to narrow it down. It's a good problem to have – but a problem nonetheless.

So, I'll start with the big picture. First and foremost, I thank God. Without Him, none of this would be possible (and go ahead and read that "none of this" as broadly as you can). He is the Alpha and the Omega. Enough said.

That was the easy part; here's where it gets tough. It would be a futile effort to try and list by name everyone I am indebted to for helping me along. Just know – and you do know – those of you that listened, edited, read, rejected, embraced, reread and encouraged – you all hold a dear place in my heart, and there aren't enough words to express my gratitude.

There are some folks, however, who I must acknowledge with a higher degree of specificity, for I know not if I'll have this chance again, and I don't want to squander the opportunity. So let me first thank those I have never met.

To those of you who left your families, jobs, homes and schools for days, weeks and months at a time to come down to the Mississippi Gulf Coast to help us after the storm, I thank you. To those who sacrificed summer vacations, spring breaks, birthday parties, long weekends, ball games and holidays to relocate in Gulfport to help rebuild, I thank you. To those of all faiths who truly demonstrated service in God's name, I thank you. To our national, state and community leaders who showed the country and the world how to handle and react to a catastrophe with grace, leadership, thanksgiving and determination, I thank you. To those in the military who patrolled our streets, guarded our homes and protected our businesses, I thank you. To our Gulf Coast churches who threw open their doors, coffers and kitchens to feed those who were hungry, clothe those who were naked and visit those who were destitute, I thank you. And to my friends who live on the best street in the world – Second Street – for never losing hope, for coming back stronger than ever, and for epitomizing the true meaning of the word neighbor, I thank you.

We can be an insular group down here in South Mississippi. No doubt about that. But I can't tell you enough how much we – our communities, cities and people – appreciate the outreach shown by the citizens of our great nation.

Now to family. First off, to Granny, God rest her soul. She loved reading more than anyone I've ever seen, and she would read three and four books at a time. She made reading fun and cool, and passed her love for books down to my mother, who in turn, passed it down to me and my brothers. If it weren't for them, this wouldn't have happened. Mom probably read more drafts of this book than anyone, and even though she would have given the story high marks if I had written it in crayon on a cereal box, her willingness and eagerness to keep going back to the well means a lot to me. Thanks also to Dad, Billy, and Charlie for providing the foundation, support, moral compass and sense of humor that carried me through childhood and continues to shape me today.

I can't think of any individuals, however, who have had a greater impact on my life than my beautiful wife Kay and our three sons, Holden, Jack and Rush. You all bring color to my days, light to my eyes and laughter to my heart. I love you all dearly. You are a constant source of inspiration and joy, and for that, I am forever thankful.

Finally, I thank you, the reader, for picking this book up and for spending some time with it. I hope you have enjoyed reading it as much as I enjoyed writing it.

Be good.

Made in the USA
San Bernardino, CA
13 December 2016